Shady Cosgrove lives in the Illawarra and teaches Creative Writing at the University of Wollongong. Her book *She Played Elvis* was shortlisted for the *Australian* Vogel Literary Prize, and her short stories and articles have appeared in *Best Australian Stories, Antipodes, Southerly, Overland,* the *Sydney Morning Herald* and the *Age.*

Dear Christine —
Hope you enjoy.
To funny !

what the ground can't hold

SHADY COSGROVE

PICADOR
Pan Macmillan Australia

First published 2013 in Picador by Pan Macmillan Australia Pty Limited
1 Market Street, Sydney

National Library of Australia
Cataloguing-in-Publication data:

Cosgrove, Shady.

What the ground can't hold / Shady Cosgrove.

978 1 7426 1273 7 (pbk.)

Secrecy—Fiction.

A823.4

Typeset in 12/16 pt Minion by Post Pre-Press Group, Australia
Printed by McPherson's Printing Group

Papers used by Pan Macmillan Australia Pty Ltd are natural, recyclable products made from wood grown in sustainable forests. The manufacturing processes conform to the environmental regulations of the country of origin.

For Scott and Serena

Contents

1 EMMA WOODS   1
2 HANS 'JACK' MEYERS   69
3 CARMEN GONZALEZ   123
4 PEDRO CARIMÁN   177
5 WOLFE GOLDBERG   235

1

Emma Woods

I was walking back to the cabin to knock snow off my boots when the cracking roar echoed across the valley behind me. It sounded like splitting timber giving way. Turning around, I could see snow breaking loose high along the Cerro Blanco ridge, dropping down in a majestic, lolling rhythm. At first it moved slowly but once it fell over a rock ledge it gained momentum and power, like a giant wave bearing down the mountain. The sheer force was hypnotic – beautiful, even – and plumes of ice-powder billowed up like smoke. The avalanche dropped lower, swallowing up trees and boulders. It was exciting and frightening, and for a moment I didn't even think about Jeremy and John. And then I scanned the mountain frantically, unable to place them. Time warped – those six or seven seconds stretched out and then compressed – and when that giant surge of snow swept across the trail and over the cliff, I had no idea if they'd escaped.

Pedro didn't look at me; he just pulled the binoculars over my head and stared at the trail. We were in the middle of the Andes, a six-hour hike from Bariloche. No road access. No helicopter. Our stillness was making me panic – we had to do something. Finally Pedro thrust the binoculars at me and ran inside. 'Look for their red jackets.'

Sliding the view into focus, I could see where the cornice had fallen into the ravine but my hands were shaking. The wind had blown the snow into a frozen wave – a Japanese woodprint etched against the sky. It shouldn't have been so lovely. There was no sign of Jeremy or John.

Pedro leaned out the front door. 'Did they have transceivers?'

I didn't know what he was talking about.

Pedro's voice was urgent. 'Avalanche signals give us their location. Strapped to their chests? Anything?'

I shook my head and he disappeared again. When he emerged, he was pulling on a pack loaded with poles and a shovel. 'It's only us.'

I knew that. Everyone else was hiking around the lake. 'How much time do we have?'

'Fifteen minutes, maybe twenty . . . They could be in an air pocket.'

It would take that just to get to the slide, but he was already running ahead and I had to work to keep up. I slipped at the river crossing, clinging to the overhead cable, but Pedro pulled me to the bank. We set off again and when we were within fifty metres of the rubble, he started shouting out for Jeremy and John. The avalanche had taken most of the snow, and a big slab of trail, into the ravine. We were faced with jagged blocks of ice and uneven piles of snow.

I had no idea what to do but Pedro was already climbing onto a mound of compacted snow. 'Do you know how to search for someone?'

'No.' I scrambled after him.

'We imagine a grid. That rock: the top corner. That tree, the bottom. We walk back and forth and explore for anything solid. Take this—' he handed me a metal rod that looked like a collapsible tent pole. In his other hand, he had a long piece of bamboo. We combed the closest pile, moving in line with each other, probing as far as we could, about seven or eight feet down. It was a relief to have something concrete to do.

'Something here,' Pedro said. He grabbed one of the shovels and began digging, shifting the snow in fast, clean arches. I tried to control my chest, filling it slowly with air. I needed to keep it together.

Copying Pedro, I pried up blocks of ice that were in the way.

'Come on, Jeremy and John,' I said under my breath. 'You fucking dickheads need to be alive.'

My shovel scraped a hard surface and I was certain we'd gotten to one of them. But Pedro jumped forward and pushed away the snow to reveal the waterlogged bark of a tree. I yelled out in frustration.

Pedro stood back up. 'Keep going. Work perpendicular to the fall line – the debris path is usually safe but we don't want another avalanche.' Pedro knew the terrain – he'd lived up there for years, managing the cabin.

I clambered over the rubble and kept searching. The quiet was cold against my ears. Only a faint murmur sounded from the wind.

I pushed down and hit something about three feet beneath me. 'Oh!' I was hopeful.

Pedro whipped around. 'Solid?'

I nodded.

Again, Pedro started digging. I scooped the snow away with my gloves and pried back pieces of ice like rock. Everything could still be okay. We would find them and they'd be alive and we'd carry them back to the cabin. But then Pedro's shovel hit something hard, a heavy clank, and we unearthed the top of a boulder.

We were working ourselves closer to the ravine. I tried to keep calm. Maybe the boys had run clear of the slide. The incline was too steep for us to check if there were footprints at the other side, but surely it was possible. I could imagine them hiking along the main trail – laughing at their close call with an avalanche. Punching each other and mucking about.

Pedro called out. 'John? Jeremy?'

I began to call out too and he shushed me, listening. But the air was empty.

Pedro had stripped down to his flannel shirt. Time was passing and it made our search even more desperate. The mountain was too huge. All I could see was snow. We worked the grid until we reached the sharp incline of the cliff and I didn't have a choice; I had to stop. My arms felt like they were going to fall off.

It was sinking in: we were out of our depth. The avalanche wasn't going to be undone by me and Pedro and a couple of shovels. Jeremy and John had made a stupid decision and now they could be over the edge or trapped under snow and there would be no helping them. I buckled over, throwing up.

'You okay?' Pedro asked.

I nodded, wiping my mouth. 'We can't leave them.'

He looked at me – inquisitive, calculating – and I wondered how much he knew. I wondered if Jeremy had said anything. But Pedro glanced back towards the cabin, wiping the sweat out of his eyes. 'It's not safe. We risk a collapse.'

'Please?'

Over an hour had passed and our mission had shifted from rescue to recovery. It was subtle – a bird crossing the sky: at what point is it directly overhead, at what point has it passed? Even if they were dead, I needed to find the boys.

Sighing, Pedro forced the bamboo pole down and I followed, giving us another two rows in the grid. 'Then we go back,' he said.

'Thank you.'

We were about halfway along when I felt the snow shuddering beneath us like an earthquake tremor.

'Up there, move up there!' Pedro yelled. Tiny creaking sounds echoed beneath us like breaking glass. We needed to get off the snow mound before it caved in. I scrambled as fast as I could, jumping over an ice ledge but I didn't know where to go. The whole ridge could cave in on us.

'That open area,' Pedro called out. It was twenty metres ahead, out of the mountain's steep shadow. Sunlight was pooling onto it as a loud groan shook beneath us. The pack was ready to fall and it wanted to take us with it.

My thighs were burning as I pushed through each step but I didn't seem to be making any distance. This was it. I'd been too careless, urging Pedro to go further, and now we were going to die. I felt Pedro shove me on. We were running but in slow motion. I had no sense of what the mountain was doing behind me. I focused only on the flat, level section waiting for us. We were ten metres away, then five. And finally I threw myself down on the ground just in time. A chunk of snow, about fifteen metres across, sloughed off and teetered down the mountain. I'd never been so scared in my life.

'I'm sorry – I didn't want to leave them.' I was gasping for breath but there was no excuse for my stupidity.

Pedro was beside me, both of us staring at the empty air where we'd just been standing. 'I'll radio down. Club Andino will know if they arrive in Bariloche.'

'What are the chances?'

Pedro shook his head like he didn't want to promise more than he could deliver. He helped me to my feet and we started back towards the cabin. I could barely walk, my legs were shaking so badly. I was glad when he took the lead and we were forced to move in single file along the trail. I wouldn't keep my composure if he tried to talk to me.

For the last two years I'd been planning to backpack through South America, and Argentina had been on my list of countries to visit. But a month before I left, it became my focus: I found out I was adopted. I was twenty-nine years old and giving blood, the bag rocking back and forth on the scale, when the nurse made a bland comment about how the bank needed more AB. She said my parents should donate because blood type was hereditary. I knew Dad was O, but the nurse said that wasn't possible. When I got home, an internet search proved she was right, leading to a series of exhausting confrontations with my parents. Turned out I'd been born in Argentina and my biological parents had died in a plane crash.

I didn't handle this revelation gracefully. I ignored Mum and Dad's phone calls as I packed and finalised bills. I couldn't figure out how much I'd known, how much I should have known. My parents were both pale and that inspired niggling suspicions when I was a kid, but doesn't everyone have those – don't we all fantasise of another tribe waiting for us? Mum told me I took after Grandma Gilly.

When I finally boarded the plane and found my seat, I fell into a deep sleep that was closer to passing out, and the air host had to nudge me to put on my seat belt. My first days in Buenos Aires were spent walking around, reeling. It was a city of monuments and statues. Modern skyscrapers tucked next to gothic domes. Gargoyles staring out over excavators and building works. I roamed the streets, staring at the majestic crumbling apartments, wondering if I could have lived in them, peering down hallways when anyone opened their front door.

Three shopfronts down from my hotel, in the ultra-bright florescence of the chemist, my lips formed the words *cepillo de dientes* – seven syllables for toothbrush. It seemed crazy that this musical, macho language could have belonged to me. The city's rhythms were also strange: I would wake at one in the morning, absurdly alert with jetlag, and listen to the Argentineans wandering home after dinner on a week night.

On my third morning I wandered into Recoleta with my daypack. I thought I'd visit the National Library and research the crash that had changed the course of my life. The library was hard to miss: it looked like a cubed UFO with landing gear had dropped onto the lawn. Inside, the detectors were out of order, and the security guard raised his hands in a gesture that said 'All this technology and what is it good for?' We laughed as I walked around.

The stairwells were patterned with repeating circle motifs. Upstairs, rooms jutted out over an open work area so you could look down at people below, sitting at the long timber desks. Beyond them, a huge expanse of windows let in the winter light. The space overhead, all that air, made me feel small.

In Australia, I was a research librarian. I loved libraries – they were epic buildings. All those books, floor-to-ceiling. Each volume a physical manifestation of an idea. It was humbling in a way that made me think of cathedrals. And all that organisation: if you knew what you were looking for, you could find it. Didn't matter if you were in another country with another language – it was all Dewey decimal.

There wasn't a line at the information desk so I walked straight to the counter, dropping my pack on the floor. The woman behind the computer didn't seem to care that it took me a moment to gather my thoughts. She wasn't in a hurry.

My Spanish was passable – Dad was a director in the Department of Foreign Affairs and had been stationed in Peru and Mexico when I was growing up – but I asked if she could speak English.

'*Claro*. Yes.'

I told her I was looking for information about family friends who had died in November 1977. A plane crash.

She nodded. With black metal glasses that matched her suit, she reminded me of my mother's friends: competent and stylish. She must have been in her late fifties. 'We have newspaper archives online and in microfiche. Can you read Spanish?'

'A little.'

'You can search the obituaries. Check the English-language ones first. My name is Julia.'

'Thank you.'

It was a quiet morning so she walked me to a computer terminal in a windowless room. I sat down and she reached over me for the mouse, entering a password and following links to the archives. She smelled of pressed powder. 'Good luck.'

I searched for my birth parents' names. Eduardo and Maria Menendez. Nothing.

Then I looked for articles about plane accidents, narrowing the date of publication. Still nothing.

Next, the obituaries. I scrolled through every edition of the English-language *Buenos Aires Herald* between September and December 1977. Then the Spanish equivalents – *Clarín* and *Crónica*. Two people with the surname 'Menendez' had died but one was a teenager in a car accident and the other an elderly man who suffered a heart attack.

I stopped at Julia's desk and thanked her.

She smiled. 'Any luck?'

I shook my head.

Her eyebrows lifted as though my lack of success reflected on her and the library. 'Who were they?'

'Friends of my mother,' I lied.

'And they died in an accident of airplanes – you're certain?'

I wasn't certain about anything. 'No.'

Julia was frowning, her forehead creased above her glasses. 'Were they political?'

'What?' I asked.

She studied me for a moment. 'Do you know about the Process of National Reorganization?'

'The "Dirty War"?' I knew a bit from my guidebook. Thirty thousand people had been kidnapped and murdered by the government in the 1970s and '80s for being left-wing.

'It might be worth talking to the Madres of the Plaza del Mayo,' Julia said.

I was confused. The Mothers of the Disappeared used to march in front of the presidential palace to protest the disappearance of their children.

Julia nodded. 'They coordinate all the records. I can call them.' She scrolled online as she picked up the phone. Her Spanish was quick and she motioned for me to write the names I was searching for on a piece of paper. She recited them clearly into the phone, spelling them out. Covering the mouthpiece, she looked at me. 'They have databases.'

'For what?' I asked.

She opened her mouth to answer but then grabbed my pen and began scribbling on the piece of paper. I couldn't read her writing or follow what she was saying – she was speaking too fast. Her voice would lift as she asked a question and she'd nod her head, eyes trained on me. I smiled, trying to convey a sense of appreciation, but I wanted to know what she was saying. Then she covered the mouthpiece. 'You should speak to them yourself.'

'Why?'

'Your mother's friends were held at La Cacha, a detention centre.' She glanced at her notes. 'According to records, police raided their home and took them into custody on 2 October 1977 and that's the last time they were seen. Their names appeared on a prisoner list that was smuggled out. Eduardo was a teacher at the university. He and Maria were members of the Revolutionary Workers' Party. Maria was eight months' pregnant . . .'

'What happened to the child?'

She looked up and I wondered if I'd been too careless – but she shrugged, the phone still tucked between her head and shoulder. 'It's in the courts now. Babies adopted in secret.

People in their thirties now, forced to take DNA tests, finding out their parents aren't really their parents. Imagine that. The Grandmothers established a national register to help families find each other. There's about five hundred missing children.'

❋

I had to sit in one of the red chairs in the study hall. It was too much to think about. My biological parents had probably been murdered and somehow I'd ended up with Mum and Dad. A couple of Australians. If it were true, and they had a friend who organised the adoption, you had to wonder how much they'd known. Were they having dinner parties with people who ran death squads? It didn't make sense – Mum had set up micro-enterprise schemes so women in the third world could start small businesses. Dad had overseen the establishment of twenty-five rural schools in Asia. We'd had arguments around the dinner table about paternalism – how much are you really helping a country when you try to fix their problems? – but my parents believed in free speech and the right of protest. They wouldn't have conspired with a military dictatorship. It wasn't possible.

I searched the library for English books about Argentina's Dirty War, and stashed them in my backpack. I walked around the detectors, smiling at the guard like we were still sharing the joke. Usually I hated people who stole books but I reckoned the library gods would forgive this one.

❋

In the outside foyer, a teenager with heavy eyeliner stood in the telephone booth, shouting at someone – a parent, I guessed – and snapping her gum. When she slammed the phone down and scurried out, the booth smelled of artificial strawberries and grease. I punched in the numbers on my card.

'Hello?'

'Hi, Dad.'

'Oh Emma.' An uncertain pause, then: 'How are you? How's Peru?'

The silver shelf beneath the phone had messages scratched into the surface. *José es un cabrón* – José is a prick. And then, below: *Te amo* – I love you.

'Changed my ticket. I'm in Argentina.' I had a clear view out the window to the street. It was a grey day but the sun was trying to push through the clouds. The lawn had been trimmed too close so the ground looked hard. Along the footpath, a mother pushed her pram in a slow, uneven rhythm. On the other side of the street, a teenager launched himself off the curb with his skateboard.

'You okay? Mum'll be home in about twenty minutes. She'd love to talk to you.'

I should have planned the phone call, figured out how to ease my parents into the conversation I needed to have. Instead, I heard my voice echoing down the line: 'You knew, didn't you?'

'What are you talking about?'

I kept my voice even. 'I'm at the National Library. There are no obituaries. No news reports. Nothing that corroborates the story of an airplane crash and certainly not a national disaster. But you know what? They're on prisoner lists as "disappeared".'

The silence was desperate. Hiccups of static echoed along the phone line.

Finally, 'I didn't know that.'

'You said it was complicated.'

The line was quiet for about twenty seconds. A schoolgirl with an armful of books made her way down the walkway. She stopped, watching the skateboarder. Dad sounded scared. 'Manuel organised it – he was in the government. He had the paperwork – we thought it was legitimate. Yes, it was strange that he appeared in the middle of the night with you all bundled up – but we thought that's how they did things in Argentina. And we were too busy to think about it – your mum had to run to the chemist for formula, we didn't even have nappies. You were so peaceful and assured, your dark eyes clear. It felt like you'd chosen us. And when we realised there were two birth certificates, one had been forged with our names, we figured your parents were dead. We couldn't raise an alarm – who knows what would have happened to you. You were alone. No one was going to love you more than we did.'

It took a moment to process what he was saying.

His voice wavered. 'We'd been trying for so long. You have no idea. We would have done anything for a child.' He corrected himself. 'For you.'

'What?' It'd been hard enough finding out I was adopted. This was too much.

He continued. 'I know. Your mum and I, we know. There's not a day that goes by that we don't think of Eduardo and Maria. The candles in the window, the tall thin ones your mother always burns, they're in honour of them. But Emma, the most horrifying decision of my life is the one I least regret. It brought you.'

'And if anyone finds out?'

'If it could be proved we knew anything ... There's no amnesty. You could murder people in the Dirty War, torture them – no worries. Former prisoners run into their guards at the supermarket. There's nothing they can do. But if you adopted a stolen child, the Grandmothers – they go crazy.'

'You wouldn't be extradited.'

'It's happened.'

'It's the press you're worried about.'

'What do you want me to say, Emma?' He was too defensive and I had to lean against the plastic booth behind me. I could feel the cold through my coat.

'The truth. I want you to tell me the truth.' I was shouting and begging at the same time.

'Yes, I'm scared this could get out. The *Herald* would run with it and it'd mean the end of everything.'

I thought of our fancy house on the north shore of Sydney and wanted to be sick. 'Helps when you have money, doesn't it?'

'I'm not going to apologise for loving you. If I were faced with the decision to make again, I wouldn't change anything. I wouldn't. Emma?'

I hung up the phone and stood there. The mother had parked her pram on the grass and was handing a sippy cup to her toddler. The schoolgirl was gone. The teenager was still trying to get his skateboard to spin beneath his feet. I didn't want to be in Argentina. I didn't want any of this.

I walked back to my hotel room and started reading more about the Grandmothers of the Disappeared. They'd lost both their children and grandchildren. Some of the women abducted were already pregnant, and others were raped in jail. From what I could tell, the Catholic Church had sanctioned the Dirty War – provided small or unborn children weren't targeted – so the guards had a situation where the parents needed to 'disappear' but not the children. They were illegally adopted out, many with no idea that an adoption had ever taken place.

I read through the testimonials. The Grandmothers knew their children were dead but they were banking on their grandchildren being alive. So, for the past thirty years, they'd been searching. One had worked as a maid in the house of someone suspected of an illegal adoption. Another had stalked a family for five years, sitting in the park across the street, while she waited for lawyers to find enough evidence to take it to court. I could imagine her, arriving early, claiming a green park bench with peeling paint, a thermos of coffee beside her. She'd watch out over the swings – sturdy black seats dangling from chunky metal chains – and wait, sometimes all day, for her grandchildren to sit in them. She'd hold her breath as they climbed the slippery dip and only exhale when they were released onto the safe patch of sand at the bottom. She learned early she had to bring needle-point and knitting because the longing was too apparent on her face – she needed to focus on something tangible to keep steady.

✳

The next morning I walked the same path back to the library, aware of how many people had tanned complexions like mine. Inside, Julia wasn't on shift – an uptight uni student was sitting behind the desk, with glasses so large they overwhelmed his face – and I didn't have it in me to lie through my story again. I left and walked aimlessly through Recoleta. At least now I understood why Mum and Dad hadn't told me about the adoption sooner. But it was clear my father's logic didn't hold up. Yes, my parents had been dead but that didn't mean I was without family. I could have an extended network searching for me. I might have siblings, grandparents, aunts and uncles.

And then there were my birth parents – Eduardo and Maria. What did Eduardo teach, I wondered. How did they meet? What had shaped them? The entire course of my life had followed an arc of consequence that began on 2 October 1977 – but I felt detached, like I'd been given the responsibility of narrating someone else's life. Did police ransack Eduardo and Maria's home? Were they handcuffed or did they walk freely down to the Ford Falcon that was waiting in the driveway? Fords were notoriously used by the death squads and this detail, something I would have skimmed over in a newspaper or journal article before, seemed ferocious and haunting.

I came upon Recoleta cemetery by accident. A small crowd were watching a pair of street performers in front of the cemetery gates. The couple were frozen, with wires in their clothes, coats bent out behind them as though they were facing into a windstorm. She was holding an umbrella that had blown inside out, his arms were reaching forward. They were completely still and yet it seemed they were being blown off their feet.

The blond man standing in front of me jostled his way to the front and dropped a fistful of notes into their hat. I was impressed with his generosity.

After watching the frozen couple work their way another five metres along the footpath in glacial increments, I decided to offer my respects to Evita, who was entombed in the cemetery. I paid extra for a map.

Inside, cats were lying in the winter sun like lazy protectors of the dead. Alleyways of graves stretched for city blocks. It was cleaner than the streets outside: the rubbish bins packed full, the ground swept. I meandered through the tombs until someone came up behind me and touched my arm. It was the blond from out front.

'Do you speak English?' He was so serious, so American. I must have smiled because he broke out in a grin. 'What, you think English is funny?'

My voice was deadpan. 'Hilarious.'

He had a round face and blue-green eyes that studied me for a moment like my sarcasm appealed to him. 'Australian?'

'Well done, usually I get asked if I'm a Kiwi. Hurts the national pride, that.'

He laughed, lifting his cap and smoothing the hair out of his eyes. 'Better a Kiwi than a Canadian.'

I wasn't flirting but the conversation was effortless. 'Don't know about that. I've always wanted to check out the Great White North. Beautiful mountains.' I pulled my scarf tight.

'If you want mountains, Argentina's the place.' He glanced behind him – another man, his friend I assumed, was studying a gravesite. 'Hey – did you get a map? We can't find Evita.'

I shook my head with exaggerated sincerity. 'I think she's dead.'

His eyes went wide with concern. 'Fuck – when did that happen?'

I couldn't help laughing and was surprised by how good it felt. My laugh erupted out of my throat – it was always too loud – but he didn't seem to notice. His offbeat humour was exactly what I needed after all the chaos with my family. I reached for the brochure that was stuffed in my daypack.

He smiled. He had big teeth, perfectly aligned – the product of braces in high school. 'I'm Jeremy.'

'Emma.'

'Nice to meet you.' His friend approached us and Jeremy held up his hand in introduction. 'This is John.'

'Hi.' John's voice was quiet. He wasn't as tall as Jeremy but he was trim, muscular. He wore loose jeans and a thin long-sleeved shirt as though he didn't feel the cold.

'Should we pay our respects?' Jeremy asked.

'Lead the way.' John's eyebrows lifted. He had an intensity about his angular face that made him seem prickly even when he was smiling. I liked that.

The three of us started walking along the tidy dirt path – Jeremy in the middle, setting the pace. We moved through the maze of gravesites, past an angel on top of a pillar. He was pointing forward like a compass – one arm outstretched, one foot lifted – directing the dead towards the afterlife. Something about the straight line of his body made me feel guilty for my earlier banter with the Americans. It wasn't respectful.

'When did you guys arrive here?' I asked.

Jeremy took a photo of the angel with his phone. 'A couple of days ago. We're headed to the Patagonia.'

'You been here before?'

Jeremy turned to me and snapped a photo before I had time

18

to argue. 'Third time. I'm writing a book about adventure sports in the Andes.'

John stood in front of the monument, reading the plaque. His dark hair fell in front of his face.

'How do you know each other?' I asked.

John caught up to us. 'Friends in high school.'

'Yeah and John's followed me like a bad smell ever since.' Jeremy waited as his friend punched him on the arm.

We found Evita's site – a white marble tomb the size of a small room. Someone had tucked carnations into the front gate and they were wilting. An Irish couple asked John to take a photo.

Jeremy looked at me and raised his eyebrows. Behind him, a jagged skyline of apartment boxes loomed in the distance. I thought we were sharing a joke, laughing at the tourists, but he said: 'What are you trying to escape, Emma? What did you leave back in Australia?'

I was appalled by my transparency. I didn't realise Jeremy was fishing, that this was the kind of question he asked people in an effort to catch them off guard. I would never have said anything but he was a stranger and that somehow made him feel safe.

'I just found out I'm adopted.' It was the first time my mouth had formed those words and I listened, amazed and relieved they could be dropped so easily into a conversation.

'Intense.' He spoke like my secret mattered but wasn't surprising – it was something to reckon with but it wasn't the end of the world. It made me want to tell him more but I wasn't sure where to begin.

There was a long pause as I grasped for something to say. 'How long are you guys here?' I couldn't remember if he'd told me or not.

'Another couple of days, then we're catching a train to Bariloche. We're going to hike the Nahuel Huapi circuit – a five-day walking trail through the mountains. There are cabins but we're going to camp. Most beautiful place in the world, they say.'

Jeremy waved towards John like he was ready to wrap things up. He glanced back to me. 'Hey, we're getting pizza. You want to join us?'

❋

I spent the next few mornings researching at the library. I arrived first thing, made my way to the databases and deciphered court transcripts with the help of my Spanish–English dictionary. Some children had always suspected they were adopted and undertook DNA testing themselves. Others were forced by judges, and wanted nothing to do with their newfound families. There was a famous pair of siblings who had been adopted by a media mogul and the Grandmothers were taking them to court. I spent hours poring over their story, staring at paparazzi shots of the brother and sister. Both had olive skin. He was balding – brown hair receding evenly over the dome of his forehead. She never wore make-up, her shoulder-length hair falling in her face. I liked her for the practical collared shirts she wore – she looked wholesome but tired. I couldn't imagine that kind of media frenzy.

At lunchtime, I'd meet up with Jeremy and John. We'd order takeaway *milanesa* sandwiches while Jeremy opened his guidebook to a random page, letting chance decide our next venture. We scoured the San Telmo markets and toured the soccer stadium at La Boca. We visited the brightly painted buildings on the wharves and watched tango dancers performing on the sidewalk. I liked being with the Americans because I could see Buenos Aires as a tourist – nothing more – and that was a relief.

John didn't talk much about himself but he told me he worked in construction and lived in the same town where he'd grown up. He spent a lot of time in New York with Jeremy, and I envied them their friendship. I'd gone to a private girls' school that could be characterised by its netball team: brassy and vicious. I know I didn't help things – I'd come straight from Bangladesh where I'd been volunteering with my mum in a women's refuge, and it'd been hard to take the North Shore seriously. But still, a friend who knew you in high school and loved you anyway? That would be nice.

Jeremy had no hesitation in talking about himself. He'd gone to Oxford for a Masters in Theology to spite his atheist parents and graduated a session early. He'd bought a subscription to the *Wall Street Journal* and started trading stocks – in less than a month, he'd made enough money to buy a flat off Times Square and the rent it brought in was paying for his trip. Now he was writing and self-publishing adventure guides.

'What about you?' Jeremy asked. We were standing in front of the tango dancers at La Boca. John was buying a photo at a street stall. 'What's so interesting at the library?'

I'd reached saturation point with it all and the words fell out of my mouth: 'I think my parents were killed in the Dirty War. I think my adoption was illegal.' I stood there, stunned that I'd said it out loud.

'That's horrible.'

Immediately I regretted saying anything. Of course it was horrible but I didn't like the way he said it. My Australian parents weren't monsters. I thought of Mum and her ugly Uncle Sam sweatshirt that said 'Support Your Radical Militant Librarian' and was surprised by how protective I felt.

'What happened?' Jeremy's voice was quiet and I realised he was just trying to be nice.

'Found my birth certificates.' I emphasised the 's'. 'Apparently there was a black market and my parents were supposed to destroy the original.'

'Why didn't they?'

'I don't know.'

'You going for a DNA test?' Of course he knew about Argentina's history – he was researching the place.

'I don't know.'

❊

The night before John and Jeremy were due to leave, we met up for dinner near Retiro station. It had been raining all day but the clouds had lifted in the late afternoon, giving the city a fresh, tangy smell. The restaurant was tucked in a winding alleyway littered with advertising brochures and grimy newspapers.

Jeremy held the glass door open for me. 'You are going to love this. It's a festival of meat. Platters of it.'

The place looked like a seedy diner even though white cloths covered the tables. The bar was packed with people, sitting in ones and twos, most of them with a silver tray between them. The bottom halves of the walls had been painted a garish shade of pink and the air smelled of onions and charcoal.

Jeremy ordered for the three of us without looking at the menu – the barbecue platter and a bottle of Mendoza Malbec. 'Just wait. Trust me.'

Once the food arrived, I could only focus on eating. The marinated beef was sliced thin so it was delicate, dissolving in my mouth – the smoky taste like an afterthought. The chicken was both tender and hearty. While I wouldn't have picked venison, the combination with the other meats was earthy, primal. I helped myself to seconds, then thirds.

Jeremy refilled our wineglasses. The red was a perfect complement for the meal. I wasn't drunk but the evening had a sense of quiet exuberance about it. Despite this, I was sad the Americans were leaving. They'd kept me sane over the past few days: a welcome distraction.

'I'm going to miss you guys.' I'd thought about asking to join them – I could have used some time away from the library. I wasn't sure what I was looking for anymore and the real question – whether or not to undertake a DNA test – wasn't going to be answered by spending any more time in the stacks. My guidebook raved about the Nahuel Huapi circuit. Cabins, known as refugios, were built along the path, each one a day's trek from the last. The hiking was manageable and the views were glorious: it sounded amazing.

'It's been good meeting you, Aussie.' Jeremy had a piece of meat caught between his teeth that he picked at with his finger.

John made a face at Jeremy's manners and turned to me. His dark eyes were intense. 'You should come with us.'

I waited, gauging Jeremy's reaction, and gestured like it was all a bit much. 'I don't know a lot about mountains.'

Jeremy rolled his eyes and it was obvious he was on board. 'You're an Australian. I'm surprised you even know what a mountain is. You can rent all the gear you need in Bariloche. We'll help you.'

Both men nodded. It seemed to make perfect sense: I should go to Bariloche.

❋

We caught the first-class double-decker bus first thing in the morning. As soon as we pulled out of the station, a steward trolleyed down the aisles, pouring glasses of champagne for all the passengers. The seats on the bus were extravagantly large with footrests that pulled out at night so you could lie horizontally. Their fuzzy fabric reminded me of the carpet in an RSL club.

We were on the upper floor. John had insisted on sitting alone so Jeremy and I were side-by-side, Jeremy next to the window. A few hours into the trip, the city buildings had dwindled and we were on the edge of the Pampa – the flat, empty fields in the middle of Argentina. Our bus felt vulnerable with the huge open sky overhead and I missed home. It was fucked, really. I missed my parents, and yet I couldn't stop thinking about that grandmother in the park. I could see her on the bench, legs crossed beneath her, eyes downcast, watching the knitting needles in her deft hands. All day, a shawl growing and growing. And then at night, after she was home, she'd unravel all her work so she'd have yarn for the morning.

Jeremy had fallen asleep and his leg was pressing against mine. I moved away but a few minutes later his knee was back, touching my thigh. I pushed him off but just as my hand touched his jeans, his eyes sprung open and he grabbed me by the wrist. 'What's going on, Emma?'

'What? No, I . . .'

'Hey, you can grope me anytime. Just wait until I'm awake, okay?'

I laughed. 'I'll try to control myself.'

'Hard, I know.'

We talked for a couple of hours – his hopes for the guidebook, the places I'd lived growing up. He asked about Dad's work with foreign affairs, Mum's business, her position on the board of the National Art Gallery. It was nice talking about them. And then the row of TV screens overhead switched on and opening credits to a Peter Sellers movie began to roll – it was in English. Jeremy high-fived me and we reclined our overstuffed chairs to watch.

❄

Bariloche was more of a town than a city, set on a beautiful smooth lake. Most of the buildings were rendered, many with off-white scallops etched into the cement. Their trims were dark brown and it seemed like we'd disembarked in a Bavarian village, especially with all the snow banked up on the footpath. We stayed at a hostel on the main street while we organised for the trek. Jeremy scored some pot and we spent our last night in town watching round robin games for the soccer World Cup.

The next morning we were up early, on the trail as daylight broke over the mountain. We were headed to Refugio Frey, the first cabin on the circuit. The opening stretch was steep and it took effort not to lag behind. The trail was marked with red circles painted on trees and rocks, but sometimes they were covered by snow, or the path forked. At these intersections, the Americans would stop to consult the map and compass, and I'd take advantage of a moment's rest.

For the most part, we shuffled on top of the ice in snow-shoes. After the climb, the path stretched through forest and I was able to stop concentrating on the physical mechanics of walking, and enjoy the place. The trees were stark against the white snow: ominous and beautiful at the same time. It was hard to imagine the foliage that must arrive with spring – the frost felt permanent and impenetrable. Then, well after lunch, the wood thinned and we dropped into a series of hollows, each bigger than the last.

The trek ended up taking eight hours. When we scaled the last peak, I was focused on my feet, thinking about my mother and how she'd been lighting candles my whole life – she'd find a windowsill in each house we moved to, as though sending a message out to the night. And I'd never asked why – that was the bit that got me. She was an atheist, I knew she wasn't praying. My adoption had been right in front of me, and I didn't even see it.

We were level with a cloudbank and it made me feel airborne. The proportions of land to sky had changed – trees had thinned and we were exposed. Standing on that cliff, with the valley spread out beneath us, I could just see the cabin below. It was tiny, barely visible – two hundred metres down – set in the middle of the basin floor, next to a lake. Its lights were glimmering in the late afternoon dusk, a beacon drawing us to safety. But you could see, even from where we were, its perimeter of safety only extended so far.

'Amazing,' John said, walking ahead.

The cold was throbbing in my fingers but I didn't want to leave the view.

Jeremy stood beside me like he was waiting to say something. 'Frightening, isn't it?'

'What do you mean?' It was frightening: how tiny we were in the grand scheme of things, how huge the snowscape was.

'All this quiet. All the nothingness. And we're alone. If something happened to you out here . . .'

It was true – if you slipped off the trail, who would know where to look? It was a disquieting thought.

We started walking after John, and I was relieved to be moving. The trail down had been cut into a cliff; even though the path was plenty wide, the steep drop gave the impression we were balancing on a precipice. I walked on the inside and we followed a series of switchbacks down to the river crossing. It was harder than I expected to navigate the steep pitch, and at one point I had to scoot across the snow on my bum.

At the river, there wasn't a bridge so we took turns stepping across the uneven stones, holding on to a chain that stretched overhead. We'd dropped in elevation and I could see the refugio better now. It was compact but sturdy. Two floors, each about thirty metres square. Rock walls and tomato-red shutters angled towards us. A heavy wooden door that could have belonged to a castle. It took another ten minutes and we were in front of it.

Jeremy dropped his backpack on the ground, unstrapping the tent.

John pushed his beanie back. 'You sure, Jer? Maybe we should check inside.'

'They might have a designated place,' I added.

Jeremy waved his hand, dismissive, and scanned for a good spot. 'It's getting dark. I don't want to do this by flashlight.'

John and I stood there for an awkward moment as Jeremy assembled the frame behind a rock wall. Finally John shrugged and we took turns pounding tent pegs into the frozen earth with a hammer. The novelty soon gave way to frustration but Jeremy and John were committed to sleeping outside.

'Think of back home – telling them about this,' John said when we finished the last one.

'Telling them what? I could have stayed inside, with a warm fire, but I chose to freeze to death instead?' I shook my head and we both laughed.

When the tent was up, I tramped across the snow to a large boulder. It was a good few feet taller than me and oblong, covered with icy patches. I scrambled up to have a look at where we'd come from. The path disappeared about halfway along, into a clump of green-black treetops. The sun had disappeared and the sky was intensifying into a lilac colour that was reflected in the snow. A tiny moon was hanging on the other edge of the horizon and I could feel the cold air in my chest.

I was so taken with the view I didn't hear anyone approach. It was only when I turned around that I saw a man of medium build talking to Jeremy. His face was round and reassuring. His eyes and hair dark. Our eyes met and I knew he'd seen me taking in the mountain. He nodded like he understood how beautiful this place was and knew the strength of the wilderness. I walked over and Jeremy introduced me to Pedro.

❄

Inside the cabin, the bottom floor was separated into a kitchen and a dining room, which served as a common area for guests. Two wide tables were tucked under the window.

Pedro introduced us to the German family sitting at one: Hita and Erik, and their three boys. They were playing a game of Monopoly. One boy was a teenager, fifteen or sixteen; and the others were younger, about six and ten years old. They'd been living in San Francisco before their big South American tour. It was weird seeing a family up there – like some Wizard of Oz cyclone had picked them up from a suburban yard and dropped them in the middle of the Andes.

Jeremy and John sat at the other table. Except for the games shelf, most of the storage was built-in cupboards overhead.

'You want a beer, Aussie?' John asked and I nodded.

A woman in her early twenties was standing in the door-way to the kitchen. It looked like whoever built the place had never bothered with a door – there was just a beaded curtain tied back with a hair ribbon between the two rooms. The woman walked over to perch on one of the benches next to the Germans. She had a long, thick braid, and moved with an air of entitlement I recognised from my private school days. I didn't like her.

'Emma, this is Carmen. She's a tango dancer from Buenos Aires,' Pedro said.

I nodded. 'Hi.'

The woman sniffed, staring at me. Her gaze was shrewd and she didn't say anything. About ten seconds passed, and I was surprised by her rudeness. But then I realised she probably didn't speak English and I was the jerk in the room – not her. She watched me like my thoughts had telegraphed across my face, and she wasn't impressed.

'Hola,' I stammered. But she stood up and walked back into the kitchen.

'O-kay . . .' I said, under my breath.

John plonked three cans of beer down and Jeremy leaned back against the plywood wall. It was covered with magazine photos of snowboarders and mountain climbers. The cabin felt masculine – the posters, the foreign beer cans balanced on the window ledge – but tidy. Someone had draped an Indonesian sarong in one of the corners.

We played cards and worked through a few more beers and a bottle of wine, and when we'd polished that off, John tipped the bottle upside-down. 'Another?'

'Why not,' Jeremy said.

John brushed himself off before ducking to the toilet. It was a separate building, about fifteen metres from the refugio. Pedro was in the kitchen and everyone else had disappeared upstairs to bed – Jeremy and I were alone. I was thinking about my parents back home – I was grateful Mum and Dad had raised me. I liked my life but it was a life predicated on death. That thought scared me.

Jeremy stood up. I thought he was headed to the kitchen but then I felt a pair of hands kneading my shoulders.

I shrugged him off. 'What are you doing?'

'Emma, you're so pretty.'

My voice was wry. 'It'd have nothing to do with those beers tonight.'

He raised his hands in surrender, but then smiled like he'd had a really good idea. 'John could sleep inside tonight.'

I shook my head. 'No way.'

'I'm serious.'

'So am I, dork.' I was laughing but he was creeping me out. I didn't want to deal with this.

He was staring at me. 'You're not seeing anyone.' It was more statement than question. I'd dodged the topic in Buenos Aires. It'd been a couple of years since there'd been anything of substance on that front but I wasn't going to tell him that.

He climbed over the bench and sat down, his leg pressing against mine. 'What are you going to do about being adopted?'

I edged back. 'What is there to do?'

'You going to get a DNA test?'

'No. I don't think I can.' I was surprised by my certainty. A DNA test seemed like the ethically sound choice. Mum and Dad should be held accountable. That grandmother, sitting in the park: she haunted me. But a DNA test would become the defining moment in our family history. A landmark case for international lawyers. A feeding frenzy for the press. No matter how angry I was with my parents, they were good people. I couldn't do that to them. I thought of the brother and sister I'd read about at the library, shielding their faces from the paparazzi as they left court.

Jeremy brushed my arm with the back of his hand. 'There's a lot at stake, Emma.'

I wanted to push him away but I couldn't move. 'What are you talking about?'

'Your parents sound important. All it would take is a phone call. If the Grandmothers have a suspicion, they can take it to court.'

'What?'

He raised his eyebrows and it dawned on me: Jeremy was capable of anything. I couldn't believe how stupid I'd been. I couldn't believe I'd trusted him.

His hand was resting on my arm, his gaze trained on my face. 'Think about it.'

I shook my head and laughed like he was joking, but inside I was panicking. I couldn't figure out what, exactly, was being negotiated. 'I'm going to the toilet.'

On my way back, I shifted my stuff in the tent so I'd be sleeping next to John.

❄

The following morning, we'd planned to hike to the next cabin but there was a warm snap, which meant avalanche danger, and all of the guests were bound to the area around the lake where the gradation was less than forty-five degrees. I was re-thinking the trip – I didn't want to spend any more time with Jeremy.

The Americans set up court in the dining room. We weren't paying to stay inside but Jeremy had claimed one of the tables anyway. It was the slow season, he said. No one would care. But I wondered how much Jeremy wanted to be sitting in the dining room and how much of it was proving he could. It may have been winter, with fewer guests, but there was no escape and every bit of space mattered.

The Americans befriended the German teenager, Jack, and the three of them disappeared to smoke pot while I read in the dining room. Later they went sledding, and when they didn't invite me I was glad. I spent the afternoon in the kitchen, sitting on the counter, while Pedro cooked dinner and tallied up bills, counting out change from an old cigar box. It didn't look like the refugio was turning much of a profit. I'd decided to play it cool with Jeremy and John, pretend everything was fine, but I'd have to tell them sooner or later that I wasn't hiking on.

After dinner, we were sitting around the table when Pedro bustled by, his arms full with freshly washed serving plates and bowls.

Jeremy was looking at the map and planning the next day's route. 'We head back along the refugio trail and hook up with the main one. That'll take us over the next ridge. With snow-shoes, we're looking at another eight hours.' He didn't notice when Pedro needed to shift in front of him.

Pedro waited another moment, then stepped forward. He was polite but it was forced. 'Excuse me.' His voice was low, his black hair pulled back in a short ponytail.

Jeremy moved so Pedro could edge ahead, but he rolled his eyes and made a fist behind Pedro's back like he was going to take him down. I knew it was a joke but there was aggression to it and I wondered if Jeremy was pissed off that I'd spent the afternoon in the kitchen, helping Pedro cook dinner. I finished off the dregs of my beer and shook my head.

At the second table, the German family was playing another game of Monopoly. The three boys had tried to get Carmen, the tango dancer, to join them but she'd gone to bed early. That was the thing with the refugio – it was so small you couldn't help knowing what everyone was doing. I wouldn't want to be here in summer: with any more people, they'd have to eat in shifts.

Now John was staring at the map. He sighed and gathered the cards to deal another hand. Jeremy took this as a sign to continue. 'After that, we follow the markers.'

Pedro stepped back and his voice was louder than before. 'You shouldn't leave.' He pointed at a series of curves on Jeremy's map. 'The snow isn't stable here right now. I'd wait a couple of days. See what it does.'

Jeremy made a face. 'I did a shear test this afternoon. It came in at grade yellow.'

Pedro looked at him like everyone was in agreement. 'Yes. Yellow – moderate danger.'

Jeremy laughed. 'Yellow's nothing. I've hiked through grade red.'

Pedro picked up the empty beer cans in front of us. 'Then you're lucky to be here.'

'Maybe.' Jeremy broke off the ring of his Quilmes can and dropped it inside. His tone was light, joking.

When I took our camping plates to the sink, Pedro was wiping down the counters. We were the same height, our eyes level, and he moved aside so I could get to the sink. He smelled of campfires and wool, and when he smiled his top row of teeth showed.

Pedro cleared his throat and looked up from the pocked wooden counter. 'Behind the refugio and around the lake – the slope is gradual. But the track back to the main trail, the one you came in on, it cuts into a cliff that is almost vertical ...' It was steep: I remembered scaling down it with the boys when we arrived.

Erik, the German father, ambled in with a red mug and filled it straight from the twenty-gallon water drum. He had big ears that made it hard to take him seriously but he was an outdoor nut, keen on teaching his boys to cross-country ski. He leaned against the counter, his tall frame clumsy in the small kitchen. 'Pedro is right. Cerro Blanco is not stable. Layers of snow are like sedimentary rock. One metre solid, like fudge. Under that, soft powder. If that solid piece cracks ...'

Pedro hung his dish towel on a rusted nail. 'Snow falls in layers. Maybe the top one looks fine but there are more below. A warm day melts them ...' He balled his fists together, one slipping off the other to demonstrate. 'It's weather that tempts avalanches. Tell your friends it's not safe to leave.'

'Okay.' I had no intention of doing this. I wanted Jeremy out of the refugio. If the Americans were stupid enough to hike into an avalanche that was their problem.

Pedro tossed the sponge into the sink. 'There's room upstairs if you want to stay.'

'Thanks. I will.' It was a relief to have this sorted. I wasn't trapped with Jeremy and John. They'd leave. I'd stay and hike down in a few days with Pedro or the Germans. Everything would be fine.

Pedro looked at me for a moment without speaking, then smiled. 'Okay then.'

Back at the table, Jeremy was reclining and John was staring at the four piles of cards in front of him, kings on top: he'd finally won.

John grabbed his hands behind his back to stretch. 'Is there another way out?'

Jeremy made a face. 'Not if you want the luxury of a trail. Don't worry, Pedro's just looking to keep us here, make a few extra bucks.' Jeremy reached over and drained my beer, slamming the can down.

I took a deep breath and tried to keep my voice light. 'I'm not feeling so well. Think I'll stay at the refugio. Hike back to Bariloche in a couple of days and meet you guys down there.'

Jeremy looked up and winked at me, his eyes smooth like washed sea glass. 'Come on, Emma. Where's your sense of adventure?'

I shifted my gaze between the two of them. 'You guys'll be fine. I'm not worried about avalanches. But the climb was a bit much for me – I don't want to slow you down.'

Jeremy rolled his eyes. 'Seriously?'

John twisted his leather bracelet tighter around his wrist. 'Are you worried about the snow?'

I was frightened by the landscape – it was so striking and foreign – but I didn't want to give the boys any reason to stay. Before I could answer, Jeremy breezed in. 'Nothing is stable, my friend. This place is Pedro's life and it's winter. It totally makes sense he'd want us to stay a couple of extra days. Well, I feel for him and all but no can do.' He held up the beer can and crushed it as a joke. He continued. 'But I want to know: why is our dear Australian deserting us?'

'I'm not.'

Jeremy watched me. 'You think I'm going to tell everyone you're adopted?'

My mouth opened.

'Don't worry, Aussie. Your secret's safe with me. And John.'

I looked at John, who half-smiled. He'd known. He'd known and hadn't let on – that felt as sinister as the fact Jeremy had said anything.

Pedro came in from the kitchen and bent down to check the

stove. Above him, boots and socks were hanging from a metal shelf, drying out. A homemade guitar was hooked on a peg to his left. As he loaded more wood onto the fire, I cleared my throat. 'I've told Pedro I'm staying.'

'Really?' John asked.

Jeremy leaned towards me. 'Come with us.'

'I told you, I'm not feeling well.'

'We'll take it slow.' I didn't like the way he was sizing me up. I didn't like the sexual innuendo in his voice.

I smiled like I had no understanding of subtext. If I pretended things were fine, they might end up that way. 'I'm going to miss you guys. I'll wait for you at the hostel and you can tell me about the rest of the hike.'

❄

Preparing for bed was uneventful. We burrowed into our sleeping bags and the boys were soon snoring, but I couldn't get comfortable. I could imagine Jeremy contacting the Grandmothers whether or not I slept with him – he was the kind of person who liked to see his effect on the world. I'd been an idiot for telling him anything. A judge would order me to take a DNA test. I'd have to face a family I wasn't ready to know, and my parents could be extradited. Dad was a public servant – there would be an inquiry at the very least. We would lose years of our lives fighting this.

My sleep was filled with night terrors set in courtrooms. When I woke, clammy and exhausted, the boys were already bustling outside. I dressed inside my sleeping bag, pulling on my thermals and a heavy wool and cashmere sweater Jeremy had given me back in Buenos Aires.

Outside, the clouds were thick and low, which kept things moderately warm, but it hadn't begun snowing yet. I hoisted my pack out onto the dirty white ground while John ducked in and fished out the last of their stuff.

'We're ready to take her down,' Jeremy said, pulling out a peg and collapsing the back half of the tent on John.

'Hey fucker,' John called, climbing through the fabric, while Jeremy gathered the tent pegs.

'You going in for breakfast?' I asked.

'Already eaten.'

I grabbed my pack and made my way along the makeshift rock wall. The dormitories were upstairs, one on either side of the stairwell. I pushed open the right-hand door. The room was dark and smelled of wet clothes and wood. Beneath that, the odour of mould. There were bunks against one wall, with foam pads laid side-by-side on each level, nothing between them. If the place was packed, your neighbour could just roll on top of you in the middle of the night – whoever designed it had no concept of personal space. Argentina was a funny place: part first-world, part third-world. There was a thin corridor to the far wall where a tiny window looked out towards the toilets. I lifted my gear onto a top bunk and dust motes drifted up from the battered mattress. The rails were round and uneven like little tree trunks.

Pedro had been right, there was space: only one sleeping bag was stretched out on the bottom bunk. It must have been Carmen's. I wasn't eager to share a room with her but pulled my bag out of the stuff sack, and laid it above like I was claiming some sense of home.

I'd just unpacked a wet jumper and hung it on the rail when Jeremy called out from below. 'You going to see us off or what?'

I eased down the uneven stairs, bracing my hands on the low ceiling. Jeremy was waiting with his arms stretched across the open doorway, cold air gusting past him.

'That was quick,' I said, as though this were disappointing news.

He grinned and stepped forward, wrapping his thick arms around me. His voice, muffled into the collar of my sweater, was final. 'It's been fun.'

John was standing just behind, outside. The snow had started, making a soft shell on his beanie. I hugged him – his arms gripped me back, forcing the air out of my chest. 'You don't have to worry – Jeremy won't say anything. He's got your back.'

I forced a smile.

'We'll see you in Bariloche? At the hostel?' John asked.

'Sure thing,' I lied.

Pedro's voice cut across the snow. 'You guys, it's not safe to leave.' There was a second entrance to the refugio, connected to the kitchen. Pedro was standing on the lip of the doorway.

Jeremy ignored him and pulled on his pack. Pedro walked across the gravel snow and grabbed his arm. 'Only a total *imbecil* would walk into that.'

Jeremy just stared at him. 'Let go of me.' There was violence in his voice. His opposite hand was clenched.

Pedro was at least four inches shorter than Jeremy, without the swagger, but he wasn't backing down. I wouldn't have picked it, but the Argentinean seemed ready for a fight. His intensity was frightening. The two men stood motionless as the snow floated around them, breath steaming from their nostrils.

John glanced at me. For a crazy moment, I had no idea what was going to happen – I was fascinated and appalled. It wasn't until Jeremy stepped back and rolled his shoulders that the air between them relaxed.

I wasn't happy. I thought he'd decided to stay another night. But Jeremy turned to the path. He glanced at me and set one foot down as though trying it out, seeing whether the icy snow could hold him. Then he moved forward again. 'What are you going to do, little man? Just what are you going to do?'

I was cheering inside. Go, I thought. Leave.

Pedro shook his head like he couldn't believe their stupidity. But there was something else in his expression, and I wondered if he was disappointed things hadn't erupted with the Americans. Something had gone down between them earlier, it seemed, something I didn't know about.

Jeremy only paused to look over his shoulder at me, winking. 'Have fun at the refugio, Aussie.'

His stride was long and certain, like he was proving something to the world, and John followed behind.

❄

And then, two hours later, Pedro and I were back at the cabin. I couldn't believe it all – the avalanche, the search, the possibility that John and Jeremy could be dead. Pedro ducked upstairs and I traipsed into the dining room. It was empty but I could hear energetic footsteps overhead – the Germans. That morning the Americans were packing their stuff and messing around in front of the porch and now they were gone. I told them it'd be fine. I wanted them to leave. If they were dead, part of that was on me. I was too exhausted to cry but I was crying anyway. The door creaked open behind me and I felt Pedro's arm around my shoulder.

'I'll check the radio. Talk to Club Andino,' he said.

I didn't want him to leave. I was afraid of being alone, stranded in the middle of the room. Spasms were jerking through the muscles in my legs – but sitting at John and Jeremy's table felt disrespectful so I tottered over to the other one.

Outside, the snow had started again – quick and heavy. Pedro ducked out of the kitchen. 'The radio's broken.'

'What?' I said.

He was rubbing his forehead like he couldn't believe it himself. 'Someone's opened the back, pulled the wires out. Your friends, I think.'

I was surprised – why would Jeremy and John do that?
'Maybe it was dropped.'

'No. This was deliberate.'

'Can it be fixed?'

'I'll try.' He didn't sound optimistic.

'What about a back-up?'

'This is the back-up. The other one is in town being repaired; it kept losing signal.'

My voice was too loud, an alarm. 'We don't have a radio? We're fucked without a radio.'

Pedro opened his mouth like he was going to try and talk me round but then nodded instead. There was no chance of help for the boys, and we wouldn't be able to get word on weather conditions. The bottom line: we had no connection to the outside world.

'I'm going to talk to Erik. Maybe he brought a radio,' Pedro said.

Two of the German boys traipsed in then, leaving the door to the stairwell open. Pedro nodded to me over their heads and pulled the door closed behind him. I couldn't let the kids see my terror. The youngest, the six-year-old, stripped off his hand-knit sweater and unlaced his boots to join me at the table. He was grinning like I'd made some gesture of friendship by sitting in his spot.

'Dad says there could have been an avalanche on the trail.'

'Yeah.' It took effort to get that one syllable out. 'What are your names again?' I asked to change the topic.

'I'm Felix and this is Klaus.'

I smiled, concentrating on that, anything to bring me back to the reality of the dining room. I tried to remember the last time I'd spoken to someone under twenty. 'Emma.'

'I know.' He rolled his eyes and started cracking up like adults were just too funny. Both boys had their father's ears and gangly arms – no chance of them being adopted – but Felix had dark eyes that gave his face warmth. His cheeks were covered in freckles and his top front teeth were growing in – big, jagged squares.

Felix was staring at me. 'Where are you from?'

'Australia.'

He scratched his head. 'I've never been to Australia. Do you have chess there?'

'Yeah.'

'Do you want to watch? I'm playing Klaus.'

It was disturbing, the idea of watching something as everyday as a chess game when Jeremy and John might be under all that snow, but there was nothing I could do. I'd told them to go.

Felix said something in German to his brother. Klaus sighed, shifting the chessboard into position.

During the game, Klaus moved his pieces quickly while Felix concentrated on each move, staring at his brother's hands as though they might give something away. After fifteen minutes, when Klaus pounced on Felix's king, the little boy smacked himself on the forehead and said 'Aye, aye, aye . . . I have fallen for his charms again,' and rolled onto the floor, pretending to be dead.

A few seconds later, the door creaked open and he squinted one eye from the grave to see who was coming in. It was their elder brother, a teenager with an angry eyebrow ring. His hair was verging on dreadlocks, tied back with a piece of string.

Felix peered up from the floor and croaked: 'You have to call him Jack.'

Jack kicked his brother lightly and rebuffed him in German.

Felix translated. 'He says it's bad manners to pretend you're dead when real people could be dead. *Ich bedaure.*'

Hearing it said aloud made me feel sick.

'And Pedro says we don't have a radio.' It wasn't clear if Jack was talking to me or not. His English was strong, fluent even. He pulled his brother up, moving with surprising grace, his slender torso emphasised by his snug Jimi Hendrix t-shirt.

Beyond the dining room window, the lake was frozen and dark. Snow dusted its surface and hung in a careful shelf along its edge, making a crisp line. There were a couple of iced-over shrubs dotted around the lake's circumference but the boundary was severe. The lake was the only flat place out here, defensive, like it was trying to hold back the mountains.

Pedro bustled through to the kitchen, making eye contact with me.

Felix slapped at Jack's back. The teenager spun around, catching his brother. 'Come on, let's sit down.'

I stood so they could have my spot and shifted to the kitchen doorway. Pedro didn't look up as I stepped inside. He was already making lunch, onions simmering in a big pot over the gas stove. The smell of garlic caught an invisible current; it was warm and comforting.

'I should have told them to stay,' I said.

He watched my face as he moved from the stove to the herb rack, picking out the oregano. 'They're adults.'

I wanted him to keep talking, distract me from the three or four seconds when I was standing on the front porch and heard that roar. The details were so careless: the dirty can of cigarette butts by my feet, the slippery wooden mat. All of it so everyday and ordinary, and then that ear-splitting moment that made me look up.

'Can you set these on the table?' Pedro handed me a stack of mismatched plates and I carried them out.

'We going to eat here?' I asked the boys. I wanted to leave the other table open, uncluttered, but Felix moved his chessboard onto the bench where John had sat. I waited for a supportive smile from Jack but he just scowled. I didn't like the spiked dog collar around his neck, and the interaction – or lack thereof – left me feeling uneasy.

A little while later, Hita, their mother, came in. Her straight-leg trousers made from quick-drying adventure fabric emphasised her large, flat bum but she wasn't the kind of woman who cared. She surveyed the table. 'We ready?' Her words were like a command.

I nodded.

She summoned everyone and we crowded around the table. The room felt smaller and stuffier. The Germans hovered at one end, and I sat at the other, across from Carmen. My new roommate was tall, with posture so straight it gave the impression she was profoundly uptight. She looked at me without smiling.

Pedro came in and stood at the head of the table, clearing his throat to hush Felix and Klaus.

When everyone was quiet, he spoke. 'There was an avalanche this morning. We don't know – it might have taken the Americans. Emma and I saw it. We searched for over an hour but we triggered another slide. No one will be able to leave until the snow pack stabilises. Please don't hike in front of the refugio, along Cerro Blanco, where it is steep. Stay near the lake.'

Erik leaned forward. 'Maybe we dig for them?'

'More weight, we can't risk it.'

Jack smacked the table with his hands. The wood was heavy, dulling the sound, but he made sure he had everyone's attention. 'You're going to let them die?'

Pedro kept an even tone. 'We don't know. Maybe they've hiked out.'

'But—'

Erik interrupted. 'It's much to risk, Jack. Pedro is right. It's most safe to hike in places that are flat, where the incline is less than forty-five degrees and—'

If Erik was trying to turn this into a lesson on snow survival for his kids, Hita wasn't going to have it. She wanted clear answers so she could make a clear decision. 'How long?' She leaned forward as though the conversation were just between her and Pedro. 'How long will we be here?'

'A couple of days, maybe longer.'

'I think longer,' Erik said. 'Maybe we stay one week. Maybe two.'

Hita shook her head, her green plastic glasses emphasising the slow movement. A lock of wavy red-blonde hair fell out from her clip.

Pedro glanced back to the kitchen.

Jack sighed. 'So we're trapped. We come around the world and we're stuck on the side of a mountain – and we're the lucky ones. Some holiday this turned out to be.'

I was having trouble taking it all in when Felix picked up his plate and moved so he was right next to me. He tugged at my sweater and I lowered my head. His voice was scratchy in my ear: 'I love the spaghetti. L-O-V-E.' He grabbed my hand under the table, squeezing it.

Pedro walked to the kitchen and came back with a giant bowl of bolognese.

'Boys, wait until everyone's served,' Hita said, before adding something in German. Even though we were in Argentina, the refugio had become an international, or extra-national, place and English was the only language we all had in common.

Hita stretched across the table for the jug of water. Her tone was like a reprimand. 'Are you cold, Hans? You want a sweater?'

'It's Jack.'

She took a patient breath. 'Jack. You want a sweater?'

He stared back at her, haughty. 'Thank you, *Mutter*. I'm fine.'

She shook her head and her whole body seemed part of the motion. She and Erik ordered beers, and I nodded along.

Jack clacked a tongue piercing against his teeth. 'I'd like a beer, too.'

Hita spoke sharply in German and Jack looked out of the window without replying.

The pasta was rich and warm; Pedro had done well. But I didn't feel like eating. Every time I reached for something across the table, my shoulder ached from digging and that reminded me of John and Jeremy.

Pedro set the beers down one at a time. The lager was soothing, its bubbles light on my throat. I drank almost half the can in one go; weariness and warmth pooled through my body.

Felix and Klaus were seeing who could get the most spaghetti onto their forks and into their mouths. Felix was looping the thin tentacles with his finger before they could fall off.

I caught Carmen's eye and said 'Hola' quickly.

She gave me a wary look across the table. Her heavy acrylic nails and purple eye shadow were distracting. 'I can speak English.'

I waited for her to continue but she didn't. Her palms were pressing flat on the table.

'Have you come here before? To the refugio?' I asked.

Carmen waited, as Jack handed her a plate with spaghetti. He was sitting next to her and whispered something in her ear – it was unsettling. She looked at me. 'Your friends, the Americans, you were close?'

She watched me like my answer mattered, like I was being judged, and I wondered if she'd spent time with Jeremy and John. Maybe they'd become friends.

'We met in Buenos Aires.' I got up to see if I could help Pedro in the kitchen and found him staring at the overturned radio. It was an old machine. One of the knobs rolled loose and fell on the floor. He cursed and I slipped back into the dining room.

Jack watched me sit down. 'You think they're dead?'

Everyone at the table was staring at me. Of course I hoped they were alive, I had been out there digging in the snow with Pedro. But then I thought of Jeremy at the dining table, his leg pressed against mine as he talked about my adoption. It was appalling but part of me felt safer with him dead.

'They're alive.' My beer can was empty, but I pretended to take another sip as though the conversation were finished.

Jack leaned forward. He'd been hanging around with Jeremy and John, talking about ski resorts and snowboards. 'Wouldn't listen. You heard them last night – wouldn't listen to Pedro.'

I was grateful for his words. I wanted him to tell me they made their own choices, they were fools and I wasn't responsible for them. But it was too much power to give a teenager and for a weird moment it was like he knew it.

Jack opened his mouth but his mother cut him off. 'Hans.'

'Jack.'

Felix clapped his hands together twice. 'He likes to be called Jack because that's his favourite writer. Jack Kerouac.'

Jack ignored everyone else at the table and kept his eyes focused on me, like I was something that had finally proved interesting. 'You told them it was safe to leave. You said they'd be fine. Why did you do that?'

I didn't know what to say: I was afraid they were dead and I was afraid they were alive. Outside, on the other side of the lake, sun glinted off the small peaks. I turned back to Jack. His silver eyebrow ring caught the light, giving the left side of his face more weight than the right. My voice sounded like it belonged to someone else. 'Whatever I'd said – it wouldn't have made a difference.'

❄

I took a dreamless nap that afternoon and slept straight through, waking briefly in the middle of the night. Outside, the moon hovered beneath the clouds, lopsided, like someone had pressed into the sky with a rubber stamp. I could hear Carmen breathing but otherwise the refugio was still. When I woke again it was light and Carmen had moved up to a top bunk. She must have been quiet climbing the ladder because I hadn't heard her. A book was open on her lap.

My arms stretched out of the sleeping bag. 'What are you doing up here?'

She smiled like I'd just told her how beautiful she was. She was pretty – there was something shiny about her eyes that would suit diamonds.

Carmen slammed her book closed, a bookmark poking out. Her head nodded towards the window. 'Needed light to read . . .'

She pressed the lobes of her ears, tugging on her earrings, and then drew a breath like there were other things to consider. 'The snow last night, it was falling and falling. We might not be able to leave the refugio – even to walk outside . . .' She watched me like this news had some deeper meaning but I was still stuck on the fact that she was talking to me. I didn't trust her.

'No.'

'We might be trapped. It could be weeks. You must return to Australia, no? Your family would worry?'

I didn't want to talk about my family. 'Where did you grow up?'

'Recoleta.'

She must have been rich if she came from Recoleta. After the cemetery, I'd explored the neighbourhood with Jeremy and John. It was all boutiques and cobbled streets. The hotels had lobbies so fancy we toured them like museums.

'You're a dancer?' I climbed out of my sleeping bag and hopped down. Even inside, my breath fogged into the air. I reached for my beanie and started layering up with long johns.

'Modern and tango.' She kicked her feet out in evidence. 'I love it. Four evening shows a week. And when I'm waiting for the music to start, everything falls away.'

'What are you doing here?'

Carmen rubbed her forehead like she was trying to erase something. 'At the refugio? I used to come to Bariloche as a child. It's a holiday place for *porteños*, people who live in Buenos Aires. My family would catch the plane here. But now . . . it's just me. Your parents, what are their occupations?'

I didn't like that she kept bringing up my family. 'Dad's a public servant. Foreign Affairs. Mum runs a company.'

'Ay . . . You are close?'

I didn't know how to answer that. I felt betrayed and protective in degrees that were catastrophic. 'Yes.'

She sighed. 'Perhaps it's too easy to judge our parents. My father destroyed himself for work. My mother lives in denial. I judge them. It's that simple. But you must ask yourself: how much do you forgive your parents when they carry guilt? How much do you protect them?'

It hit me: Jeremy had told her everything. I tried to swallow but my mouth was dry. I watched her, horrified, but she just edged to the rail and hung her legs over. 'The decisions you make determine the person you are. People think it's the other way around. No.'

I tried to focus on what she was saying but my mind was spinning. 'You knew the Americans?'

She seemed surprised but her gaze zeroed in on me, her eyes narrow. 'Better than you, I think.'

It didn't make sense. 'How? When did you talk to them?'

She shook her head like it wasn't worth the time it would take to explain, and jumped off the bunk. 'See you at breakfast.'

❄

In the dining room, Jack was reading on the floor while Felix and Klaus pushed for a game of snow soccer – they wanted to pitch broom handles in the snow for goals. The conversation took place in German, but they were gesturing, and Klaus was balancing a ball on his finger.

Carmen was right: Hita wasn't taking chances with the weather and everyone was staying inside. This wasn't welcome news – the only heated areas were the dining room and kitchen, and they were connected by the open doorway. I sat far back in the corner, holding a plate with my toast. Carmen must have been in the kitchen: I could hear her talking about the World Cup soccer with Erik and Pedro.

A few minutes later Pedro emerged with a mug of tea, and set it on the red-and-white plastic tablecloth before me. I piled in a heaped spoon of powdered milk, crushing the biggest lumps.

He pulled out the bench and sat opposite, his elbows on the table. 'I'm glad to see you awake.'

'Good morning. Any news?'

'Radio still broken.'

I stirred the tea. 'Anything I can do?'

'Talk to the heavens about this snow?'

'I'll get onto it.'

Pedro smiled. In front of us, Klaus pretended to throw the ball at Felix, who reeled over to our table as though he'd been struck. 'Doh, I've been hit.'

He raised one hand and whispered behind it. 'Don't worry, I'm not dying. Don't tell Jack I'm dying because I'm not. It's only a surface wound.' He tried winking but just blinked his long lashes.

Pedro pushed the sleeves of his sweater along his forearms. His skin was smooth, his digital watch small on his wrist. 'I'll let you know if anything changes.' He stood, and I concentrated on spreading jam on my toast. I didn't want him to leave. I felt safer when he was in the room.

Pedro disappeared into the kitchen, squeezing past Erik, who was standing in the doorway. Erik crossed the room and pulled another chessboard from the games shelf. 'You boys are ready?'

Felix started groaning. 'Not again.'

His father stopped, like he was consulting a long list of indoor activities. 'Hmm . . . I challenge Klaus to chess. What do you want to do?'

'Draw. I want to draw with Jack.'

Jack bent down a page of his book and grabbed his little brother around the neck. 'Where's your paper, Little Fox?'

'On the games shelf.'

'We can't draw if it's over there, can we?'

Felix bobbed across the room and returned with an unlined notebook and a bundle of bright felt-tip textas held together with a rubber band. As he opened the pages, he watched the blank paper as though its potential had dramatically increased now that Jack was involved. 'Show me some magical shapes.'

'I think I can manage that,' Jack said.

I stretched, watching the two of them with their heads bent over the notebook. Erik and Klaus were beside them, with chess pieces at attention.

The morning moved slowly, following an uneasy rotation. I'd get fed up with the boys clamouring in the dining room and I'd move to the kitchen where Hita was revising the family itinerary on the counter. When I lost interest in that, I'd go upstairs and crawl into my sleeping bag to keep warm. Perhaps a trip outside to the toilet. Then I'd head back to the dining room and start the cycle again. I had too much time to think – wondering if the Americans had made it out, wondering if we'd make it out. A sense of dread hung over the refugio.

Finally it was afternoon. I was downstairs in the dining room, which was empty except for Jack, who was reading at the other table. Felix and Klaus were upstairs with their parents – I could hear them jumping off the bed, landing directly overhead – and Carmen was in our room. I was giving her a wide berth. Pedro brought out a battered kettle filled with hot water and set it on a tea towel. 'You want a *maté*?'

I tried to smile. I'd been playing solitaire with a deck I'd just put together from spare ones on the games shelf. John and I had made one our first night here, piecing together cards to make the full fifty-two. The backs were varied – some showed British country landscapes, others tropical fish and, my favourite, Las Vegas showgirls.

'Look at you, all the way in the Andes,' John had said to a black-haired beauty named Scarlet, her autograph splashed across the bottom corner of the card.

Our deck was still on the games shelf, but I felt superstitious using it and had counted out another. It made me wonder: was John at the next refugio, counting out cards, or was he just outside, trapped under the ice?

Pedro set a silver cup on the table. It was shaped like a stocky hourglass, rounded in the middle, and already packed with *yerba maté*. As far as I'd been able to tell, the loose leaves were an Argentinean equivalent of tea. He shook the contents against his fingers to clear out any dust and pushed in the *bombilla* metal straw. The set-up looked like an elaborate prop to smoke hashish, as Jeremy had wryly noted in Buenos Aires, but Pedro treated it as a ritual. In Argentina everyone who drinks from the *maté* cup shares the straw.

Pedro poured the water in and air bubbles sprang to the surface. He drained the cup with one long sip and filled it again, passing it to me. The hot straw burned my tongue and I took a slower, more tentative sip. The *maté* was cut with peppermint so it was less bitter than the other times I'd tried it. I liked it for the strong buzz, but that afternoon, it felt like I was drinking high-powered agitation. Pedro glanced over to the stove.

'I put a log on before,' I said. 'It's fine. What's it like here in summer? Must get crowded.'

'It feels like that now because we're trapped inside. With warm weather, people come to be outside. They camp, they cook. There's a lot of space around the refugio. It's busy in summer. The dormitories fill. But people only stay one night, maybe two.'

His fingers drummed the edge of the table.

'Where are you from, Pedro?'

His hands stopped moving and he made a face like I'd asked him something awkward. 'What do you mean?'

'Did you grow up nearby?' Pedro was the one person here who seemed solid to me, who I could trust. I wanted to know more about him.

'I'm from the mountains. Not these ones – but I wanted to come back to the land. I needed to get away from the city.' He glanced at the kitchen like he was afraid of being overheard but no one was in there.

'Why?' I asked, quieter. But Pedro shook his head like life was a series of departures and there wasn't anything interesting about another person leaving another place. 'I grew up in the province of Neuquén, five hours north of here. A town. Then I moved to Córdoba, a city in the middle of Argentina. And then I came to Bariloche. Not too interesting.'

He stood, clearing his throat, and I returned to my game of solitaire, hoping for a bit more time in the dining room before everyone crowded in again. I couldn't imagine the refugio with more people. It was already claustrophobic, all our bodies sharing the same space, breathing the same air. You could smell Carmen's perfume even when she wasn't in the room – who brings eau de cologne and cosmetics up a mountain? Then there was Hita, talking under her breath, irritated with her husband. And Felix and Klaus with so much energy – they were like snapping rubber bands. I took a deep breath and focused on my cards, bracing myself for the sound of feet stomping down the stairs and the next rotation.

❄

That night, after dinner, everyone was in the dining room. Felix was sitting by the window, drawing magical shapes, while Carmen explained Truco to Jack. Jeremy had mastered it in Bariloche, playing it in the bar with a group of backpackers from Buenos Aires. I'd sat with John that night, both of us dealing separate hands of solitaire. From what I'd seen, Truco was a boisterous game, played in teams and based on bluffing.

Jack was holding the cards and staring at me. 'Do you know Truco? We need more players.'

I should have joined them for the sake of refugio camaraderie, but I was thinking of Jeremy holding his cards and downing a shot of vodka.

It was in that hesitation that a knock sounded on the dining room door. Jack turned around and scanned the room. Everyone was accounted for – Felix was beside him, the rest of his family at the other table, Pedro in the kitchen fiddling with the radio, and Carmen next to me. Jack's eyebrow ring tweaked upwards and my mouth went papery dry.

The revelation came in slow motion – as though we'd been sitting there, waiting for it: Jeremy or John was alive and had come back. Klaus, who hadn't heard the knock, was asking his mother for an *alfajor* – an Argentinean biscuit layered with caramel. Hita shushed him and the room was heavy with silence.

I had the sensation it was snowing inside and I was covered in a dusty layer of relief and dread.

Felix and Klaus broke the eerie silence, chittering in German.

'Shit . . .' Jack said.

Pedro hurried into the dining room, clutching a screwdriver and watching the door with visible relief.

Everyone was waiting.

When the door finally eased back, it wasn't Jeremy or John but a tall man wearing a beanie. Even in his padded grey snow gear, his slender frame was evident – thin legs and arms. And he reeked of cigarettes; from the other side of the room, the stench came in on the cold. He must have smoked one just before he'd knocked. It was creepy – this stranger standing outside, beyond the refugio light, waiting.

Stepping into the room, he pulled off his hat, exposing a crop of curly brown hair. Pedro stepped back and the screwdriver clattered onto the floor but all of us were focused on the man. I pegged him to be in his mid-forties. His face was tough but strangely beautiful – like the bark of a tree. His scraggly beard had about five days' growth to it and the wrinkles around his blue eyes weren't from smiling. He looked at each one of us like he was thinking of purchasing the refugio and we were all included in the bargain rate. He didn't seem to think he'd gotten a good deal.

'Phew.' He waited a moment and then said, 'Well?' His voice was haughty, expectant.

We all stared at him. Even Felix had stopped drawing and was watching, transfixed.

Pedro moved into the middle of the room. 'What are you doing here?'

'Nice to see you too, Pedro.' The man was American. His accent was sure and strong like Jeremy's. He glanced at the rest of us.

Pedro rested his hand on the edge of the table as though to steady himself. 'Is anyone with you?'

The man took a moment to answer, enjoying Pedro's suspense. 'No.'

'It's late to be trekking. Which way did you come?'

The newcomer shuffled in and threw his gloves on the table; they were puffy and oversized. 'Past the Alpine Cabin.'

'The trails are closed.'

'I came cross-country along Cerro Negro – I had some steep ice climbs. Thought I'd drop in and see how you're doing. You got any dinner?'

He'd come from a different direction than Cerro Blanco, where the avalanche had fallen, but if he'd been outside, he was closer to Jeremy and John than we were. I waited until he glanced at our table and then spoke. 'Did you see anyone else? Two men in red jackets?'

'No one out there. Just snow.'

We all seemed to sink lower with that news, nodding our heads as though we were in collective agreement.

Jack waited a moment, his fingers tapping at the Truco cards. Then, answering a question the man had no intention of asking, he said: 'Avalanche. We think two people were swept away.'

Our arrival just sniffed and lowered himself onto the bench at our table. Pedro came back with an extra pizza from dinner. They'd been cooked in a frying pan, the lid making an impromptu Dutch oven.

Jack gave up on recruiting me for his game and turned back to Carmen. Felix straightened his line of markers and watched the American sawing into his pizza with a bread knife.

That's when I noticed the newcomer was missing two fingers off his left hand – his index and middle ones. The bone had been cut clean at the knuckle. He paused and glanced at Felix, then me. 'You guys hard up for fun? Surely you've got something better to look at.'

Felix set his elbows on the table, leaning into them. 'What happened to your fingers?'

Jack stopped talking. Both he and Carmen stared at the man but he was watching his pizza, cutting it into bite-sized pieces. After swallowing, he leaned back. 'Frostbite. Sometimes the mountain calls and it's hard to say no.'

Pedro was fiddling with the screwdriver but his eyes were shifting between Felix and the American. Something was going on – he seemed afraid or excited.

Felix pursed his lips. 'The mountain *called* you?'

'Not on the telephone, stupid,' Klaus said.

The man ignored him and zeroed in on Felix. 'You go higher and higher – maybe you're skiing, looking for the perfect clean sweep and you see it: a long stretch of powder that just drops away. You're in the middle of nowhere and it's fresh – no sign anyone's ever been there – but the incline is steep and you're in avalanche territory. So you dig a test pit just to be sure. But it's silly because you know, whatever that test pit says, you're going to ride down the mountain. And maybe you even want an avalanche to come. Maybe you're ready for it.'

Erik looked up in horror. I could imagine a long family discussion before bed about the importance of mountain safety.

Pedro had inched around the table and I thought he might interrupt, but Felix twisted his mouth to one side and looked right at the American. 'What's your name?'

'Wolfe.'

Felix's head bobbed back and forth. 'Like the animal?'

Erik swung his legs around so he was fully facing our table, eager to install himself into this conversation. '*Nein*, it would be short for Wolfgang. German?'

'German–Jewish, actually. It's not short for anything and we've been in the States five generations. Lucky for us.'

I looked at Carmen to see what she made of our newcomer but she'd pulled Pedro back and was asking him in Spanish about the radio. Her voice was urgent but he answered without meeting her gaze; he was still watching the American. Wolfe cut another delicate square of pizza, his fork clinking against the plate. His fingers and teeth were stained with nicotine.

'You know, we have chess and Monopoly,' Felix said.

Wolfe stared at him for a moment as though he were an insect that had crawled onto his plate. 'I don't play board games.'

'Oh.' Felix shrugged his tiny shoulders and shuffled through his pile for another sheet of paper. He was rattled. I wanted to ignore the newcomer out of loyalty to Felix but Wolfe was a welcome distraction from thinking about Jeremy and John. He smelled of snow and cigarettes, he was traipsing around in avalanche conditions and he was a caustic piece of work.

I took a deep breath. 'Where are you from?'

'New York.'

'New York City?'

He glanced at me like I was a moron and then ate the last bite of his pizza.

I tried again. 'What are you doing here?'

He sighed, disbelieving, and it occurred to me that if he had a rock in his hand he would have thrown it at something – a bird, the lake, my head – to distract our attention from him. 'What do you think? Climbing mountains and skiing.'

It was Carmen who spoke next: 'I'm here and I'm not skiing or climbing a mountain.' Even though she was backing me, her confidence was grating. She seemed to like the new arrival.

Wolfe tweaked his mouth to the side and the rest of his head followed. 'Well you had to climb one to get here.' There was an implied democracy to him, which I appreciated: he thought we all were idiots.

But Carmen wasn't finished. 'I did – but that's not why I'm here.' She was disagreeing with Wolfe in a way that was charming at the same time. It didn't make sense – she'd been downright rude to me before we'd even spoken. Why would she be nice to Wolfe?

Wolfe didn't care. His face creased as he lifted one eyebrow. 'Why on earth would you come up here in the dead of winter? Surely that's the only thing to do up here?'

'It's far away.'

'From where? That's the question.'

For a moment, she didn't say anything. Her gaze was sturdy – she could be tough when she wanted. 'How do you know Pedro?'

He glanced at the Argentinean. 'I'm a regular up here.'

The conversation was left hanging but Wolfe didn't say more. He was staring past us to the reflection in the window glass.

Usually I'm comfortable with silence but something felt wrong about Wolfe's arrival. I turned to Jack. It was the first time I'd seen him without his book nearby. 'What were you reading this afternoon?'

He sighed. '*On the Road*.'

I'd tried reading Kerouac years ago but had found his writing verbose and self-indulgent.

'Beat poets. Anti-consumerism,' Jack said, waiting a moment. Then he swore under his breath like explaining anything so obvious was physically painful. But still, he wanted to be understood. He couldn't stop himself: 'Jack Kerouac, Hunter S Thompson, Charles Bukowski, Chuck Palahniuk, Haruki Murakami. It's about questioning capital, globalisation.'

'Art shaping the world,' I said.

Wolfe glanced back from the window and pushed his plate away. 'Art? Sounds like adolescent chaos. Oh, things are unfair until you get a job that profits from global capital. That'll change your position. And who needs women for the revolution? For someone concerned with global inequities, there weren't a lot of women writers on that list.'

Jack stared at him. 'What do you do for a living?'

'Journalist. I used to be a foreign correspondent, then an editor. *New York Times.*'

'Used to be?' Pedro asked.

'Yeah. My father was sick. Then he died,' Wolfe said, meeting Pedro's eyes.

Pedro glanced down at the screwdriver in his hands. 'I'm sorry to hear that.'

I was wary of Wolfe but I was wary of the other guests, too – Carmen and Jack, especially.

Erik was getting another round of beers and I nodded. Carmen signalled she wanted one too, raising her hand. I'd assumed she didn't drink but Erik set an armful of cans on the table and she opened two of them, passing one to me.

I didn't notice Wolfe had stood up until he walked towards the window. He was staring outside as though judging the texture of the snow through the glass. Then he looked down and coughed. He was watching Felix draw and shaking his head, the gesture soft and patronising.

'Oh how nice,' he said, his tone bland and sarcastic at the same time. 'The German child is drawing swastikas. It's so nice when tradition is maintained, don't you think?'

Hita shot up from the other table and I thought she was going to shove him. Her glasses had slipped down her nose and her woollen sweater was too small, riding up. 'What are you saying?' Her accent left uneven pauses between her words, which made her seem ineffectual against Wolfe.

Felix looked up, confused. He had a white piece of paper with an outline of a large swastika. It had been drawn with dashes and he was inching his way around it, the pen gripped between his fingers. 'It's just a . . .'

Hita stepped over and snatched the sheet away from him. Jack was staring the other way, giggling to himself. 'Family tradition,' he said, between breaths, talking to me in a voice loud enough for everyone to hear. 'You should have seen the ones down in Bariloche. Great-uncle's house, picture of Hitler on the fireplace.'

Hita hissed something in German and smacked him hard on the head. He turned around and she grabbed him by the ear, tweaking him to his feet. He wrestled free and rubbed the side of his face. 'I didn't realise we had such an upstanding family until we arrived in Argentina.'

She grabbed him by the ear again and he twisted around to look at her. They were like figures in a grotesque renaissance painting until Hita pulled Jack outside. The door let in a sharp gasp of air and fell closed behind them.

Erik came and sat at the table, wrapping Felix in his arms. The boy's chin was quivering. His father rocked him back and forth, and whispered in German.

When Erik looked up, he was calculating how much to tell us. 'I apologise. We met distant family in Bariloche and they're . . .' He paused but not because he was looking for the word. '. . . sympathisers. What do you say to someone like that? To someone you're related to?'

He was shaking his head. Carmen's mouth had dropped open and I didn't know where to look. Wolfe opened a beer and began drinking it. 'German guilt – long history of it. I'm sure you'll be fine.'

Erik continued, his long fingers spread out on the table. 'Jack is angry with us. He thinks we should have left. Refused the hospitality. Maybe we should have. Hita was polite because Heinrich was my great-uncle.'

No one said anything. Carmen was twirling a piece of hair between her fingers, looking for split ends. I tried to make eye contact with her, but she didn't look up.

'At least Jack has conviction,' Wolfe said, eventually.

It had nothing to do with me but I felt curiously envious of Jack. How nice to know exactly what you think about the world and your place in it. Around us, the windowpanes were black and cold; the night was seeping into the room.

I reached for a deck of cards and flicked through a game of solitaire. Carmen sat next to me, watching the cards. A couple of times, I waited until she spotted a move. 'There. The red nine on the black ten,' she said, as the door opened.

Jack eased in. His mother stood behind him, a subtle and insurmountable wall. He stood just inside the room, his gaze settled on the boxes stored overhead. 'I'm sorry.'

I wasn't sure who he was apologising to – Felix, Erik, all of us in the refugio? Everyone waited for the rest of his speech but he only shrugged. A half-hearted movement that said he wasn't sorry and he wished his parents, his mother especially, would fuck off. 'I'm going to bed now.' When the door closed behind him, it felt like he'd taken all the oxygen in the room. Everyone looked tired.

Hita's mouth set in a grim line like Jack had followed the rules of a contract but it wasn't the outcome she'd been expecting.

'I'm going to bed too,' Carmen said, yawning. It seemed she'd given the signal for everyone to disband for the evening. There was an exodus to the toilets, led by the Germans. On their way outside, Klaus accused Felix of stealing his toothbrush and Hita glanced at Erik, shaking her head with a weary expression.

❄

The next morning, Carmen's bed was empty so I made my way downstairs to a breakfast of plain oatmeal with powdered milk, and instant coffee. I took my bowl and sat outside on the stairs. The cloud cover was high and the filtered sunlight was soft. We were having a reprieve from the snow and my gratitude was intense. Even with the faint waft from the toilet, it was beautiful – staggering and open – but my appreciation felt like a betrayal. John had hugged me right here. This was the last place I'd touched him.

When I'd finished my breakfast Pedro came out, tossing a tub of warm water on the ground. It steamed up, melting a puddle of snow. 'I'm ahead of my schedule. Lunch is already prepared. You want to see an ice waterfall?'

'Sure.'

He ducked back inside. When he returned, we headed along a trail behind the refugio. My heels angled into the snow for grip but I slipped anyway, grabbing Pedro's arm. He held me, keeping balance for both of us. The lake was to our left and in the sunshine, it wasn't the enormity or the stillness that was so exquisite, it was how safe we were, cupped between the blank, frozen water and the easing slope.

'See that?' Pedro pointed to a rock face in the distance. 'A winter cathedral.'

'You religious?'

The trail narrowed but we kept walking side-by-side. I could smell sunlight and snow.

'Sometimes I offer prayers to the Virgin. But I'm Mapuche. Our folklore is about the land.' He gestured up a sheer rock face, pointing out a rippled formation.

He continued. 'You wanted to know where I come from? I was born at an *asentamiento* – the name for our community – in the province of Neuquén. North of here. My people were given a land grant in the early 1900s. An apology, making amends. But then over the next century, four different owners lived on the land next to us. Each one redrew the boundary. One shifted the fence in the middle of the night. Another tilled land that didn't belong to him. My grandmother and mother filed documents for the community. They organised meetings, journeyed to court. But that never led anywhere . . . We lost three hundred hectares.'

'What happened?' Despite the sun, I could feel the cold in my toes and the tips of my fingers.

'We took it back.'

'What do you mean?'

'With machetes. Guns.' Pedro had stopped walking. 'I don't remember much . . . I was a baby at the *asentamiento*. But apparently they were the golden years. And then the military took over. The Dirty War made it hard for *indígenas*. Thought we were subversives. Opened all the windows so everyone could hear the "questioning". It was torture – electric, mostly. And soon we were relocated. But you can't exchange one piece of land for another. It splintered the community, making us move like that. My mother, brothers, we settled in town.'

'Torture?' I would never have asked but I was thinking of my birth parents in La Cacha, the detention centre.

Pedro was watching the path ahead of us. 'I was never taken in but my cousins were. Sometimes the guards would use an electric prod. One of them rewired kitchen appliances to shock prisoners. That way, if the prisoner were freed, they'd never forget. Every time they used a blender or a coffee grinder, they'd remember being tortured. My cousin would laugh, though: the guards were wasting their time, we didn't have money for blenders.'

'That's sick,' I said.

'Worse if you were a unionist. Most of them didn't come out alive.'

I thought of my adoption – I didn't want to be related to this history. I was feeling shaky. 'What did your family do? When you were forced to move?'

'My uncle started a junkyard in town and my mother has a plot behind it. That's where I grew up. I got a scholarship to a fancy school in the city, over an hour on the bus each way. But I learned English. I suppose I wouldn't be here now, with tourists, if we hadn't moved. What about you?'

'Me?'

'Where are you from?'

I didn't know how to answer that. My stomach was churning.

Pedro touched my arm and pointed to our right. 'Look—'

It was the ice waterfall. The water was frozen solid and it was like witnessing a freeze-frame version of a waterfall. About three metres wide and fifteen high, the middle was rough-white and thick. Its edges were riddled with icicles. Pedro was like a kid showing me his treehouse, his breath catching on the air. 'I pump water up from the lake with a hose. It flows down and freezes. I didn't bring my gear but we could climb it. Maybe tomorrow.'

My head moved up and down, but I couldn't match his enthusiasm.

❄

By dinnertime it had started snowing again and the icy powder was like a layer of insulation against the rest of the world. We were locked in together. When we'd finished eating and cleaning up, I'd already had three beers and, with each one, the Americans seemed to slide just a little bit further away. After the fourth, I was buzzing. The walls had relaxed and the floor was buoyant. Shadows from the overhead lamp textured the room and there was a faint smell of mothballs and onions.

I pushed in next to Carmen on the bench. 'Tell me. How many people can say they were stranded in the Andes? This is life experience. We're doing this for life experience.'

She scooted over to make room for me, and Wolfe, who was standing at the other table, rolled his eyes. 'It only counts as life experience if you live through it.'

'What did you do today, Wolfe?' My voice was cheerful and patronising like a camp counsellor and he smiled in spite of himself.

'I climbed Little Cerro.' Little Cerro was a mountain peak about halfway along the lake.

'How come we can't leave but you can climb Little Cerro?' Carmen asked.

'The incline of the mountain,' Jack called out from the floor in a textbook monotone. 'Little Cerro is gradual, the slope is less than forty-five degrees. Safety is never guaranteed but if you pay attention to the terrain and dig test pits, you can usually gauge how stable it is. Cerro Blanco is too steep, much more dangerous. Unfortunately, we have to pass it to get to the main trail. Bad luck, that.' He was making fun of his father.

Pedro turned to Wolfe. 'Did you go up the back?'

'Yeah. Wanted to get a sense of the terrain. The wind was something nasty.'

I was still confused. 'Why can't we leave the way Wolfe came in?'

Pedro shook his head. 'He didn't follow a trail; he hiked through back country. It's too dangerous – especially now with the weather.'

Carmen finished her beer and stood up. She stretched her arms over her head in a smooth languid movement. In my beautiful alcohol cocoon, I decided no one had ever been lovelier and we should become friends. We just needed to let go of whatever craziness was between us.

She was pointing at the stereo. 'Music?'

I nodded, following her. Someone, surely an Australian, had left a scuffed cassette of 'ABBA for Adelaide'.

Wolfe rolled his eyes but I cranked up the volume anyway, leaning back and forth in a way that approximated dancing. Carmen joined in. She was graceful, but not quite sexual. Her thin limbs made the display look delicate, but there was something about her chest and neck that seemed strong, fearsome even.

She reached for Jack's hands. 'Come.'

He wouldn't have joined in for anyone else. When he stood up, he let go of her hands and began jerking to the music. His movements seemed frustrated and yet he understood rhythm, his feet hitting the ground in perfect time. It was an awkward and compelling thing to watch. His little brothers followed. Hita and Erik held hands, making a bridge for the younger boys to traipse through. Felix began strutting back and forth behind Jack, pausing to thrust his bum out until his brother batted him away.

My face was warm from the beer. My shoulders had relaxed, my arms loose, swaying with the beat. Pedro was leaning against the window.

The refugio felt like a meeting hall. And that makes us villagers, I thought.

'To global villagers.' I said this aloud, during a lull between the songs and Wolfe raised his beer in a toast.

Pedro picked up the few remaining glasses and disappeared into the kitchen.

The Adelaide mix wasn't confined to ABBA and soon I was teaching Carmen the arm gestures for 'YMCA' and shouting over the music. 'A classic. If you want to immigrate to Australia, you have to know "Waltzing Matilda" and "YMCA".'

'Sophisticated place,' Wolfe piped up, and I steadied myself against the table. He was holding a pack of cigarettes, peeling the plastic back, curling the wrapper between his fingers.

That was the moment when Pedro marched back into the living room and smacked the ghetto-blaster, silencing the room. At first, I thought it had something to do with Wolfe but he scanned the room, looking at all of us. 'My money from the refugio is missing.'

Pedro wouldn't have misplaced it. Even drunk, I knew that much.

'I want it on the table tomorrow morning,' he said.

Wolfe leaned back, his cigarette pack on the table in front of him. 'Fifty bucks says it was Jack.'

Jack's eyes widened. 'What?'

'Why you'd steal money in a place where you can't spend it has me beat, but there you go.' He offered a condescending nod to Erik and Hita. 'Teenagers. What can you do with them?'

Erik looked down at Jack. 'Did you take it?'

'Of course not.'

Wolfe pulled out one of his cigarettes and tapped it on the table. 'As if he's going to tell you.'

Erik gripped his son's wrist and spoke to him quickly in German.

'*Nein!*' Jack squeaked, wrenching his arm away.

Erik stared at Wolfe as though he were the deciding force in the refugio. 'If my son says he didn't take it, he didn't take it.'

Wolfe scoffed and Erik stepped closer. It was the first time I'd seen the German worked up – his jaw was clenched and his chest puffed out. Wolfe shook his head dismissively and this seemed to infuriate Erik further.

Pedro moved between them. 'Let's just wait until tomorrow and see if it appears.'

I didn't want to wait until the morning – I wanted a search that night. It was one thing to be wary of the mountain. It was another to have the threat inside, among us. If we couldn't trust each other, what hope did we have?

❈

When everyone was awake, Hita organised a search of all our backpacks. Whoever had taken the money wasn't going to keep it in such an obvious place, surely. But after breakfast no one was allowed upstairs, and Wolfe took the boys in front of the refugio to build a giant car out of snow. He wouldn't have been my choice for a chaperone but no one argued. Even Jack followed outside without grumbling.

I was well into my third round of solitaire when Hita came downstairs with Pedro. The two of them stood in the doorway, Pedro in front, hands resting on hips. He held up an old-fashioned airmail envelope with red and blue stripes along the perimeter. 'You know this?'

Hita was watching the creased envelope.

I looked at them. 'The money?'

Pedro sighed like he couldn't believe anything anymore. 'There's no money in it.'

'Where was it?'

'In your backpack,' Hita said. Her lips made a thin straight line. She was waiting.

I was so edgy my first instinct was that she'd planted it on me. 'I didn't take it.' I was careful with my face – concentrating on keeping my mouth still, my eyes level. I was telling the truth but the fact I was under suspicion made every movement a sign of my guilt.

Pedro shook his head and walked into the kitchen. I stood up and followed, brushing past Hita. I was shocked: could he really believe I'd taken the money? He was the one person I trusted in the refugio, my only friend. And then a more unsettling thought: someone was trying to frame me. Someone wished me harm.

Pedro picked up a chopping board and set it down to fill the washing basin. He picked it up again. He didn't know what he was doing, I realised. He was flustered.

I took a deep breath. 'Why would I leave the envelope in my backpack? It doesn't make sense.'

He looked at me like he had no idea who I was and grabbed two onions from a box on the floor. His knife sliced cleanly into the skin, and he peeled it back. His jaw was clenched. 'That is everything I have. You don't understand. You people can all go home and make more money – this is just a holiday. My whole life was in that envelope.'

The onion flesh was exposed, the yellow skin glistening. Pedro turned the chopping board and began rocking the blade through the onion, slicing it in long thin strips. 'Either return the money or leave.'

2

Hans 'Jack' Meyers

I was having sex for the first time in my life. Isobel's parents were working late and we were in her room, this crazy attic triangle with a window that looked right over San Francisco. Down below us, all these old pastel buildings and, across the water, a thin crust of dirt that was supposed to be a park. From her bed, I had a straight view of her walls, all layered with anti-globalisation posters, ticket stubs and notes like she was giving the finger to her neat-freak parents. Every bit of space was covered.

She unbuckled my belt. Her arm got caught in her shirt and she made a face, which got us both laughing and the whole thing made me think of my little brother, Felix, who loved to strip off his t-shirt, inside out, so its round collar circled his forehead and the body of the shirt trailed behind him like a wig. Isobel was unclasping her bra, and I was still thinking of my little brother. Obviously in a moment like that you don't want to be thinking of your little brother – but there I was, thinking about how he was playing soccer at home and how home felt so much further away than a twenty-minute walk along 18th Street – so when Isobel's mouth landed on mine, I was grateful to be brought back. She was right there. Whatever happened, I was ready: I'd been waiting for this.

'You okay?' she asked and I was thankful one of us knew what we were doing. I nodded. The mattress was a raft, and she pulled me to the middle and rolled on top of me.

Her breasts were small and rounded with pale nipples; she drew my hands towards them so I could cup them in my palms and the only thing I could think was: how could you wash the dishes, how could you go grocery shopping or wait in line at the cafeteria when you could be doing this?

That evening when I got home for dinner, my parents were already seated at the dining table. It was a piece of shit that was way too small and falling apart but it'd been given to us by one of my dad's colleagues so of course we had to cram around it for family meals. My younger brothers were sitting down and arguing about whose television night it was – everything, even the minutes spent in front of a digital screen, had to be sanctioned by my mother. But really, that night, I didn't give a fuck – I felt detached from it all, like an alien sent to planet Earth to document human behaviour.

'Something with lots of fighting.' Klaus, hardly the family intellectual, was pointing a finger gun at a make-believe bad guy in the kitchen and making sound effects: *pow-pow-pow*. It was worth suffering the noise for the pained expression on my mother's face.

As I pulled my chair in to the table, she bumped my arm and watched my brother with an expression that was all cow – jowls and neck, chewing – until she spoke, straightening up. 'Klaus, manners. Sit up and hold your fork properly. This is dinner.'

I smiled, egging my brother on. His gun magically changed to an AK-47 and he started mowing down his imaginary enemies – it was great but I was willing him to take aim at our table because nothing pissed my mother off more than being imaginarily assassinated.

Our father set his cutlery down. 'Klaus, listen to your mother.'

Felix was humming and thwacking his feet against his chair like he was making a joke at our family's expense – adding more mayhem to annoy my mother – and it made me snicker. We had them outnumbered. If Felix was sitting at the table, it always felt like there was someone on my side – he had this uncanny ability to make you feel understood, make everyone feel understood, and so he was the favourite. Klaus, our parents: we all liked Felix the best and no one was too bothered about it.

My mother was watching my father with the expression she used when he needed to be authoritative, but the whole thing was pathetic – the guy would be wearing mismatched shoes if it weren't for her. I thought he was going to grill me on being late – I'd borrowed books from Isobel for my library alibi – but he wasn't looking at me. His hair had been cut, probably by my mother, and there was a wispy bit she'd missed near his ear; it twitched as he cleared his throat and I just focused on that unruly piece of hair. The man looked ridiculous. His voice lifted as he tried again: 'We have an announcement.'

The boys stopped horsing around and I put on my 'listening seriously' face.

'My contract has been cut short – we'll be leaving the United States. But we won't go straight to Germany. We'll take the time to travel.'

'Travel, where?' Felix tilted his head.

Klaus started belting out 'Ticket to Ride' as some kind of family joke because our father played the Beatles all the time, and of course our dad grinned like this was a bonding moment. I wanted to chuck my knife and fork at them. My father for being stupid. My brother for being a traitor.

That's when my mother cut in. 'To South America.' She was holding a spatula like it was a weapon.

'What do you mean, South America?' I asked. Suddenly I was listening seriously.

My dad shrugged. 'There have been changes in the department and my supervisor feels horrible but an early departure works better for all of us. So we're leaving – at the end of the school year.'

'That's only a month away!' They couldn't do this to me, not now, surely not now. Jesus fucking Christ, why did they have to ruin everything?

Klaus set down his imaginary microphone. 'What about the World Cup? What about the football?' He glanced at Felix and the two of them turned to my mother in a united front. Germany was hosting the competition: we'd been planning a family trip back home to coincide with it, and Felix had been anticipating it for as long as he could remember – they'd made the announcement almost six years ago.

Our mother's lips tightened into a thin line. 'It doesn't make sense to fly all that way when we have the chance to travel. I'm sorry we're going to miss it.'

❋

We'd been in the Bay Area of the United States for almost five years – we were living in the Castro because my parents have to turn everything into a cultural experience, even gay people. We'd come for my dad's sabbatical and he loved it so much, he organised a teaching exchange so we could stay on. But the point of going to San Francisco had been so my dad could check out geographic fault lines. The trip to South America didn't make sense – Dad wasn't going to collect any data, he wasn't even going to any conferences. It seemed like our holiday had more to do with some giant bee that had crawled up my mother's butt than with anything else. I think it was Isobel – after we got picked up for disturbing the peace at five in the morning, my lovely mother made it clear Isobel would never eat dinner at our table again. I wanted to tell my mother we'd been lucky: disturbing the peace was nothing compared to larceny and drug possession.

Isobel and I had been smoking weed and 'shifting' cars that night, which was one of our favourite post-midnight pastimes: hotwire anything we could and move it half a block down the street. That way, the owner gets a shock and appreciates the role of the motor vehicle in their work-life routine but no harm's done; they just have to walk an extra hundred metres in the morning. We always left little business cards on the dashboards: 'Appreciate every mile – you're driving us closer to global warming.' San Francisco was full of phonies – people who 'cared' about the environment but only as long as they were comfortable.

That night, we'd gotten tired of cars and raided the second-hand bins where people drop off shit they don't want.

'Fucking hell, check this out,' Isobel said, shining her flashlight at some stacked boxes next to the bins. They were full of romance novels – I'm talking at least two hundred, maybe three hundred, from the '70s and '80s, before we were even born.

'This is too good.'

We piled them into the tray of a 'borrowed' pick-up truck and Isobel drove, clutch-hopping us through the 3 am darkness to Golden Gate Park. It was dead quiet so we dumped them on the damp lawn near some kids' play equipment.

'What do you think? A question mark?' I asked. The park smelled of freshly cut grass.

Isobel reached into her backpack and ripped open a bag of gummy bears, pushing a handful into her mouth and staring out over the lawn. 'What about a roman candle in honour of Jack Kerouac?'

Isobel had written out that passage from *On the Road* and stuck it to her wall: it's better to be interesting than boring, even if it means you die early like an explosion from a big firecracker. It was cool – the idea of shooting yellow lines across the sky and everyone down below appreciating the view. But how could you render that with romance novels?

She passed me the bag of gummy bears and I put a rubbery orange one on my tongue, sucking at it. 'Maybe we just make a big rectangle. People will think it's some kind of comment on structure but we'll know it's a tribute to the beats.' It was about honouring our anti-establishment pioneers who knew that bastards were running the show.

Isobel was already reaching for the books. 'We'll have to start in line with the sidewalk.' That's why I loved Isobel: she didn't fuck around – she got straight into things.

The gummy bear slid down my throat and I popped three more in my mouth, gnawing at them, as we set about making a huge romance-novel rectangle. The covers were all facing the sky: distant castles and sweeping-font titles, waiting for some desperate reader to look down from the clouds.

'It's getting too wide. We need more there,' Isobel said, pointing to the bottom.

She bent down, her jeans straining through the thighs, and I watched her for a moment, fascinated, until she cleared her throat and I blushed, moving to the lower edge like she'd suggested.

Light was beginning to creep into the sky when we were finally finished and Isobel gazed over our work. 'It's street art.'

Buzzing on sugar and darkness, I tried to wrap my arms around her but she grabbed my hand and wrestled it back, laughing. She smelled of cloves and patchouli and all I could think about was sex. I pushed her over and we both fell on the ground, and she yanked a fistful of grass out and stuffed it in my face. I spit out a piece of grass and she reached for my other arm, pinning me down.

'I win,' she said, pushing herself off the ground. 'Now come on.'

We didn't get busted until we were walking home – we'd just parked the truck and were making our way along her street. Isobel was laughing so loud I didn't hear the police car behind us: it was only when the spotlight flared on that I realised we weren't alone. The officer couldn't get us for vandalism or car theft, which was lucky because Isobel and I didn't have licences yet, but he insisted on driving us home: Isobel first. I waited in the back of the car, watching as she strode up her front steps. Even though we were in the Mission, her house seemed secluded, with these tall trees close in on either side like security guards. Her family had a whole mansion to themselves because her dad was loaded from Google or Apple or something. The door opened as soon as the automatic yard light clicked on as though her father had been awake inside, waiting; he peered out at me, sending some kind of warning through the upper-end urban darkness.

I was thinking he could fuck off if he thought he'd stop me seeing his daughter and then the officer slipped into his seat and slammed the door closed. 'You ready?'

Before I knew it, I was standing at my apartment block with its ugly brick façade, watching the officer's finger press our number again and again until my mother's voice answered on the intercom.

Once my parents made the announcement we were going to South America, my father finalised the paperwork from the university so we could leave on the last day of school. In protest, Klaus and Felix refused to wear anything besides their football jerseys, which my mother was forced to wash during bath time. I'd looked into staying on in San Francisco under the guise of scholastic commitment, but my mother didn't even hear my arguments out: 'No, Hans. Families do things together.'

Over the next four weeks, Isobel and I spent every spare moment together but we weren't allowed at each other's houses so that curbed our sex life until I found a vacant apartment that was in-between rental tenants. We'd climb in the bathroom window and go at it until she had to get back for dinner. The carpet was some acrylic scratchy blend that made me break out in hives so I had to stash a blanket there – some quilt from my mother's side of the family that I forgot on our last visit.

And then, after the shittiest goodbye ever – at school of all places because Isobel's family was going away for the weekend – I was on a plane, packed between Klaus and my father, with some jerk in front of me leaning his chair all the way back. All too soon we were arriving in Buenos Aires and crammed into this tiny room with a fold-out cot and two double beds (I got to share with Klaus, who kicks in his sleep: delightful). The nights were unbearable, everyone in my family snores, but the city was pretty cool – so of course my mother had to ruin things, renting a banged-up car and making us leave sooner than planned, because she didn't like the smog. Buenos Aires has public art on the streets and tango dancers doing their thing, and there's my mother, hiking around with a handkerchief over her face, complaining about the air: it was too embarrassing. We drove up and across the middle of Argentina with this nothing terrain – all grass and sky – to Córdoba, and then the wine country in Mendoza, and then south to Bariloche, where the illustrious Nazi-loving incident happened. Then, like we needed a family excursion to distract us from Uncle Heinrich, my father came up with the genius idea of hiking up to the refugio for a few days. He should have had enough of mountains – we'd spent lots of time going to the Sierra Nevada – but as we drove around the outskirts of Bariloche he'd gasp in wonder at the rocky outcrops, pointing towards a cliff face like we'd just had a close encounter with a wild animal. On one stretch, he got so excited he started veering off the road and my mother had to take over driving.

I usually sat in the back seat, next to Felix, listening to playlists that Isobel had made for me on my iPod, and having imaginary conversations with her about what I was reading. We were interested in the world and perplexed by the concept of political optimism so we downloaded everything we could, reading Bukowski and Ginsberg in an effort to be ready. We'd gone to anti-globalisation rallies and boycotted fast food chains, we used cloth bags for our shopping and hated cars with needlessly large engines. If I were elected to government I'd put every SUV owner into their car and blow up the lot of them. You can't tell me the world wouldn't be a better place. Isobel and I were bound in our distrust of global capitalism so I was thinking of her when I met Jeremy and John.

Jeremy was a pompous loudmouth who just happened to be the walking personification of the enemy – he raved about Wall Street, for fuck's sake. Most of the time it'd been easy to ignore him, but one morning when no one else was around he sat at my table while I was finishing Chuck Palahniuk's *Fight Club*. Usually I kept the same book jacket – *On the Road* – for whatever I was reading to mess with people's heads but I'd left it upstairs.

'Book's better than the movie,' he said.

'Yeah, but the movie's pretty good.'

'Depends if you're a book person or a movie person . . . You want to smoke some grass?'

I was impressed he'd read the book and didn't side with the movie like most of my friends. I checked for my parents just to be sure but the coast was clear; they were cross-country skiing around the lake. 'Definitely. Not in here, though.'

My mother had been watching me closely since Córdoba because she thought I was trying to score ecstasy. We'd been sitting at this outdoor café in the pedestrian-only part of town and my dad had come up with this great plan that we'd all share mains to cut costs. Like, we'd order three dishes for the five of us, maybe Felix and Klaus could share something and Dad and I'd share something. And I couldn't handle it, sitting there, watching my dad grin like he'd really gotten one over on the system and my brothers fighting about *carne* or *pollo* – beef or chicken. Even Felix was annoying me – fiddling with his asthma inhaler, tromping it back and forth across the edge of the table like a robot – so I left for the toilet.

Inside the restaurant, the waiter was sitting in front of a wall the colour of baby shit, folding cloth napkins – he wasn't much older than me, wearing a gold chain and his hair all gelled into place. I asked for the bathroom and he gestured down the back, past the empty wicker chairs and table settings. When I returned, he called out – '*Amigo.*' He was holding a plastic baggie with two small white pills. I wasn't stupid – they could have been anything – but I just wanted to talk to someone who wasn't related to me, even if it was only for five seconds. I stepped closer, asking how much. The waiter brushed his hair out of his eyes like we were getting down to business when someone cleared her throat in the doorway. My mother – eyes blinking, chins quivering. She hissed my name, not once but over and over like she thought I'd developed some kind of spontane-ous hearing loss. And so for the next two weeks I hadn't been allowed out of her sight – only at the refugio had she given me a bit of space and that was because there was fuck-nothing I could get up to out there.

Jeremy gazed around the dining room like he was taking in a panoramic view from a cliff top. 'Amazing country, eh?'

'I guess so.'

'You guess so? We're in the Andes. We've hiked up to no-man's land. How many people are here? Dead of winter? This place is crazy. This is why people live, my friend. They live to come to places like this.'

I'd been thinking people live to have sex with their girlfriends and travelling with your family in a beat-up station wagon so you can hike into the wilderness has to be about as far away as you can get from that, but I nodded.

'You spend time in the capital?' he asked.

'Yeah.'

'Us, too.' He said this like we had so much in common and for a weird moment maybe we did. It felt unbelievably good to be talking to someone new.

I turned down the corner of my page – a habit that irritated my mother no end. 'You guys heading off – back to the States?'

He liked that I knew this and grinned. 'After we hike around the circuit – time's ticking. Let's celebrate this glorious country, get into those joints.'

My brothers had gone skiing with my parents but I looked around anyway – Felix could keep quiet but Klaus was a tattletale. Thankfully the dining room was empty.

Outside, the sun was glinting off the ice on the ground. Emma was walking down from the toilets but she didn't follow us – she headed inside with a book. Jeremy took two big steps and slid across the melting layer towards his tent. I followed: my feet had no traction, it was all about balance. Just as I was sweeping up behind him, Jeremy hit a slick patch and fell onto his butt, and I swerved into a pile of snow that Pedro had shovelled off the roof. We hadn't made contact, I was pretty sure, but I watched his face anyway – he seemed like the kind of guy who could get pissed off easily. He just burst out laughing.

Jeremy kicked his shoes off at the tent and lifted the doorway flap. I could smell smoke. John was sitting in the apex of the tent, Indian style, with a sleeping bag over his legs and a joint in his fingers. He smiled and passed it to Jeremy, who climbed in and closed his eyes to concentrate.

We were quiet, focused on the joint as it went around the three of us. When it came to John a fourth time, he nudged my arm. 'Pretty up here, isn't it?'

It all looked the same to me but I shrugged, thinking of my father peering through the windscreen, pushing the sun visor back, and I had this weird pang of scorn and love for my dad because he was the kind of man who could be happy looking at a rock.

Jeremy inhaled and punched John on the arm. 'Okay, John. Don't get all righteous. But you know what this place needs? A Denny's. Think of that. You hike all the way up here, slide down that last section, and then you get a grand slam combo. How great would that be?' It took a moment to understand what he'd said, like his words were balancing on the smoke around us, and I knew I was stoned. It always happened fast.

'What?' I said.

'You know, Denny's.' Denny's was a diner chain in the States – my family had eaten there a few times before I swore off globalised fast food.

I cleared my throat. 'Whoa, that's intense.'

I meant the word 'intense' in a bad way but Jeremy didn't hear that. He just started grinning and handed me the joint. 'The German gets me. That's totally what I mean. Intense. That's the word.'

It wasn't the word, I thought, but I was lifting the roach to my lips and smiling anyway, shaking my head or maybe nodding it. I could imagine Isobel, peeking out from a room tucked in my brain. Her arms folded across her chest, her mouth scowling.

Jeremy sat forward and hit John again to make sure he was listening. 'Why can't you enjoy nature *and* a breakfast combo? What's wrong with some bacon and eggs to go along with your exquisite view?'

John grinned like he was being knowingly conned into something. 'I like their bottomless cups of coffee.'

'That's exactly what I mean.' Jeremy looked at me like a fellow conspirator. 'What do you want?'

My voice was croaky. 'Like food?'

'Yeah, from Denny's or wherever. If you could order anything right now, what would it be?'

Make-believe Isobel climbed out of my ear and crouched beside me. Her voice was clear: 'What are you doing with these losers?'

'I don't know.' I must have said this aloud. I was talking to Isobel but Jeremy nodded like I'd just posed an in-depth philosophical dilemma.

'Too much selection. I know what you mean.'

John was shaking his head. 'He's just fucking with you. He hates the capitalists as much as you do. Except when he's busy being one of them.'

Jeremy tried to punch him on the arm but John blocked it and gave Jeremy a shove. Both of them were laughing but I didn't care if they were making fun of me – this beat hanging out with my brothers or tallying the number of days it'd been since I last had sex: I was up to twenty-seven. I cleared my throat and could feel my chest; it was sore. I must have missed something because Jeremy was talking about Emma now, the Australian who'd hiked up with them. I didn't like her – she seemed like she thought she had something to offer the world.

'She's a librarian, dude,' Jeremy said.

'Really?' I couldn't believe a librarian would have such a loud laugh. That would have to count against you in job interviews, surely. 'Is she your girlfriend?'

'Nah.'

John smirked. 'Jeremy just likes to help the ladies out.'

'Not like I get any thanks for it. But you know who I'd really like to get it on with? The chick from Buenos Aires . . .'

Carmen, the tango dancer. We'd eaten dinner together, all of us crowded in the dining room, but I'd never spoken to her, nothing more than asking her to pass the salt, anyway. Pedro had gone down for more supplies and came back with her, found her on the trail. Jeremy was right: she was pretty.

But Isobel was now slapping my shoulder and grimacing at the Americans. 'Get away from these fucking pigs.' I couldn't make myself stand up – maybe it was the weed, maybe I'd spent so many hours cooped up with my family that talking to anyone else, even corporate Americans, was better than sitting through one more retarded chess game. Seriously, the tables were always piled with my brothers' shit – fucking board games and candy wrappers and coats – so you couldn't sit down without having to clear a place for yourself. The only good thing about all the mess was knowing it pissed my mother off more than me.

Or maybe I actually liked the Americans. Maybe I liked the way Jeremy elbowed me like we were in cahoots. The image of a caramel sundae, capped in a plastic fortress, hovered in my mind. They used to come with nuts. When Felix was still a baby, my dad used to sneak me and Klaus to McDonald's and I'd always order a caramel sundae with nuts and extra sauce. I leaned back on my elbows and pulled a green sleeping bag over my legs. Isobel was right in my face now but I closed my eyes and concentrated on fazing her out.

❋

It didn't matter that the flesh-and-blood Isobel was thousands of miles away, probably carving her name into a summer school desk, without any idea that Jeremy and John existed: it felt like I'd betrayed her by becoming friends with them. That afternoon, before we all went sledding, I tried to explain it to her inside my head but she didn't answer, and for the first time since we left, Isobel felt far away.

We headed towards a clear stretch about halfway along the lake. Jeremy led, his feet crunching through the frozen layers, and John and I followed, carrying our plastic sheets rolled up, on our shoulders. I was excited to get away from Klaus, who'd started strumming the silver guitar that had been hanging over the fireplace. I don't think the instrument was supposed to be played, it looked like a sculpture project – a metal replica of a guitar rather than an actual one.

About three-quarters of the way up, Jeremy paused. Before we'd left, he told me to bring snacks so I'd stolen some granola bars from my family's food stash. Being the miser my father was, he never planned on ordering breakfast at the refugio so we'd carried up these bars that tasted like horse feed and were full of these black seeds that went straight through you. Klaus was the one who first noticed the seed-poops and this had us all cracking up for days – all except for my mother, who just sighed at the reproductive gods who'd failed to give her a daughter. The funny thing was, eating them now, out in the snow, they didn't taste so bad. Jeremy tucked into his and half of John's while we were all sitting on our plastic sheets.

Jeremy spoke with his mouth full. 'Where'd you get these?'

'Bakery in Bariloche, the one near the vegetable shop.'

'I might get some of these back in town.'

It was a throwaway line. I only remembered it because I thought he was crazy – my jaw was sore from crunching into them every morning – and the idea of going out of your way to buy them started me laughing. Of course, it might have been the pot we'd just smoked but soon Jeremy was giggling too, and even John cracked a smile.

After the avalanche, I thought about that granola bar and how Jeremy took John's. It was such a nothing moment, but when we were up there, spitting crumbs at each other, it was obvious Jeremy had no idea what was coming.

'You're joking. They taste horrible,' I said.

'I'll be the judge of that.'

I was facing down the gradual slope of Little Cerro, perched on my sheet and trying to catch my breath. Without warning, Jeremy gave me a big shove and I was careening along the slope. It was faster than I expected: my fingers gripped the plastic through my bunchy gloves and I was in danger of sliding onto the snow. My hat flew off, ice was spitting up in my face and my weight kept shifting towards the edge of my sheet – it was liberating and freaky and almost too much. I watched the lake swerve closer and closer. My foot trailed in the snow, skid-breaking, but that veered me towards a bank until I caught air and waited, suspended for a long strange moment, before thumping down hard on the ice. I listened, to hear if Isobel might have forgiven me, if maybe she was laughing at me, but the air was silent and cold. As I stood up and waved to John and Jeremy, my thigh was aching from where I'd hit the ground.

❉

After John and Jeremy left, I wished that Emma had gone with them. In the refugio, playing cards in front of the fire, she was living proof that things could have turned out differently. I didn't have any optimism: I knew they were dead, I could just feel it.

At breakfast the morning they'd headed off, Jeremy grabbed my hand in some kind of thumped-up bro shake and I laughed, letting him pat me on the back. 'It was nice to meet you,' I said.

'Yeah. Travel safe.'

'You're definitely going?' I asked. I knew my dad was a peanut but he'd been droning on about safety and conditions and how the Americans shouldn't leave.

'We've got places to go, cabins to see. Sadly we must bid goodbye to Argentina's lost orphan,' Jeremy said.

'Who's that?' I asked.

'Emma.' Jeremy grinned.

'What does she have to do with anything?'

John shook his head. 'She doesn't. Jeremy's being a jerk.'

Jeremy shot him a look. 'If she asked us to stay, I would.'

'She's not going to fuck you.'

'Her loss.'

'Her loss, all right.' John was laughing and after a moment Jeremy joined him. Then he pushed his blond hair back into his bandana like there was more important stuff to get into. He pushed two joints into my hand before sitting down. 'You'll need them more than us.'

'Thanks.'

My family was waiting outside so I stashed them in my pocket and pulled on my gloves, trudging after them on yet another excursion. I didn't even look behind me as we zig-zagged down in front of the refugio; I just followed along, all of us boys marching in single file because 'families do things together'. The air was so cold my lungs ached and I had to wrap a scarf around my mouth and breathe through the wool. The only thing that made it bearable was Carmen – she joined us down near the lake.

We were about halfway around – tromping single file in our snowshoes – when we heard the avalanche. From where we were, it sounded faint, a slight cracking in the distance. Dad said it was nothing to worry about – probably a snow collapse high up on the Cerro Blanco ridge. It was only an hour later as we pushed through the front door of the refugio, Klaus carrying on about his *alfajores* and *dulce de leche* caramel sauce, that I knew something was wrong. The place was cold, the fire had burned out, and Pedro's cassette player was click-ing over, unable to change to the other side. I turned it off and the silence was eerie.

Felix and Klaus ran upstairs but no one was in the refugio. My parents checked the dining room again and, after sizing up our options, decided the thing to do was wait. They faced off against each other in a rare chess match – my mother doesn't have a lot of patience for board games – and I went outside. There's probably a good explanation, I thought, staring at the jagged mountain, but I couldn't see Pedro anywhere. Eventually my mother herded us all upstairs to clean our dormitory room.

❄

That afternoon, after lunch, my father was fussing over the radio in the kitchen and I was trying to ignore him from my perch in the dining room. My book was open in front of me but I hadn't been able to read. The thought kept beating through my head: *John and Jeremy are dead, John and Jeremy are dead.*

The door opened and Carmen interrupted my mantra. She walked by the table and then came back like she'd decided to tell me a secret. 'I need to radio my family.'

I wanted the news to come from me – like I understood the place. 'Radio's still broken.'

'What?' She hung up her coat and untied her hat from beneath her chin. Her thick hair was pulled back in a braid.

'My father's trying to fix it. Pedro's in there, too.'

Carmen strode into the kitchen where a flurry of Spanish erupted. I couldn't understand what Pedro was saying, but Carmen seemed anxious. Her voice was loud and Pedro was trying to calm her down.

When she came back out, she was almost crying. I motioned to the seat opposite but she sat down beside me. Her arm brushed mine as she settled into the bench and my first instinct was to rub her shoulders and warm her up as though she were Felix or Isobel. I tried to keep my tone neutral – whatever I said, I didn't want her to remember I was sixteen years old.

'I wouldn't be here if it weren't for him,' Carmen said.

'Who?'

'Pedro. I should never have trusted him.'

'Why do you need the radio?'

'Family.' She stared at me as though thinking about them pissed her off – she had these eyes that were brown-black, so dark you couldn't even make out her pupils. 'My father's dying.'

'Shit. Really?'

I regretted how quickly my words had fallen out, how thoughtless they were, but she smiled like I'd said something right and I prodded her along. 'You need to visit him?'

She held her hands up in a helpless gesture. 'That's what I'm trying to understand. I don't know.'

'But he's your father.'

She frowned and her mouth opened as if she were about to say something but Pedro and my dad cut through the room then, talking about the trail.

Carmen leaned forward so our faces were only centimetres apart. 'We haven't spoken in eight years. Since I was fifteen.'

I was impressed and kind of frightened by that – who doesn't talk to their parents for eight years? The most I'd lasted was eight days, probably not even that. I wanted to say something so she'd touch my hand or brush against my arm again but it was like the silence was too much for her and she sat up.

'I feel trapped in here. This room grows smaller and smaller. I need a walk.'

I thought maybe Carmen could tell I was checking her out and she wasn't impressed, but then she nudged my side with her elbow. 'You want to come around the lake? You know the path?'

'Yeah. Meet you outside?'

I darted upstairs for my jacket, and when I came down Carmen was bundled up, sitting on the front step and staring at Cerro Blanco. That's where two bodies are buried, I thought. You'd want it to be quick – nothing would be worse than waiting for help that didn't come.

Carmen was wearing her hat – a pink thing with a huge glittery pompom. 'We're safe around the lake?'

It was maybe three miles and we'd need snowshoes but the lake was set within a wide, open valley. We'd be fine.

'If the angle of the mountain is gradual, we're safe. My father took us hiking this morning and he doesn't go anywhere that's dangerous.' I was acting as a tougher version of myself and watched her out of the corner of my eye to see if it was working.

She didn't seem to notice or, if she did, she didn't care. 'It's nice to be outside, isn't it? I'm going *loca* in there.' She rolled her eyes all crazy, making me laugh, and then she joined in, both of us giddy as we strapped on our snowshoes. The walk was slow-going, each step took effort in the powder, but we held onto each other for balance.

'What are you going to do about your family?' I asked.

'What can I do?' She didn't seem to want an answer so I nodded as if I understood and she spoke again. 'What do you want out of your life, Jack?'

The trail was clear enough. I could see where my dad's skis had left a swish-swish track in the snow. And there I was, plodding right along in his path. It depressed me, like I couldn't escape him, but then Carmen stepped ahead and her pink jacket was bright against all that snow.

I spoke up so she could hear me. 'I don't know. There has to be something better, right?'

'So you're an optimist?'

'I don't know if I can find something better. I just know it's out there. That's why I get frustrated.'

Carmen turned around and sighed, her breath making a little cloud in front of her face. 'When I dance, I know where I'm supposed to be. I went to university in Córdoba to study science but I missed the tango.'

She circled her arm through mine. 'The movement becomes the moment and that's all that matters.'

'An escape?'

'The opposite. When you're dancing, you have to be inside the moment. But you are not alone, in fact you cannot be alone – you share it with your partner.'

'Will you teach me?' I tried not to act too excited but the idea was genius: learning to dance with Carmen would give me the perfect excuse to spend time with her – and we'd have to touch.

She started laughing like Isobel – a quiet flirty laugh – and I felt guilty. I didn't have a chance with Carmen, she was at least seven years older than me, but Isobel seemed so far away and for the quickest moment I didn't know or even care if she was waiting for me.

Carmen was watching the path. 'You want to learn the tango?'

'What else is there to do?'

We had a good view of the refugio against the mountain but all that white just made the place look desperate and bored.

Carmen sucked in her cheeks and then her face relaxed. 'Okay. I'll teach you. Maybe tomorrow.'

❋

But the next day we were trapped in together because of all the snow, everyone in the dining room, so we didn't get a chance. I wasn't going to let it go, though – the thought of dancing with Carmen was the only thing that kept me sane – the boredom was so intense in the refugio I would have gouged out my eyes with Klaus's bishop if anyone had dared me. Anything to break up the monotony.

That night, after dinner, I took Felix to the bathroom and used the opportunity to sit next to Carmen when we returned. We were going to play Truco but I was really trying to guide the conversation to our tango lesson when Wolfe knocked on the refugio door. My first thought was that it was Klaus, doing something silly, but he was sitting at the other table with my parents. Then I thought it was one of the Americans – or maybe both of them.

But when the door opened, Wolfe stormed in and he was on the offensive. He had this jittery presence so that even when he was still, it felt like he was moving – breathing over your shoulder or pawing through your things: it wasn't that I was scared exactly but there was something unsteady about him. Even Emma didn't like him, I could tell, and it's not like we agreed on stuff. The swastikas didn't help but I'd just been trying to make the point that my parents were hypocrites – they could have all the family heart-to-hearts they wanted about history and guilt and persecution, and it wouldn't change the fact they stayed at Heinrich's house for cookies and tea.

It was obvious there was something else going on too – something with Pedro. Wolfe may have been an experienced mountaineer but he wasn't a regular at the refugio – I heard him ask Pedro where the bathroom was after everyone had gone to bed. I'd come down for a cup of tea and had been standing in the stairwell when they headed outside.

I snuck into the kitchen – I don't know why I was so secretive, I just liked the idea of doing something without everyone in the fucking refugio knowing about it – and filled my mug with hot water and waited for my tea to steep. I was just poking through the kitchen, looking in cupboards, checking out Pedro's cookbooks, and there, hidden under a piece of cloth, behind a crusty flour container: the cigar box. I pulled it out – just ordinary wood with a tacky golden clasp – and swung the lid back and saw the envelope with the money. It was never about the cash, it was like moving cars with Isobel – I wanted people to question what mattered in the world: money is just a symbol, a way of valuing things, and if some money disappeared for a little while, maybe people would think about how much power they gave money in general. That was the hope anyway. I was never going to keep it – that would have defeated the point. And if the disappearing money made things more interesting around the place, if it started a witch-hunt, then that was an added bonus. No one could pin anything on me: no one would know I'd ever been alone downstairs.

❄

The morning after Wolfe arrived, Pedro was in the kitchen, staring at the two-way radio splayed out in front of him – back off, pieces and wires on the counter. He was watching the plastic casing as though it might just give up and tell him what was wrong.

I edged into the kitchen. 'Were you scared?'

He looked up, surprised, like he'd forgotten part of his job meant talking to guests. 'When?'

'After the avalanche.'

He stared at me like he had no idea how to deal with such a fuckwit. 'What do you think?'

If he wanted me to leave the kitchen, I wasn't going to budge. I didn't trust him, not if Carmen didn't, but I wanted him to know the story behind the swastikas. 'You from Bariloche?' My voice almost cracked.

Pedro took a deep breath and rubbed the side of his face, his voice relenting. 'North of Bariloche – a village in Neuquén.'

'Well, in Bariloche they've got this statue in the main square. General Roca. Beneath, the plaque says "Death to the Nazis". Graffiti. When we were visiting my uncle I realised Nazis really came here after the war.'

'They did.' His voice was matter-of-fact, as though it wasn't a good thing or a bad thing he was saying. 'Perón pardoned the Nazis. Our president was intrigued by them – their promise of nuclear power. Do you know Huemul Island, closest to Bariloche?'

I nodded.

'Perón gave the island and millions of dollars to a German, Richter. He was supposed to develop nuclear *fisión*.'

'Did it work?'

'Richter was a fraud. But you wonder: how many countries would support Germany after World War II? What does that say about Argentina?'

'Bet you don't get a lot of Israeli tourists.'

'Actually we do. Many German immigrants met mysterious deaths here in the 1970s and '80s. Even now, the Israelis come to travel, especially after their time in the military.'

Out in the dining room, Klaus was playing the same space-alien riff over and over on the metal guitar. I think it was supposed to be 'Lucy in the Sky with Diamonds'.

I didn't want to leave – there was something I needed to explain to Pedro and I couldn't put it into words. I waited, but he didn't look up.

❊

I think I wanted to tell Pedro how I'd been in charge of the map. In Bariloche, everything was measured in kilometres from the centre of town, and the town sat on this big-ass lake – Nahuel Huapi. The family hostel where we were staying was at kilo-metre 3.6 and my father's great-uncle lived at kilometre 15.8 with views right over the water.

The lakes in the province all looked the same to me, still and dark, and Nahuel Huapi was no exception – it was like someone had spread out a big plastic tarp so you couldn't see what lived below – and it didn't help that it was the local landmark, the one sure-fire way to find yourself on the map. It was creepy, that much empty space in the middle of the mountains.

We were in the rental car and I was navigating from the back seat because my parents are all about life skills. My mother was driving along Avenida Costanera and, because she wouldn't know how to speed if her foot turned to stone, we were being passed by every car and motorbike that zoomed up behind us. Drivers would wave at us all smug as they zipped by: oh-my-god embarrassing.

I knew ex-Nazis had immigrated to South America, but I didn't really think about what that meant for day-to-day life – Nazis at the supermarket or Nazis at the gas station – and I certainly didn't think my father would be related to one of them.

We pulled up in front of this A-frame cottage with a dark grey Ford Falcon parked in the driveway. Dad's great-uncle Heinrich was staring out the window, curtain pulled back, when we arrived. He let us in, white hair all wavy, and shook my father's hand before gripping each one of us boys around our shoulders and staring us in the eyes. When he reached for me, I was surprised by his strength. He smelled of cigars and leaned in close like he was going to say something but he just peered at me instead – his eyes glassy blue and thin, like mine. I'd always thought I had my mother's eyes.

Heinrich showed us into his living room, walking with a gold-tipped cane that seemed like an accessory more than anything else. My family all perched ridiculously close on this leather couch in front of a fire that was blasting out a ton of heat. Felix sat on my lap, sliding his hand back and forth along the armrest like an airplane taking off.

There's nothing more awkward than meeting people for no other reason than you're distantly related, and my mother wouldn't shut up – the flight from San Francisco, increasing fares, changes in altitude. You would have thought she was the one who'd just discovered her long-lost relations. My father sat on the other side of her, smiling and piping in whenever she paused for a man's input into things.

When Heinrich pushed himself out of his chair to get more anise cookies from the kitchen, my father followed to help. Felix was crushing my leg so I shifted him and stood up, walking towards the fire. On the mantel there was this series of photos – a wedding shot, a couple of family portraits, and then on the end: an old black-and-white of a crowd, a huge crowd, and in the background, a large Nazi banner. It looked like an image from our German history books and my first thought was that Heinrich produced textbooks, that's how far away World War II seemed, and then I looked closer: it was Hitler staring out from behind the podium. He looked small, dwarfed by the immense crowd, but his slick hair and stern eyes were unmistakeable. The frame was solid pewter, heavy, and the back was crushed velvet. It unlatched, and I realised the photograph was an original, a processing stamp had been pressed into the paper – someone had taken and processed this photo. Someone had been at a rally and here, over sixty years later, the image was preserved in a thick silver-grey frame. My mouth gaped open and my mother was suddenly behind me, taking the picture out of my hands.

'Shush,' she said. But I hadn't said anything. And after everything that we'd heard and everything we'd learned in school – the field trip to Dachau; the reading lists with Anne Frank and Elie Wiesel; the never-ending, never-get-over-it guilt – when it came to facing our past, my mother hushed me. The hypocrisy is what got me. Her fingers tried to reassemble the photo and the frame, fumbling with the latch, but her hands were too large and she tried to push the photograph at me.

'I'm not touching it,' I said. When she set it back on the mantelpiece, the image was at an angle inside the frame.

'What are you going to do?' I asked.

She swallowed and I realised she was incapable of rudeness,

even to a Nazi: the woman had as much conviction as a beige wall. Her mouth opened into a perplexed circle and then closed. Before she could reply, I stormed out – I wasn't going to sit there, making small talk with a long-lost uncle who thought it was great to kill millions of people. The front door was too heavy to slam but I did my best and then I was left standing outside where it had begun to snow.

I waited. Surely the rest of my family would be following. But after ten minutes, the door still hadn't opened. Shivering, I began to pace the street. Heinrich's neighbours lived in similar log cabins, all the orange-yellow colour of carsickness with smoke drifting from their chimneys. I stared at the windows, wondering how many of them knew Heinrich's past, how many of them shared it. It was on my second time around the block that I heard Felix pattering behind me, and turned to see the hood of his parka pulled close around his ears.

He was holding a key chain. 'We can wait in the car if you want. Heater.'

He unlocked the door, using both hands, and we sat together in the front driver's seat with the blowers on high. Felix didn't say anything; he just nestled close into my chest. Even with the air gusting from the front vent, our breath fogged the windows.

'It's bad enough that the adults in this world are still putting in nuclear power plants and digging up coal and fucking over the planet with more cars and massive office blocks. On top of that, they're hypocrites who can't deal with the past. I don't fucking get it.'

Felix clasped his arms around my neck, and I was just glad someone understood.

❄

But of course I couldn't put this into words for Pedro and I couldn't quite leave the kitchen. Pedro had given up on the radio and was standing at the counter, sizing up the ingredients for lunch: a bundle of meat was wrapped in plastic, thawing. I leaned against the window and could feel the slick chill of the glass through my sweater. When Wolfe walked in, he was full of aggression but the man was as helpless as the rest of us – what use is a journalist on top of a mountain? What use is a journalist anywhere, really? They're just go-to men for the corporations. Wolfe leaned against the doorframe, checking out the kitchen. 'I can cook here?'

If Wolfe were a regular, he'd already know the rules: he could cook in the kitchen but he'd have to wait for Pedro to finish. Maybe something deeper was going on because Pedro didn't look up, he was concentrating on the potatoes – his knife was so dull he had to saw into them. 'Just give me a bit of space.'

I was surprised. No one else got to do that.

Behind Wolfe, Klaus was strumming away in the dining room with our latest game of Monopoly abandoned beside him.

Pedro moved onto the meat. The ground beef was still semi-frozen so he hacked it into smaller chunks. 'Can I buy powdered milk from you?'

Wolfe's voice was gruff. 'Why?'

Pedro still hadn't looked up. 'How much food do you have?'

Wolfe didn't reply.

Pedro continued: 'We don't know how long we'll be here. In autumn, the horses didn't come as planned. Then snow arrived early . . .'

Wolfe's three fingers were tapping at the dark wood. 'I carried my food in, I'll eat it. Last night, you had enough supplies. Certainly enough alcohol.'

'I have root vegetables. Wine and beer, fine. But otherwise . . .' Pedro looked up, watching the American for five or six seconds, crazy-slow seconds, and then moved to the sink to wash his hands.

Wolfe just shook his head like it wasn't his problem, and that pissed me off but I didn't have to worry because Pedro was onto it – whatever Wolfe might have had on him, the Argentinean was ready to beat it. 'We don't have a choice. We need to combine supplies,' he said.

'I don't have to do anything.'

Pedro smiled like he had Wolfe at checkmate. 'If you want the protection of the refugio ...'

Wolfe scratched his head like he was trying to pause the conversation. 'What?' He fully entered the room then and dropped his knapsack behind him. 'Are you threatening me?'

Pedro looked like he was ready to spring at Wolfe and beat the shit out of him. And weirdly, if I needed to back one of them, my money would have been on Pedro. But the Argentinean just looked back to the dishes, his voice super-smooth. 'Think it through: that's all. It's better if we're a group.'

Wolfe didn't move; his eyes were still trained on Pedro. 'I'll bring down what I have,' he said, and I could feel the tension in the refugio rising in certain, bored increments.

When Carmen came in, I'd settled in front of the fire with my book, imagining myself riding on the back of a truck across America and leaving love notes for waitresses. Pedro and Emma were hiking to the waterfall, my family was out around the lake and Wolfe was fuck-knows-where – probably chain-smoking up a mountain and telling himself how smart he was. We had the dining room to ourselves.

'You ready?' She'd found a cassette tape with dramatic accordion music that could've been a soundtrack to smoky rooms and gangsters; it was the same kind of stuff my family had heard at the Café Tortoni tango show in Buenos Aires. Carmen picked up the end of one of the tables, and we edged it back to the window and stacked a couple of the benches on top. As I swept the floor, Carmen straddled one of the remaining benches.

'The tango is a negotiation. You plead your case with me. Perhaps I understand. Perhaps I forgive you. But then I plead my case with you. The crossover step is where that negotiation happens. We are both powerful and vulnerable. We are fighting and reconciling. There is nothing that hesitates in the conflict. And whatever comes, it must always be honest. Sit down,' she said, counting out the eight beats and patting my arm in time. 'Now join me.'

We ran through the numbers again and again before she stood up and held the imaginary hand of an imaginary partner. It was only eight steps – an extended rectangle – and her feet always started off the same way: first the right goes backwards and the left takes you around the corner, then the crossover step. I pretended to focus on her feet – I *tried* to focus on her feet – but her legs, shimmering in black leggings, kept drawing my field of focus further up. If she noticed me staring at her, she didn't let on. 'It's easy. Here.' She counted off.

We were both barefoot with our hands clasped and elbows bent to ninety degrees. She moved in slow motion and I followed, aware of the hot stove – our full dancing area was no more than fifteen or twenty square feet. When I'd been sitting on the bench, the progression seemed obvious – but moving with Carmen, I couldn't mirror her steps.

She nodded like she was thinking to herself and pressed play on the cassette machine, her voice carrying over the accordion. 'Five, six, seven, eight . . .' The music was forceful and I had trouble stepping off on the first count so she waited and counted in again. This time I was ready. We marched through the eight beats so I could learn them by rote, drilling the numbers into my head and counting my feet into place. Again. And again.

When my feet followed naturally, she said, 'Your hand must press between my shoulders. I should know what to do by the way you touch me. I can teach you steps but I can't teach you to lead. You must do that yourself. Try it again . . . six, seven, eight . . .'

When our feet pushed off, I realised she was right about losing yourself in the tango – the only thing I could focus on was dancing: I was aware of her breath, her arms, the way her feet marked time. The music was all I could hear and for the first time since we'd arrived at the refugio, I forgot I was in the mountains, I forgot I wasn't getting laid and I forgot I hated my family.

In our first lesson, we drilled the eight steps over and over until my forehead was sweaty but thankfully my hands stayed dry. After an hour, I could almost lead, migrating our little box around the open area.

'Next time, we go further,' she said and sat down to rest.

'Why did you come here?' I asked.

'To the refugio? It wasn't my intention.' She glanced around the dining room like she still couldn't quite understand how she'd ended up there. 'I was going to a little cabin. You can find it through the forest. Two, maybe three hours from here. Off the path. I used to go there as a child. It's—' she swallowed, '—beautiful, quaint. I'd gone there to figure out what to do about my family, and Pedro came, walking with supplies. I thought I was doing the right thing. I needed to get away. I didn't realise . . .'

She'd become so sad all of a sudden. I knew about that cabin: my dad had been keen to go there before the weather changed – it was on another trail. If you crossed the creek and went right, instead of left, over Cerro Negro and into the woods, and kept going past the cabin, you'd link up with the main track near Bariloche. But I didn't want to think about my dad and the stuff we weren't able to do, I just wanted to make Carmen feel better. Things had been fine between us when we were dancing but that familiarity had disappeared – I shouldn't have given it up so easily, I should have fought for it, given her a hug, but instead I picked up a ballpoint that had been used to keep Monopoly score, and flipped it around my thumb in a move Isobel had taught me. Carmen and I both watched the pen whipping in tight circles, balancing against gravity.

❊

After we pulled the tables and benches back into place, Carmen disappeared upstairs to read and I was sitting at the window, waiting – waiting for something, anything, to happen – but without Carmen, the dining area felt stuffy and second-hand. Everything from the fraying curtains to the recycled plastic forks had been used and re-used, even my books and the playing cards were tattered. When the door burst open, my head jerked up but it was only my father, covered in powder, grinning like snow was the best thing that had ever been invented.

'I am digging – no, I dug – test pits out by the trail: the snow is not stable.' He said this in English even though there were no English speakers in the room – my parents had a thing about using common languages: they didn't want to be rude.

'What about Cerro Negro, the way Wolfe came in?' I asked.

'He hiked cross-country. We need to stay with a trail.'

'Any idea when we'll be able to leave?'

He shook his head.

'Great.' If I'd had my book, I would have looked down to it. My little brothers were following him in and I didn't like the way he was watching me, raising his eyebrows – like we were some kind of father–son duo who'd been put in this refugio to entertain my little brothers.

'You'll play Monopoly with us?'

I still couldn't believe someone had carried the board game all the way up the mountain: the properties had names like North Carolina and Illinois so I was assuming it had been an American, probably a tourist, which made me think of Jeremy and John and that left me feeling queasy.

I didn't look at my father. 'Nothing would interest me less, thank you.'

Klaus grinned. 'Jack is too sophisticated to play with us; he likes to avoid capitalistic greed mongering when he can.' He'd learned that expression from Isobel when she'd tried explaining the evils of chain stores to him.

'Shut up,' I said.

Beyond the window, the snow was whirling in gusts – it was responsible for everything, I thought. Without it, Jeremy and John would be alive; I wouldn't be hiding the refugio money or learning the tango; Carmen would have called her family – maybe she'd already be with them.

My brothers were now shouting out for the shoe, the hat, the car and my father, always the banker, was counting out money. Felix got so excited jumping up and down, he had to take a time-out for his asthma inhaler: he shook the powder-blue tube and held it up, sucking at the plastic mouthpiece. Klaus was eyeing off Broadway and Park Place while I leaned against the window and searched through my daypack for my copy of *On the Road*.

The game took all day and, believe me, it was a slow-moving day. When the final property had been purchased and almost half of them had plastic houses and hotels, Pedro hollered out that dinner was ready.

'Let's move down here,' my father said, inching the board towards the window.

Someone out in the hallway was stomping snow off their boots. The door opened and Emma stood for an awkward moment by the fireplace, warming her hands before helping my father and younger brothers set the table – of course my father was nice to her, asking what she'd done that day.

'Hiking around the lake with Pedro.'

My father smiled like she'd really excelled herself and I realised he liked her – not like he wanted to sleep with her or anything like that – but still he liked her. That made me hate them both even more.

I was thinking about the money, wondering when Pedro was going to discover it was missing, as Carmen and Wolfe came in, both of them laughing and speaking in Spanish. Wolfe's voice seemed louder, more emphatic than usual, and I wondered if he was trying to compensate in a foreign language or if it was Carmen's influence. He was telling a joke I couldn't understand and rubbing the side of his jaw with his hand, the one with missing fingers. I couldn't help staring – it looked so gruesome – and I wondered how Carmen could listen to him without being distracted, but he delivered some punch line and she pushed his arm, laughing.

He reached into his backpack for a big bag of rice and a zip-lock baggie of milk powder and shoved them at Pedro. 'I just want it to look like I care about the needs of the group.'

'That's fine with me,' Pedro said, taking both of the bags into the kitchen.

Emma followed, returning with a stack of plates. Felix and Klaus were busy at the table folding paper napkins into origami shapes – cranes, grasshoppers and fortune-tellers. My father was pouring everyone water.

I rolled my eyes. 'Maybe people aren't thirsty.'

'Maybe they are,' he replied, guzzling down a full glass as though it were a beer-drinking competition until Felix and Klaus started chanting, 'Drink, drink, drink.'

My mother frumped in then, shaking her head at my

brothers and hanging her coat on one of the spikes next to Wolfe's polar fleece. She squeezed in next to me on the bench while Felix climbed up on my other side. Usually I love sitting next to my brother but Carmen was at the other end, next to Wolfe. They were shifting between English and Spanish and it was impossible to understand them over the noise of Klaus and Felix arguing about the World Cup.

We hadn't been able to get any news on the games with the radio down and this was a continual point of angst for Klaus. My parents had promised – *promised*, he kept reminding them – we could stay in a hotel with cable TV during the World Cup. Surely Germany would get through to the finals, though we didn't have an easy draw. Felix wasn't as loud as Klaus but he was probably the more committed fan: his passion was a thoughtful one – when my parents read to him before bed, he wanted to hear the biographies of the world's greatest players and then the histories of their countries.

We were eating a dry potato mash with flecks of beef in it. Felix grinned, placing a big chunk in his mouth with his fingers. Carmen glanced up to catch me watching her and smiled. She shrugged and I rolled my eyes, making sure to look away first.

After dinner, when Emma was playing her crap Australian music and we were all dancing, Pedro made the big announcement that the money was missing. It was great – everyone was so worked up and suspicious, trying to figure out the culprit. They missed the whole point: that nothing had to change with the money gone. In fact, nothing did change. The refugio was so far from the rest of the world, it was an ideal place for a utopia – we could make a new way of living if we just agreed on it. It was that simple.

Wolfe was playing all Sherlock with the refugio money and I was careful of him because of that. After grilling me in the dining room, he followed me into the kitchen, sneaky, and I didn't like it.

'Why'd you take the refugio money?'

I shrugged my shoulders. 'Wasn't me.'

'Who else would take it?'

My mother followed in then and this filled me with dread – she could always tell when I was lying.

'Someone's taken the money and I'm willing to bet five hundred bucks it was one of your boys. Let's see, Guitar Man?' Wolfe gazed back into the dining room to Klaus, who'd picked up the metal guitar again. He was hammering 'Eight Days A Week' like a '90s grunge star. Wolfe shook his head, 'Not smart enough. What about Little Swastika?' He glanced at Felix, sitting on a bench, swinging his legs. 'Don't think so. That leaves our G8 protester.'

My mother peered at me then, her lower lip protruding ever so slightly in a way that reminded me of farm animals.

'Wasn't me,' I said, strolling past my mother and continuing on to the outside door. I would have stopped to see if Carmen wanted to join me for some fresh air but she was singing along with Klaus and Felix, and I felt allergic to family.

❄

The next morning, everyone was packed into the dining room when I came down for breakfast – my brothers were scooping jam onto their toast, and Emma was talking to Wolfe, with a half-finished game of solitaire in front of her: you couldn't invent a more brain-numbing game.

When my mother announced the big search for Pedro's cash I needed to stash the money quickly. So I waited until the adults were in the kitchen, washing their dishes, and pushed it behind an old chessboard at the back of the games shelf in the dining room. My brothers were in the room but I just made it seem casual, like I was looking for something, and no one noticed. Then I stashed the envelope in Emma's pack for a bit of excitement – her dorm room was open and it couldn't have been easier.

When that was taken care of, I grabbed a piece of toast and headed outside with my brothers and Wolfe. He didn't mention the money and I was civil to him. Together, we entertained my brothers by building a life-sized car out of snow – it was pretty good but the roof kept caving in on us.

When my mother came outside and announced that Emma was the thief, Wolfe raised his eyebrows and stared at me but didn't say a word. After a few minutes, I followed my mother inside. She was already busy, going through Pedro's cupboards. I stood behind her, but she was counting to herself in German.

I cleared my throat. 'What are you doing?'

She held up a finger to shush me as she finished and then jotted something on a notepad. 'Pedro and I are drawing up a log to see how much food we have.'

'What, and we could go hungry? Eat each other? Great. Nice trip, Ma. Glad we missed the World Cup for this.'

'Hans.'

Her voice was tired but I couldn't stop myself. 'Jack.'

'Fine, Jack.'

I smacked my tongue against the roof of my mouth. 'First, a warm snap and now more powder. We might be here for weeks before we can hike out. This is becoming a real adventure. Congratulations.' I didn't mean to be such a jerk, I really didn't; these things just fell out of my mouth.

I was thinking I should say something nice and balance things out a bit when she cleared her throat. 'Did you take the money?' She was watching me, her eyes flint-blue.

I crossed my arms over my chest and leaned against the counter. 'Isn't it enough that we're alive? People care too much about material possessions. We're in the mountains, away from global capitalism, and everyone still hangs on to this idea of possession. Why?'

'Pedro's asked Emma to leave.'

'What?' Emma was a tool but it never occurred to me that Pedro would ask her to leave.

'It's dangerous outside.'

I took a deep breath. 'I know.'

My mother just stared at me – all slow and careful. I didn't like Emma but I didn't want her to die. I had to get the money back to Pedro sooner rather than later, without giving myself away.

My mother pushed her glasses back into place. 'Did you take the money?'

'Wish I had. Teach people about possession.'

That's when my father wandered into the kitchen and piped up like we could turn this into a family dialogue. 'We tried that but then the '80s came along.'

My mother sighed, we were getting off track: my father didn't get the subtext, he never did – he was just smiling to himself, a big toothy grin.

I shook my head emphatically. 'No. *You* tried that. I didn't try that. I wouldn't fail as badly as you all. Look at your generation: greedy and pathetic.'

And for a funny moment, I was tempted to confess: to just blurt out that it had been me, I'd stolen the money – but of course I always have to push things to the limit so I stood there with my arms crossed, waiting.

❊

Half an hour later, I was sitting at the dining table, listening to Klaus bang out a tinny version of 'Yellow Submarine'. Outside, the snow was falling again. They say every snowflake's different but I don't buy that. There was too much of it – like the stuff was mass-produced and they couldn't get rid of it anywhere else so they dumped it all up here. Pedro and Wolfe stormed outside together – they were arguing about the money: Wolfe was telling Pedro that he'd got it wrong, there was no way Emma had stolen it; Pedro was telling him to mind his own business. The angst made me smile, a small win for the anti-capitalists, but still, I needed to fix things up.

I leaned in towards Klaus. 'Tidy-check this afternoon.' Our mother was such a fucking control freak she policed our beds and backpacks, making sure all of our clothes were folded and sleeping bags laid out straight.

'Really?' He still hadn't figured out they happened like clockwork every day after lunch. He leaned the instrument on the bench. 'Thanks, Jack.'

'Not a problem.' His guitar was giving me a headache and I had to clear Emma's name.

The door closed behind him and I counted to five before double-checking the kitchen: I was alone. Fucking hallelujah. I scurried to the games shelf, grabbed the wad of bills and ducked into the kitchen, setting the money on the fridge – but that was too obvious so I moved it to the windowsill, behind the curtain. Perfect.

I left the kitchen and waited in the dining room but I was still bored and no one had come in, so I reached into Wolfe's fleece to check his pockets. I wasn't looking to take anything – I just wanted to know his story.

Wolfe's wallet had a picture of a woman and a little boy. The woman had thin brown hair and blue eyes, and was dressed up for something – fancy shoes and slacks. She was cradling the boy, who was in pyjamas. The kid was maybe five years old and looked Native American – he was pale but with a broad nose and round face. I wondered if Wolfe had adopted him but the

American didn't strike me as an open-border kind of guy. The woman and child were looking just left of the camera as though someone else had also been taking a photo and they'd decided to focus on them first. Wolfe also had a first-aid card, two credit cards and a bunch of receipts. It was disappointing – the guy had a family, but so what? I slipped the wallet back into his pocket.

❋

After lunch, I cleared the dishes and helped Pedro wash up. I'd decided to be on my best behaviour until the money appeared. My father had found a cassette tape of Elvis Christmas carols and he kept taking turns with putting away dishes and dancing my mother around the kitchen. The dish towel was smelly but I pushed it down to the bottom of each glass and over-dried the plates, watching my parents. My mother was a schoolteacher back in Germany. My father was a geologist who'd been lumped with too much administration in the university system. If I were either of them, would I be in Argentina with three kids? Would that be enough? Would I be happy?

I'd finished with a large pot and was about to ask where it went when I saw Pedro at the window – he'd moved the curtain aside to open the glass for a bit of air and was looking down, surely at the money. I kept watching the polished tub in my hands so Pedro wouldn't think I'd known anything – it wouldn't look good to pre-empt his announcement that the illustrious money had finally been found.

'Well . . .' he said, holding it up for my parents to see. It was anticlimactic. I wanted some bigger reaction but he just stuffed the wad of cash into his pocket without counting it and I didn't feel any freer than before.

❋

I decided to smoke one of the joints Jeremy had given me – a little cigarette of bliss and escape. The front door scraped closed behind me and the cold felt liberating. I was wearing all my sweaters under my coat, but I'd need them, especially after a couple of hours outside – my plan was to waste as much time as possible. Every minute that passed took me closer to the time that we could strap on our packs and walk out of there.

I fingered the joints – they'd been crushed in my pocket, the grey thin paper stained from where Jeremy had licked it. Smoking the joints would be my way of honouring the Americans, like a memorial. I couldn't do it around the lake because someone might come across me – people kept hiking and skiing around it for exercise – and if I went behind the bathrooms, the smell might waft down. But maybe I could go up from the refugio, find a big rock to hide behind or something.

I took a couple of steps, punching into the top of the snow that Pedro had pushed off the roof – it had solidified into an uneven barrier around the refugio. I was thinking about the likelihood of Klaus and Felix following my tracks when someone grabbed my shoulder and shoved me back into the ice wall.

'You little fucker. I know you took the money.' It was Wolfe, his voice thick like sawdust. He started coughing and I stepped forward for better footing but he shoved me again, harder.

'What?'

'I know it wasn't Emma.' He leaned against me and the wall behind gave way. Tripping backwards, I tried to wriggle out of his grasp but he had me firm and his forearm was digging into my neck. 'What on earth are you playing at?'

He tightened his grip and I clutched for breath.

That was the moment Felix's voice echoed from the doorway, shouting to Klaus about seed-poops, and Wolfe relaxed his arm and pushed me away.

My hand was massaging my throat. 'You fucking psycho.' I was too weirded out to smoke the joint so I hurried back inside.

❋

The only thing that made the refugio bearable was Carmen. She grabbed my arm that afternoon and whispered that the dining room was free. I was eager to dance. I'd been practising the steps upstairs, humming the tune to myself. When I held Carmen in my arms and we moved across the floor, I was more confident. I still stumbled on the crossover step, it wasn't easy, but I was getting better. Carmen nodded her approval. 'It comes naturally for you.'

At dinner, Wolfe made a point of watching my mother when he came into the dining room. When she glanced at him, he grinned and then turned his eerie smirk to me and walked fully round the table until he was beside me. I wanted to move – the guy was a freak who smelled like an ashtray – but my mother gave me one of those looks and I stayed put while Felix nestled into my other side. Emma was at the other end of the table – as far from Pedro as possible.

'Carmen, Carmen, sit near us,' my youngest brother said when she entered the room and I nearly gave him a high five: Carmen would distract us all, even Wolfe.

She bestowed a glossy smile on Felix and turned to the American. 'What have you been doing?'

'Jack and I admired the mountains. Quite a view from the east side of the refugio.'

'Is there?' Carmen looked at me, expectant.

'Depends on what you're looking for.' If you want a view of a crazy-fuck American strangling you it's great, I thought.

But what I really wanted was to talk to her about the tango. I was wondering how to get her alone when my mother called out. 'Jack, make sure your brother eats his dinner. There's not enough to waste.'

Felix squirmed beside me, sitting up on his knees. 'It's revolting,' he whispered in my ear. Pedro had undercooked the rice and overcooked the vegetables.

'I know. Let me help you . . .'

Together we started matching each other bite for bite. After a few, he tugged on my arm and I bent down so his breath tickled my ear. 'This is really disgusting.'

I squeezed his knee. 'I have crackers upstairs. We'll pretend we're going to the bathroom and get them.'

'You're my favourite oldest brother.'

'Yeah, I'm your only oldest brother.'

A few minutes later, Felix threw one hand over his eye and leaned back. 'I'm so sorry to trouble everyone, but I must depart for the facilities.' The kid was a nut – both of us were cracking up.

My mother's mouth pursed; she knew we were up to something but couldn't figure it out. 'Can it wait?'

'I'll take him. Come on, buddy.' Before she could protest, I lifted Felix from the table by his arms and carried him over to the empty bench where we put on our boots. 'We'll be right back.'

After slamming the outside door, we tiptoed back upstairs to my secret stash of chocolate-hazelnut spread and crackers, and I ripped open a pack. Felix held his hands out – we each got five wafers. He grinned, his tongue pushing against his two new teeth, and I scooped into the spread with one of the crackers before passing him the jar. The pressure to eat quickly made it taste even better.

After Felix scoffed down his share, he hugged me and planted a slobbery kiss, full of crumbs, on my cheek. I pinned him down and messed up his hair. He giggled and tried to get a hold of my arm.

'They're waiting for us.'

He dipped his finger into the chocolate one last time and sucked on it. We jumped over the creaky step on the stairs and gave each other a quick brush-down to clear away any cracker evidence.

'Let's be tin soldiers,' Felix said. So we paraded in, with stiff arms and military gaits, and I was glad to see Wolfe had left the table. My mother, of course, was still sitting there, her head swivelling towards us as we marched by the fireplace.

'Whatever you're doing, you still have to finish your meals. No one's leaving the table until Felix's plate is clean.'

Felix sat down and stared dismally at his rice while I took a secret spoonful from his plate.

When our parents disappeared into the kitchen to help with the dishes, Klaus took a mouthful and even Carmen leaned across the table.

'Here, I'll help.' She took my spoon and pushed it into Felix's mush before licking it clean. I couldn't believe it: we were sharing a spoon. She winked at both of us then, sitting back when my mother stomped into the room to clear the remaining dishes.

'Well done, Felix,' she said.

Klaus shuffled forward on the bench, poking out his thin chest. 'Does that mean we all get a Manteca bar?' He was addicted to the sweet chalk candy that tasted like almonds.

'There's only two left. You can share one.'

I split my portion and offered half to Carmen, who smiled and placed the whole piece in her mouth. It was the kind of thing Isobel would have done. I usually took my time with sweets, savouring each bite. I thought of the night with Isobel and the romance novels, the way she ripped open that bag of gummy bears and sprung handfuls into her mouth – but I didn't want to be thinking about her with Carmen right there, so I tried to concentrate on the sweet texture of the Manteca bar. When I glanced up, Wolfe was standing in the doorway watching me, one hand tucked in his front pocket. It pissed me off, the way he was looking at me. I'd returned the money – what else was I supposed to do?

❄

The next morning, after a breakfast of rock-hard toast, everyone helped tidy up and wash the dishes except Wolfe, who just sat on the bench, reading the same *Sky-Dive* magazine that had shuffled around the dining room since we'd arrived.

Someone – Emma, probably – put on the ABBA cassette and I thought I was going to lose my mind with the saccharine pop. Instead, I focused on wiping down the tables in long, broad strokes.

Carmen's voice cut over the music. 'Pedro, the hot water's not working.'

Everyone crowded into the kitchen then, even Wolfe. Beside the sink, the large drum looked fine, it didn't smell electrical, but Pedro was able to rest his hand comfortably on the drum and this wasn't a good sign. 'Hmm . . .'

All of us were milling around like retarded cows: Carmen was holding a *maté* thermos; my father was leaning back on his heels, pretending he knew something about electricity, while my mother waited beside him, no doubt making lists inside her head about what a blown-out hot water system would mean to life in the refugio; Wolfe was perched against the far window with Emma; and my brothers were sneaking into the cupboards to see if Pedro had any secret stores of candy bars.

If it hadn't been such a perfect opportunity, I wouldn't have done it – I thought I'd learned my lesson, but the ease of it all was too tempting. One foot inched back, almost of its own accord, and then another, and before I was even aware of myself, I was back in the dining room, grabbing the first thing I could see – my mother's purse. It was an ugly thing, denim fabric, with a big pocket on the front like it had been made from the seat of someone's jeans. Ducking into the hallway, I opened the side closet and stashed the bag behind a stack of wooden crates.

I was gone fifteen seconds max and my re-entry into the kitchen was smooth. No one even glanced at me, they were watching Pedro – especially my father, who was cooing over the Argentinean's handiwork. Pedro was pulling the elements out of the heater – there were six of them, taken from individual kettles, bound with wire and strapped to the top of the drum.

'You did this yourself?' my father asked, as though hot water were up there with inventing the automobile or the internet.

Pedro reached for a screwdriver. 'That should fix it.'

I leaned in next to Carmen and she smiled. When Klaus went to the bathroom, I nudged her: 'Wonder where he's going?'

At lunchtime, the interrogations started: my little brothers were each questioned. At first, it seemed the attention I'd already received set me outside the line of inquiry but that was only because my mother was saving the best for last. I was reading – elbows on the table, shoulders hunched – when she grabbed my upper arm, her finger digging into my bicep. It was a death grip but I was feeling strong and dumb that afternoon.

Her face was no more than an inch or two from mine. 'Is it you?'

'What?'

'Don't push it, Hans Meyers. Are you the thief?'

'I told you, no.' I squirmed away, glancing outside.

My mother's hand grabbed me by the chin. 'Look at me.'

We were almost touching – her nose was big and round, sloping down her face, her forehead flaking with dead skin.

My throat was stiff. 'I didn't take your purse.'

Her grip relaxed and she smiled, tired. 'Okay then.'

'Glad we cleared that up. I'm going outside.'

It was a stupid thing, stealing the purse. I was going to have to return it or get one of my brothers to look in the closet, maybe a game of hide-and-seek. It could wait, though – I needed that joint. And I wanted a little time to think about Jeremy and John.

I went upstairs to get some crackers and chocolate-hazelnut spread for a private feast but my backpack had been cleaned out. I looked under the bunk but it was stuffed with my father's mountain gear. I combed through my brothers' bags in case they'd decided to start a family riot but there was nothing. It didn't make sense.

My mother looked up as I stomped into the dining room.

'Did you take my food?' I asked.

'We've pooled everything together.'

'What?' It took a moment for me to realise what she was saying.

'In case you hadn't noticed, Jack, we're surrounded in emergency.'

'You went through my bag? Without even asking?' It was fucking unbelievable. I thought of my mother rifling through my stuff, and wanted to ram my fist into the wall. Thank God the joints were in my pocket.

'Everyone's donated all their food. We're keeping it locked each night.'

I knew Wolfe would have kept stores for himself – there's no way that asshole would give everything to Pedro – but I was too pissed off to argue. 'Jesus Christ.'

'Hans.'

'You could have asked.'

She sighed and pushed her glasses up along her nose. 'I suppose we should have.'

'You think?' I didn't wait for a reply – I flew out of there, into the cold air outside. Hypocrisy! If I'd done the same thing to them, going through their bags without asking, taking whatever

I wanted, I'd be bailed up big time. It just wouldn't happen. Wait until I'm eighteen, I thought, I'll leave this fucking family and never look back.

The front door slammed closed behind me. I couldn't be fucked hiking too far away so I climbed to the nearest boulder, keeping on the firmer snow. I had a clear view down on the refugio and would be able to see if anyone approached. If my parents discovered me smoking some weed and wanted to cause a scene, they were welcome to it.

Carving out a hollow space beside the rock, I sat cross-legged. With snow pants and boots, it wasn't graceful but it seemed an appropriate gesture for Jeremy and John. 'Here you go, boys.'

I reached in my pocket for the joints; they were taper-thin and smooth. The lighter flicked on easily enough and the paper caught. I breathed deep and held the smoke in my lower lungs to keep from coughing – it tasted warm and soothing, and I wondered what Carmen was doing at that exact moment: this light-headed ease was meant to be shared. I'd save the second joint for her, I decided – she was probably in the kitchen, talking to Pedro as he fiddled with the radio. In the dining room, I could imagine my brothers hounding my father to take them skating. My mother would be sitting at the table, humming Elvis and looking at the South America itinerary in front of her, revising it for the eightieth time, taking our added delay into account, considering which sights to drop from her list.

In my little snow pocket, tucked away from them all, I felt distanced and omniscient. I took another slow drag and sat back – even though it was still snowing, the sky seemed lighter, the cold friendly. That was when the wailing started: it took a couple of seconds to register the sound echoing up from the refugio – it was high, almost inhuman, like a cartoon hyena – and I wondered for a brief moment if I were imagining it, but the door shot open and Klaus was outside, hands cupped over his mouth, yelling my name.

I stood up too fast and everything turned spotty; I was dizzy.

'Up here,' I called out but he didn't hear me so I started straight down the slope but the path wasn't clear and I tripped, my leg plunging into the snow. Pulling my thigh free, I concentrated on following my footsteps down and keeping my weight light.

'I'm coming.' My breath was heavy. When I finally staggered into the clear area in front of the refugio, Klaus was flapping his hands, on the verge of hyperventilating.

'What is it?' I asked. The yelling was coming from inside – it was my mother; it was louder than I'd thought.

Klaus's hands were fully tensed, his fingers rigid. 'Felix. Felix is having an asthma attack.'

'What?'

'And the . . . the . . . inhaler is in Mama's purse.' The words seemed to spin like a computer graphic, fast then slow, turning inside out, shifting backwards. It took valuable seconds for my brain to comprehend what he was saying.

'Fuck.' Already I was running inside, into the noise. My boots clomped snow and dirt on the floor. The closet door was stuck and I yanked it open, and there, behind the boxes and under the hanging coats, the purse. It was just sitting there: quiet and innocuous. I scooped it up and pushed into the dining room where my mother was holding Felix between her legs and pumping his bare chest with her hands. My father was beside her, cupping Felix's head. I knew it was Felix because he was wearing green socks and brown trousers – *Felix's* green socks and brown trousers – but that tiny body couldn't belong to my brother, surely it couldn't? What had I done? Jesus fucking Christ, what had I done?

My father glanced at me and my mother followed his line of vision but she didn't seem to recognise me – her face was contorted, eyes watery – and I knew I'd never be able to return from this. Her voice was a gruff whisper. 'Get the inhaler.'

I fumbled in her purse, ripping the zipper and throwing the contents on the floor – maps, a small mirror, a compass, her wallet. Everything seemed to be shifting in size, taking up too much space.

'It's in the side.'

Klaus must have followed me into the refugio because he tried to grab the purse and I shoved him off, tearing into the side pocket. The blue inhaler was right there and I thrust it towards my mother.

'Come now, breathe this in. You will do this.' She held it to Felix's mouth and I watched in horror. It was too much – the inhaler was plugged into his face but nothing was changing, it wasn't working.

'Dear God, please dear God.' I could have been shouting or whispering, I don't know, I was losing track of myself – everything was too big, too strong, too heavy. Breathe, I urged Felix. Breathe. I watched his thin chest and tiny nipples as my mother's hands fluttered helplessly over him, holding the inhaler, pushing it into his face. My father was yelling her name, trying to get her to calm down, and finally, like some greater power had reached down into his chest, Felix gasped at the inhaler. It was a small wheeze, but then he did it again. And again.

The medicine was getting through, his airways were opening. We all waited. After another blast, Felix pushed her hand away. He was breathing on his own.

'Oh thank God.' My mother was rocking him back and forth.

Felix's face was small with fear and tinged blue; his big ears were the only thing about him that seemed untouched. He shook his head as though to say the fuss was unwarranted and then he looked behind me, and I realised Pedro was standing by the kitchen.

I didn't know what was worse – the way Felix watched me, his eyes all scared, or the way my mother ignored me. She was staring at the floor as though it could anchor her but she wasn't the one who needed an anchor, I realised. It was me: nothing could save me from what I'd done.

'Hans . . .' she said. There was defeat in her voice. I could have braced myself for anger but defeat was too much. I'd failed us. I'd thought I was so clever, hiding those things; I'd thought I was clever lying to my parents. But I'd been there, in the doctor's office, when Felix got clearance to hike up. My mother had been worried about his asthma and the altitude – she'd wanted a professional opinion – and I'd sat there in a bony plastic chair, staring at the certificates on the wall, when the doctor said we'd need extra doses of salbutamol for his inhaler just in case. My mother said she'd keep them safe in her purse.

I backed out of the dining room and hurried up the stairs, two at a time. My long underwear was folded at the end of my sleeping bag, no doubt my mother's doing, and I shoved it in my pack, on top of my sleeping bag. My hands were shaking as I combed through the rest of my stuff for my compass and flashlight. All of us boys had been given one in the parking lot before we'd started hiking – my father pressing them into our hands one at a time as my mother double-checked that nothing had been left in the car. My father had meant it as some coming-of-age ritual but Klaus started swiping at Felix as though his flashlight were a light sabre and Felix soon unscrewed his to see how many batteries it needed and the springs rolled under the car.

I threw my flashlight and compass in the top pouch of my pack and took a backward glance at the bunks – each sleeping bag was lined up and wrinkle-free. Nostalgia was already gripping me for this room, for my family, but I had to leave. Ducking downstairs, I almost tripped on the steps and twisted my ankle but my hand gripped the railing, steadying.

It had stopped snowing outside and an afternoon moon was waiting for me like a bullet hole in the sky. My feet bit into the snow, searching for traction, and I headed across the open area in front of the refugio – the place where Jeremy and I had slid across the ice. I didn't feel the wind or the cold. Slipping over the rocks, I made my way down to the river and crossed over, holding on to the chain. It didn't matter where I was going: I kept moving, one foot stepping ahead and the other following – a shifting game of follow the leader. The path was covered in layers of snow so I followed the red markers, frantically combing ahead, searching for the next dash of colour spray-painted on a tree or a rock. Of course it was dangerous but I didn't care – if the snow was going to avalanche down and crush me, I deserved it.

3

Carmen Gonzalez

When the phone rang, a night-wind blew through the living room and rocked the windows against their frames. I thought it was my housemate Cristina calling. We were supposed to meet at the Cosmos Cinema in half an hour. I loved sitting in the middle of the theatre, submerged in the velvet darkness, with a bottle of red wine. We were going to celebrate the fact we didn't have to be at work for three days.

A weight-heavy pause then, 'Is Carmen there?' The voice was tired and slightly shrill. My mother.

We were officially on speaking terms but she hadn't called in over three months. I coughed, staring down at my painted toes as though they could secure me to the hardwood floor. 'It's me, Mama.'

'You have to come home, Carmen.'

My hand pressed against the back of Cristina's dining chair, a wooden antique she'd bought at the markets and painted bright yellow. It almost tipped under my weight and my purse hung precariously towards the floor. 'Don't start.'

'Your father's sick.'

My father had been sick since I was a child. My mother called them 'episodes' but they were like black holes – moments of stretched space that pulled us into his momentum. Everything on hold – my mother writing sick notes to my school, ballet classes skipped – so I could visit Papa in the hospital.

I cleared my throat, waiting for my mother to add something new to the conversation. There'd better be something new, I thought, or else I was going to have to start screening my calls again. She took a deep breath and I imagined the phone line between us taut, an electrical tightrope stretched across Buenos Aires.

'He's in the hospital and he's going to die. It's cancer.'

I didn't believe my mother so I reached for my purse and the nearest coat I could find – Cristina's green suede with fake fur cuffs – and began walking the fifty blocks to the hospital. Even at night, Buenos Aires is a dirty fairy-tale city. The nineteenth-century buildings seem haunted, nostalgic for wealth. Our European façades and marble statues are gritty with smog and decay. I was thankful for the recent rain as I paced along Corrientes Street, holding my breath as a bus lumbered past with a stream of exhaust. Even though it was well after ten, the night was still early for *porteños*, and I could see glittery couples waiting for dinner and teenage girls clutching each other with laughter. In front of my tango school, a man whacked his donkey with a stick and his cart teetered with cardboard recycling. Across the street, a boy was pulling open garbage bags. You wouldn't have seen that before the peso collapsed – I heard my father's voice in my head.

Outside the hospital, my faint reflection stared back from the glass doors. My hair was wild from the moisture in the air. I should have just called. But I had to see the face of the person who was giving me the news in order to believe it.

At reception, I asked if Juan Gonzalez was checked in.

The woman on the other side of the glass typed into her computer. 'Date of birth?'

'His?' My voice jerked back. 'The 26th of July, 1938.'

'Yes, he's checked in, ward nine, but it's after visiting hours. Nine to one in the morning and three to eight in the afternoon.'

I looked at my watch – it was eleven-thirty. But it didn't matter. I didn't want to visit him.

'Could you tell me, is it serious?'

The woman opened her mouth and then finally spoke. 'I'm sorry, we're not allowed to give out patient information. Only to family members.'

'I'm his daughter.'

'Do you have proof of that?'

I pushed my licence at her. She looked at it dubiously and picked up the phone, pressing the keypad twice.

Across the lobby, the front doors kept sliding open even though no one was there. It was paced, about four or five seconds between each movement, like invisible people were coming and going. Every time it opened, night gaped into the hospital's fluorescent entryway. It was beginning to rain.

The woman called out to someone in the office behind her. 'Guillermo, the door's caught again.' She looked at me. 'The doctor's not available but if you'll take a seat, an oncology nurse will be right down.'

There was no one behind me so I kept standing in front of the receptionist. She shrugged like she'd done her best with me and began reading a magazine. A few minutes later, a nurse bustled out of the elevator. She was a sturdy woman, used to delivering bad news. It had softened the lines in her face and made her thick about the middle. She stood a couple of feet from me, as though leaving clearance for my grief, and looked up to meet my eyes. 'Are you Miss Gonzalez?'

I nodded.

'My name's Luisa. I was here when your father was admitted. He has pancreatic cancer. It wasn't detected early – it never is.' Her words were quick but well-meaning.

'So he's really sick?'

She nodded.

'Thank you.'

She waited for further questions but that seemed like all I needed to know. I stumbled towards the door, where a man – Guillermo, I assumed – was standing on a chair, fiddling with the remote sensor. Later, I wished I'd asked about treatment and prognosis, but I needed to get outside – the sweet-chlorine antiseptic smell was making me feel claustrophobic.

The rain was sheeting down. A small stream rushed along the gutter, carrying candy wrappers and a plastic soda bottle. I was desperate for that rain and stepped out from the hospital awning. Within seconds my face was slick, my hair wet. My legs shuddered as I crossed the grass and sat down on a bench near the taxi stand. Cristina's jacket was ruined but I didn't care.

A couple of nurses were taking their cigarette break in the undercover alcove, laughing as an ambulance pulled into the emergency area and splashed through potholes. I ignored them and stayed on the bench while water dripped down my collarbone and soaked my shoes. And then, finally, I said it aloud to myself: 'My father is going to die.' I'm usually wary of words – you can't take them back, voice has no eraser. When I was little, my father told me to watch what I said because words had long memories and I imagined large warehouses filled with all the things ever uttered. There was no system in place to organise all those exclamations and half-thoughts but they were being stored, safe and dry, and one day someone might just find something you'd said and bring it back to you. But it was okay to acknowledge my father's impending death that night – he had larger forces to face. Our fraying family, my dead brother: all of that paled with the ghosts haunting his bedside, sneaking in and out of that automatic door.

'My father is going to die.' I said it again, staring up at the sky, scaly and black with rain, and wondered what on earth I was supposed to do next.

❋

I was used to rain. Sometimes it came so sudden and strong, it was enough to make me believe in God: nothing feels closer to holy rage than a flash flood. Watch your neighbour's car float away, watch a dead cat stream past, and tell me you haven't done something wrong. Tell me God isn't watching.

I was seven years old when I first understood this. My family was in Bariloche for the summer holidays, staying at our second house. Papa and Samuel had agreed to take me up the mountain while Mama stayed back to cook beef *asado* for dinner: it was Samuel's sixteenth birthday. We were hiking up to the Snow White Cottage – a one-room cabin built into a rock. It had been constructed by an alpine club and I was convinced it was a place that attracted elves and pixies when humans weren't around. It was set on the edge of a grass circle guarded by trees.

Despite my fear of heights, I begged Papa to let us take the ski lift over the first, and steepest, section of the hike. Maybe this was what set him off later – he'd been a pilot before his desk demotion. As the chair eased in, Samuel helped me jump on and the three of us sat side-by-side, gliding upwards. I shifted my bottom back as far as I could and gripped my brother's hand. Samuel had used some of my father's cologne and their combined scent was like a force field, an invisible net that would save me if I toppled out of the chair. My eyes were pinched closed.

Samuel's voice had broken during the school year so it was low. 'Keep a look out for baby dragons. They're known to breed here.'

'That's right,' our father said, smiling along.

I squealed. 'Dragons don't live in Argentina.' The chairlift paused and we rocked back and forth for a slow moment. The mountainside was quiet and sunlight flooded over us.

Samuel peered down. 'Well, if you're sure, keep your eyes closed. But *I'm* hunting for dragons.'

I couldn't help myself and searched the treetops; the fear was delicious.

'Maybe we'll see one because it's my birthday,' he added.

The lift started to move again and the end of the line came into view just over the hill's crest. I glanced at my father and he was staring off, upwards. At the time, I thought he was on the lookout for flying creatures but his body was tense. My father was supposed to be a round man; he had a face with full cheeks and thick lips, but his frame had always been too thin. People who just met us said Samuel and I both looked like him but I didn't see it, even as a kid.

The sky was an empty, phosphorescent blue. 'There's going to be rain,' he said.

'No Papa, it won't rain today.' Samuel shook his head. 'And even if it does, we'll be fine.'

'It's going to rain.'

I held my father's hand with both of mine so he had to look down at me and we jumped off the chair. The trail markers were easy to follow – the cabin was tucked away on a side trail. A few hours later, when I got tired of walking, my father took the backpack and Samuel gave me a piggyback ride. 'We almost there?'

'Almost,' Samuel said.

'How many steps?'

'One thousand and eight.'

'I'm counting.' It only took six hundred and forty-two and we rounded the bend and I saw the little cabin. It was in a small clearing. On the other side of the trail, a large church bell had been lodged in a tree. Tucked behind that, the familiar altar for the Virgin of the Snow. Someone had left flowers. Her face was thin and her eyes gaunt as though she knew everything that had happened. I wouldn't put it together for a few years but Samuel knew. Even back then he was saving all the newspaper clippings that mentioned our father.

I pulled on the plastic blue-and-white rope and the bell sounded. It was my own private ritual to tell any magical creatures in the vicinity that humans had arrived.

My father set out the picnic and we ate salami, cheese and bread. He peered up to the sudden clouds and I touched his arm. 'Samuel says it will be fine.'

'I told him rain was coming.'

It began in small patters and Samuel gathered our picnic, moving it into the hut. He laid out his coat on the cement floor and we sat together, with our backs against the wall.

Our father stayed outside, in the middle of the open clearing. His shoulders were arched back and his arms stiff with fear. Below his cuffs, his hands were fully outstretched, fingers spread open. He was peering up at the clouds and shouting out, telling the sky to leave. I had a straight view of his silhouette through the window, his Adam's apple moving as he cursed. The first wisps of rain began to brush against the glass and he still didn't come in.

Samuel stood. His jeans were too short; he'd gone through a quick growth spurt and all his clothes looked small on him. He tugged on the denim just above his thighs, pulling the fabric down so it hung lower on his waist. He stepped into the doorway and brushed the hair out of his face. He'd been growing it long to irritate Mama. 'I'll get him,' he said.

Usually it was our mother who brought Papa out of the rain. It had begun with oceans; he didn't like large bodies of water so we'd had to stop going to the seaside. His distrust now extended to lakes, rain and even table water – someone could always poison our drinking water. This last one wasn't paranoia: someone had tried to poison him at a restaurant a few years earlier.

By now the wind was spitting water against the cabin window. It reminded me of horses, invisible hooves galloping across the glass.

Samuel pulled on his coat and watched the showers from the doorway.

My father was shouting now. 'Do you hear them?'

'Hush now, you'll scare Carmen.'

'They're coming.'

My brother inched towards him. 'No one's coming.'

But my father took no notice, staring upwards.

'Inside now.' Samuel's voice was forceful.

Papa shoved him and when my brother regained his footing, my father punched him square across the jaw. It was a quick smack of sound and Samuel was on the ground.

'Papa!' I cried.

He was staring down at Samuel, bewildered.

My brother's head was cocked back, his leg bent. A tight smile pulled at his mouth and his eyes were alert. He was fine but he waited at least ten seconds, giving Papa time to take stock of what had happened, before he stood up and dusted himself off. My father watched Samuel like he'd never laid eyes on him before and I was too stunned to cry.

❄

Sitting in front of the hospital on that bench, cupping my rain-pruned fingertips together, I felt that same sense of wonder and confusion: the news that my father was going to die seemed just as violent and sudden as that spontaneous right hook out in the mountains. But Samuel was dead now so I'd be taking the brunt of this blow. My head shook wearily. One of the off-duty nurses was peering out at me from the hospital entrance as though I might have escaped the mental health wing. I didn't have it in me to explain why I was sitting in the rain, so when a black and yellow taxi slowed in front of me, I pushed myself up and walked to the curb. Inside, the heater was roaring and the windshield was smeared with condensation.

'Where to?' the driver asked.

'The airport.'

'Which one?'

'*Aeroparque.*'

I didn't want to make conversation. I didn't want to explain myself or apologise for dripping all over his back seat. Maybe he sensed this because he only asked me one other question: 'Where are you going?'

'Bariloche.'

❋

The Bariloche airport still only had two gates but it had been renovated with chrome and glass since I'd last been there. I could see the baggage handlers outside, setting suitcases and backpacks on the conveyor belt, and realised I didn't have any bags to wait for. I'd taken the next flight without even stopping at my house. I'd have to call Cristina – she'd be worried about me.

Soon I was facing the shop windows where wine, perfume and moisturisers waited for rich *porteños* to purchase them. Once upon a time, that had been my family. My mother loved to shop in airports. She'd sample all the testers and fill her basket with powdered cosmetics and bullet-cased lipsticks. She'd spray me with perfume and my brother with cologne. Samuel would push her away and she'd chase him around the store, laughing. That was before the peso collapsed, before my father lost it for good. I was in Bariloche because I wanted to understand what had taken us so far from where we'd once been. Maybe then I would know whether or not to see my father.

I stayed in the central youth hostel and rented the essentials: backpack, sleeping bag, stove, snowshoes, ski-shell and pants – everything I needed to get to the Snow White Cottage. I was planning on spending the night in the cabin so I stocked up on food and enough water for hiking; I could melt snow as required. I was in no way a committed mountaineer, but I did know the area. At Club Andino I scanned the young men behind the desk for Enrique or Tomás, friends of my brother, but they'd moved on. Only Carlos, the manager, was still there. I felt silly watching him help a Mexican couple plan their ski trek and didn't introduce myself. I just browsed the brochures, picking up a couple of maps, and used the phone to leave a message for Cristina: if she could cover for me this week at work, I'd be home as soon as I could.

The next morning, a *remise* taxi picked me up from the hostel. As the driver sped out of Bariloche, wheels slipping against ice, I watched the capped peaks hovering on the horizon. The cloud cover made them seem surreal, as though they were a mirage that might disappear if I stared too long. When we pulled into the parking lot of the resort – Bariloche's main attraction for the *porteños* – I motioned back to the bottom of the hill where the hiking trails started. I didn't want to take the chairlift; I wanted my journey to be physically exhausting. The taxi driver shrugged and looped around. Snow had banked up on either side of the parking lot and the car skidded through slush as he braked.

It was a warm day with thawing snow so it took about five-and-a-half hours to trudge to the cabin. I was still well below the tree line, so the wind wasn't severe, and even with two river crossings, I was fine. I might have been a *porteña* hiking into the Andes – the kind of person to inspire derision if something dire happened: 'city girl hikes to her death' – but I was careful and knew to stay on the trail.

When I arrived, the field was covered in thick snow with a powder-soft dusting on top that shimmered in the sunlight. I threw my backpack on the ground and bounded to the cabin, my boots leaving deep imprints in the wet powder. Even from the outside, it was obvious something was wrong. Someone had shattered the windows, and the door had been left ajar. The words 'Death to Nazis' had been scrawled above the middle window in red ink. I waited for a moment and approached slowly to prepare myself.

The cabin reeked of urine. I pushed the door back and almost stepped on a mound of thawing human faeces. 'What . . .?' My voice echoed with disbelief and I pulled my coat closer. My hand rested on the doorway where mounds of chewing gum had been arranged by colour. The walls were stained with graffiti and mildew, and the floor was piled with garbage – plastic bags, chip packets, used condoms. A layer of snow had blown in, melted and refrozen. The room was smaller than I remembered, little more than a grotto, and the rock wall made it seem heavy and dark. Even in the cold, the smell was rancid – shit and mould – and I had to step back.

I searched for a place to sleep, wary of venturing too far from the path. I found a hollowed tree behind the Virgin Mary shrine. The outside trunk was grey and wet but it had kept the snow out – there was a dark circle of earth inside. The inner circumference was about half a metre and I'd have to crouch to fit in but the decaying wood would protect me from the wind. I'd stay until the morning and as soon as it was light, I'd hike down. That decided, I followed my mother's tradition of avoiding the realities of life with cooking. Tonight's menu offered a *plat du jour* of packet carbonara. Surely I'd survive the one night, I thought, pumping up the camp stove. If worse came to worse, I could move into the cabin. The smell would have to fade if it got colder.

Half an hour later, a man appeared on the trail, rounding the nearest bend. I didn't hear him at first, I'd been singing to myself. And when I looked up, he'd already stopped, wary of moving too quickly as though I were an endangered creature he didn't want to frighten. He was carrying a large backpack.

'You okay?' he asked, his voice kind. 'You know the stretch to the main trail can be dangerous – avalanches.'

I didn't know this but my head tilted up and down.

'It's fine today: I've dug a test pit. But if this warm weather holds, the snow will thaw.' He glanced towards the cabin. 'Pity, isn't it?'

'What happened? I used to come here as a kid.'

'When the Slovenian alpine club disbanded, no one took over the maintenance.'

'Surely someone else would take care of it?'

He gestured like you couldn't second-guess the tiny tragedies of the world.

My throat constricted and he looked away. We stayed like that for a moment, and then he spoke again. 'You can stay at the refugio – there's room. My name's Pedro.'

I knew vaguely of the refugio but had never hiked there. 'I could return to Bariloche tomorrow or the day after?'

'Of course.' I should have thought it through – Pedro couldn't promise that. I was trusting a stranger in the wilderness.

He continued: 'There's a shortcut through the forest here but it's prettier along the main trail. That's the way I'll be going.'

'Why did you come here then?'

'I was making a detour for the Virgin.' He gestured to the wooden icon, carved into the cabin wall. It felt like he was confiding in me – people visit the Virgin when they need her help.

'Is it far to the refugio?'

'Maybe two hours.'

❄

The mountains were a dubious refuge, I realised as I followed Pedro – a place to go only when there was nowhere else. The branches were skeletal and then further on, the rock faces seemed to be whispering to each other, their voices catching on the wind. The precipices and boulders reminded me of mythological animals that had been turned to stone. A couple of times I almost turned around – Pedro could have been leading me anywhere – but I was frightened of finding my way back alone.

When we arrived at the refugio, it felt like we'd stepped into a family living room. Two boys were flying paper airplanes and making sound effects to go with them. Their parents were sitting at the table and introduced themselves – Hita and Erik. The boys chimed in – Klaus and Felix – and I concentrated on all the names. We spoke in Spanish, shifting to English when the Germans struggled to find words. I felt welcome as an airplane darted towards the window and crashed limply to the ground. Felix picked it up, bending it back into shape. When it sailed through the room, he grinned at me and cheered.

Beside Hita, an older boy was listening to headphones and reading a book. He reminded me of Samuel in the way he focused on the pages in front of him. Samuel had been able to read like that, tuning out the fights between my mother and father.

'That's Jack,' Felix said.

I watched Jack for a long moment, willing him to look up. His family were inviting and I felt comfortable for the first time since my mother's phone call, but it was more than that – I had the uncanny feeling I knew him. It was ridiculous but his posture, the way he kept reading as his hand slowly turned the page, it was familiar.

※

That first day I avoided Jack – the sense that I already knew him was so strong it made me shy – and then the Americans arrived. Jack seemed taken with them, and I wondered if I'd just imagined our connection. I didn't like the Americans. I was standing at the kitchen window when they crept in, pitching a tent, hammering pegs into the tundra, without talking to anyone. They should have cleared things with Pedro. When I walked to the bathroom, Jeremy stopped, his head at an angle. He held up a gloved hand like he was guarding his eyes from the sunlight and stared at me. I waited for him to shout out but he didn't. He just kept watching me as though trying to steady his aim.

We stayed like that for a moment. His coat was half open despite the cold and something about this reminded me of the young men who circle Retiro station in gleaming cars. I didn't realise then that he was in his late twenties; he didn't carry himself like that – there was something expectant about him that made him seem younger.

I should have welcomed him, maybe told him where the bathroom was and the rules for the kitchen, but the words did not come. Specifically, the *English* words did not come. I wasn't new to the language; I'd studied it for eight years. I went to a private girls' school where English was mandatory and I'd never lost my hold of the language. When Jeremy finally called out, I understood him but couldn't form a response. After a strange pause, I kept walking.

A bit later I looked out and saw Pedro with the newcomers. Emma was there this time, behind the two boys. She had light olive skin and a heart-shaped face. She was shorter than I was, with two braids poking out from a sky-blue hat. The colour seemed intense and artificial: I liked it. I thought she was with Jeremy because he kept reaching for her but she jumped back each time he swiped his hand through the air. Jeremy was doing most of the talking, kicking his boot against a rock. I was inside, far away, but he must have sensed me because he looked up and stared at the window, right where I was standing. I decided to give them a wide berth.

I avoided the Americans the next day but this didn't go unnoticed. That evening, as I trudged back from the bathroom, I was thinking about whether or not to visit my father. The moon was out, casting a purple-edged glow on the refugio. I could drop out of my family's life like a stone off a cliff. I could return to Buenos Aires and ask Cristina to change our phone number. My father would die and there would be no reconciliation. My mother would never speak to me and this might not be such a bad thing: she still didn't believe my father was guilty. She thought his episodes were hereditary.

My mother was not a reason to return. But it would haunt me if I didn't see my father. I wondered if the ghosts could sense he was nearing the afterlife and if they visited more often because of that. I wondered if he'd found the humility to ask for forgiveness.

The refugio light flickered and my feet crunched into the snow as someone cleared his throat. It was Jeremy, leaning against the outside wall. He'd waited until I'd just passed him and he was signalling a little victory: I hadn't been careful, I'd overlooked him.

'*Perdón.*' My throat was dry, the syllables slow like a rusty hinge being coaxed open.

'You're pretty.' He said it as an insult and moved in front of me. I didn't like that we were alone.

I smiled, pretending I didn't understand him. It was the same smile I used when patrons had too much to drink.

'Do you speak English?' he asked and I shook my head, side-stepping him. He shifted so he was still in front of me and I moved back, bumping into John, who had materialised out of the darkness. My pulse was now skidding in my veins. Jeremy stood too close – I could smell potato chips and beer on his breath. His eyes flashed in the outside light from the refugio. 'I think she likes us, John.'

They must have planned this, I realised. They'd been waiting.

John wasn't holding me but I was sandwiched between them.

I tried to step to the side again but Jeremy grabbed my waist. It was a funny intimacy, his hands didn't move any lower but they were heavy. I couldn't have broken free if I'd tried.

I didn't say anything; I just focused on our breath, shadow clouds in the night air. Jeremy leaned in against me and I twisted. My hair got caught on something – his watch maybe? – and my hat fell to the ground. I yelped involuntarily. I don't know why I didn't scream.

I could feel John behind me, waiting for some kind of signal from his friend. When Jeremy looked down at me, I thought he was going to force his mouth onto mine. This is it, I thought. I've been chosen to repay my father's debts. I don't believe in past lives but I do believe we carry the guilt of our fathers and forefathers. We cannot separate ourselves from those who came before us and all things move towards equilibrium.

Jeremy leaned in so his face was right in front of mine, eyes staring at me. I could feel his breath on my upper lip. I willed Pedro to open a window in the kitchen or for one of the boys to scurry out to the bathroom. For a place that offered no privacy, all of us stepping around each other, it seemed bad fortune that I should be alone with Jeremy and John. Any interruption would do. I was frantic.

'Do you think she's scared, John?' Jeremy's gaze was fixed on mine: he was talking to both of us.

'Um . . .' John drew the syllable out like he was pondering the question. 'Yes. I do believe she is.'

Jeremy watched me like he was waiting for me to say something but I wasn't going to give him that. I wasn't going to play along. And when he figured that out, when he knew it was pointless to wait any longer, he jumped back with a bogeyman grin. 'Gotcha!'

Before I knew what was happening, they had both let go of me. Jeremy was laughing. 'Joke. You didn't really think . . .' They turned around and started walking back towards the refugio while I just stood there. The night air was cold and spacious, taking up all the room around me.

Jeremy looked over his shoulder. He was shaking his head. 'You should have seen your face.' His voice was so easy I almost believed him. And John was smiling like we were all buddies – like I'd passed some kind of initiation.

I didn't say anything. I was still stunned. My arms were crossed in front of me. I shifted my weight to stop my legs shaking.

At the door, Jeremy called out: 'We're watching you.' He pointed two fingers over the bridge of his nose at his eyes and then directed them towards me. I just moved my lips into a violent smile – don't-ever-fuck-with-me-again-you-mother-fucking-*cabrón*-or-I'll-eat-your-heart-for-breakfast – and he pulled the door closed.

Even though I could hear Jack and his brothers arguing, I didn't go back into the dining room. I went upstairs and squirrelled into my sleeping bag.

I stroked my scalp where it was sore. The movement was slow and I remembered a police officer grabbing a woman by her hair and yanking her off the bus when I was a child. It was towards the end of the Dirty War. I'd been sitting just behind her, on my mother's lap and the woman kept turning around and smiling, hiding her eyes behind her hands and jumping out in peek-a-boo. She seemed old at the time, but she was probably only eighteen or nineteen. She was wearing a soft pink cashmere sweater that I kept pushing forward to touch. When the bus pulled in to a checkpoint, everyone reached into their bags for their identification. The woman didn't look alarmed. Even when the officer strode down the aisle and stood beside her, asking about her brother, and my mother's hands pressed into my arms, the woman didn't look alarmed. It was only when he reached for his walkie-talkie that she swallowed. And then, before he'd even heard back from whoever it was he'd called, he slapped her across the face and dragged her from the bus.

I'd cried out but Mama hushed me. Her rings glittered as her fingers pinched me hard. 'Obviously a bad woman,' she whispered.

❋

I'd been planning on leaving the refugio the next morning – organising everything into my backpack and heading off before anyone was awake. But Pedro was worried about the snow pack and I didn't want to be alone on the trail with the Americans. It seemed better to hike back to Bariloche with the Germans. They were friendly, and after breakfast I explored the other side of the lake with them. The trouble was: I needed to get back sooner rather than later. I'd decided to visit my father.

When the Americans trekked off, a shadow lifted at the refugio. If they were dead, so what? Worthier people die all the time. With them gone, I could speak English again and wondered if I'd imagined my muteness – but I remembered back to the afternoon when they arrived and how stubborn my tongue had been. I was relieved to be speaking English. It meant I had a presence in the refugio. And it meant I could talk with Jack – his English was much better than his Spanish. The first time we spoke, the radio was broken. I wanted to confide in him because he reminded me of my brother Samuel. I told him my father was sick and he seemed to understand that I was trusting him with this information, that it was potent and fragile. Jack was at a funny stage of life, he was *becoming*, and I liked that. Even though I was twenty-four, with most of my life in front of me, it felt like things had long been set into place.

That afternoon, he grilled Emma about the Americans. Jeremy and John were his friends, they were probably dead, and she was the only thing he saw to blame. But I couldn't help him. I didn't want to pretend I was sorry they left and I didn't want to mention the night out by the toilet block. I wasn't going to discuss it with him, or anyone, because I didn't feel like testifying and that's what it would have become, a *testimonio*, and then Jeremy would have carried a weight he didn't deserve and I'd be left to carry the doubt of whoever I told. And what had actually happened, anyway? A joke, Jeremy had said. Obviously we didn't share the same sense of humour.

And Emma – I had no compassion for her. She'd chosen to travel with Jeremy and John. You have to take responsibility for the company you keep. When she moved into my dormitory room, I made an effort – talking about family – but she acted like I was accusing her of something so I left her alone.

❉

The next night Jack and I had been trying to round up enough people to play Truco when Wolfe knocked. My mouth had gone dry with that hollow sound. I was certain Jeremy was standing outside. Jack had shifted closer as if feeling my dread, and I pressed against his arm.

When Wolfe stepped in, dusting the snow off his jacket, I was so thankful he wasn't Jeremy I didn't mind his off-putting remarks. But the atmosphere in the refugio changed – as though everyone realised how unsafe we were in Pedro's care. I didn't trust the Argentinean. He seemed gentle – but he was a liar. He'd known the snow pack was unstable and he'd still said I'd have no trouble hiking down. Maybe this didn't matter for most tourists – they could book a later flight – but my father was in hospital. And then, to be stranded without a radio – that lack of foresight on Pedro's part was unforgivable. Again I told Pedro this in Spanish, my voice louder than it should have been, but he just rested a hand on my arm and stared past me, to Wolfe.

The American sat at the table, eating pizza and drinking from his water bottle. Maybe I liked him that night because he made Pedro uncomfortable. But I also liked that he said what he was thinking. I was impressed with how he handled Emma's questions and grilled Jack on his reading list. He didn't back down to be polite. Wolfe saw through us and wasn't afraid to say so. He must have been through a lot, I thought, because he seemed like a hard man to surprise.

✻

When Jack asked me to show him the tango, it was like I'd been waiting for him. The tango was not something I shared lightly – in Buenos Aires, I'd had one partner for the past five years: Felipe. And though it wasn't a sexual relationship – his inclination tended towards wealthy men – I never danced with anyone else. Cristina used to say she dated enough men to count for both of us and until she learned the pleasures of restraint and I learned the pleasures of excess, neither of us would find a boyfriend. But I wasn't concerned with finding a boyfriend. Most of our friends were already married and that kind of eager devotion wasn't in my nature. My weekend nights were already filled with the tango show.

I began dancing seriously when I was thirteen. My mother loved the talent contests, recitals and commercials – a distraction after Samuel, I suppose. She drove me all over the country for auditions and always made sure to apply my make-up: 'Never trust make-up artists – they don't care enough,' she said, brushing mascara onto my lashes.

My nature was more suited to study – as a child I had wanted to be a scientist. But studying left me too much time to think and tango offered a way to escape my head.

Jack and I sat together on the bench, tapping out the eight-count rhythm and I couldn't help remembering Samuel. The gentle slope of shoulder, the concentrated gaze. The two of them shared a reluctant grace, as if they didn't want to accept a gift that had been set before them. Maybe it was nothing more than longing on my part but the familiarity was compelling. I had to control myself – I wanted to hurry Jack along. I wanted him to lead me around the small dining room before we'd even held hands. I don't know where this urgency came from – Samuel wasn't a dancer, I couldn't remember seeing him dance with anyone, but he did have that uncomplicated ease in the way he moved.

When Jack stood up, I felt an unexpected shyness and almost stopped the lesson. It all seemed too intimate, too revealing. But he took my hand and started counting off and soon we were moving around the open area in front of the fireplace. He was a quick learner. After the tango show in Buenos Aires, Cristina and I dance with members of the audience. Some of the patrons understand the tango with their heads, they know what they're supposed to be doing, but they can't communicate to their bodies. Jack wasn't like that. If I made a suggestion about the way he held my arms, it was as if I were speaking directly to his hands: they understood, tightening instinctively. Even with the crossover step – Jack kept stopping, swearing to himself in German, but his feet would fall into place when he let them. His movements were sharp and controlled: the specificity suited the tango. As Jack and I practised our eight steps, his palm pressed between my shoulder blades, it dawned on me that friendships arrive in surprising people. He was a gift.

When he could lead with confidence, we sat on the floor, out of breath. His eyebrow ring reflected the kitchen light. I leaned back against one of the stacked benches and he crossed his legs. 'Why did you come here?'

I told him about the cabin.

'What was it like?'

'Beautiful. Just as I remembered. Tucked under a rock. Brown wooden shutters and a door with a quaint latch. It's one of the only places in the world I feel safe.' I don't know why I lied to him. I think it was because Jack understood wanting the world to be a place with less compromise.

'Why didn't you stay there?' he asked.

'No electricity. No running water.'

'My father wanted to go there; he showed us the trail. And then the warm weather arrived.' He brushed his fingers through his hair; it hadn't been washed in days. 'Were you trying to figure out whether to visit your father?'

I fought back the urge to laugh. 'The man is dying in a hospital and I had to fly to the other side of the country to know I need to see him. And now I can't even call him on the radio to say goodbye.'

❉

The next day there was a reprieve in the weather. I sat out on the front steps, bundled up and appreciating the sun on my face. It was a dusty sunlight, like a light layer of sleep warming my features. The clouds retreated across the sky, following some upper-level air current that couldn't be felt on the ground. If I concentrated, I could feel the momentum of the earth falling forward.

Wolfe was entertaining the boys – building a life-sized car out of snow – so Hita could search for the missing money. But even after Hita discovered the envelope in Emma's pack, I knew the Australian hadn't stolen it. She was too preoccupied, radiating this boisterous sadness about the Americans that made me want to be kind to her even if I thought she was a fool. I wondered if Wolfe had stolen the money to spite her but then he seemed so determined to clear her name that it didn't make sense – he couldn't have taken it.

That left one of the boys. Jack was too sensitive. He may have been Wolfe's prime suspect but I didn't think he'd let someone else take the blame. And Felix seemed too young to hide things with efficiency. That left Klaus as a likely culprit. He walked with a confidence that made me think of cowboys and Indians – and I could see him appreciating a bit of lawlessness in the refugio. But I didn't think he was smart enough to get away with it for that long; I was waiting for him to brag to someone.

Jack and I fitted our rehearsals in with the spare moments when the dining room was free. He improved quickly, internalising the steps so his movements were fluid. I was impressed with his ease and posture. We'd snatch ten or fifteen minutes when we could, but I was always disappointed when his little brothers flew into the room, shouting about colouring books or Monopoly.

The next morning, Klaus and Felix were outside, building a snowman. They'd tucked an old pair of hiking boots beneath his giant girth and this gave him an air of hilarity, enhanced by Klaus, who kept farting and blaming the snowman. He let another one go and then pointed a stick at his creation. Pinching his throat he spoke in a high tone, mimicking his mother: 'Ringo, manners. That is inappropriate at the dinner table.' Felix was laughing so hard at his brother he tripped and fell over in the snow.

After looking over their handiwork, the boys pushed by me to find a pair of glove-hands for Ringo and I stood up to stretch my legs. My calves were tight. In my time at the refugio, I'd forgotten to take care of my body – I hadn't been stretching.

I'd told myself it was because there wasn't space in the refugio but I was making excuses.

Walking down to the lake that afternoon, I concentrated on my legs, feeling my quadriceps extend with each step. My feet moved as if they belonged to someone else. Despite the sunshine, the air was still sharp in my lungs – the cold like a warning. Below me, the lake's icy surface gleamed: it was a tenuous, soft shimmer as though ice mermaids were lurking below the surface and would emerge when every bit of water was frozen. My pace quickened. I was afraid of being alone here – the sun might disappear behind a cloud and I'd be stranded on the lake's shore, waiting to be taken.

'You okay?' I jumped at the voice but it was only Wolfe behind me. Even bundled up, he was skinny and that gave him an ageless air. But it looked like he hadn't been sleeping well: dark smudges had worked into the hollows of his face. He flicked a cigarette against his thumb, ashing onto the snow.

I watched his eyes – they were the shade of threadbare blue sheets I remembered from my childhood, the ones I hadn't let my mother throw away. We stayed like that for a moment, staring at each other, until I spoke. 'What were you doing?'

'I dug a test pit. It might just be possible to head out via Cerro Negro. We'd need gear, though.'

'Pedro doesn't think it's an option.' I wanted to know what Wolfe thought of our host.

He shrugged – it was a casual gesture, his shoulders barely moved, but it was obvious he had little respect for the Argentinean. 'He's committed to staying on the trails.'

'Or keeping people here. Making money.'

'He doesn't want to go to Bariloche, that's for sure.'

'But he went down the other day. I met him on his way back.'

'His circumstances have changed, I think. You watch – Pedro's going to keep us here as long as possible.'

I didn't know what that meant or how to respond. It didn't sound good. Wolfe cleared his throat, changing the subject: 'You know how some people are drawn to fire – pyromaniacs? I'm obsessed with snow. Have you seen an avalanche up close?'

I shook my head.

'Talk about sheer force . . . But, if you can read the snow, you'll be fine,' he said.

We were almost back to the refugio when Jack ran out of the front door. Sliding down the path towards the river, he stumbled but regained his footing.

'Where on earth do you think he's going?' Wolfe asked.

'I don't know.'

Jack slowed for a moment, adjusting his backpack. I laughed, tempted to call out, but he was already running again.

'I think he's afraid,' Wolfe said.

'Of what? The Americans are gone,' I said, unthinking. Wolfe laughed as though I'd made some calculated political commentary. But I watched Jack, and realised I hadn't been paying enough attention to the way he moved. He was running away from the refugio like something unearthly – vampires or body snatchers – was chasing him. I shouted but he was out of earshot. Or maybe he did hear me, and it only motivated him to run faster, because his pace increased, even as he crossed the river. Something was wrong. He was climbing upwards now – away from the safety of the lake. Wolfe and I should have followed him but we didn't know about Felix's asthma attack. We didn't understand what had happened.

❄

Four hours passed and Jack still hadn't returned. While Wolfe and Erik were out searching for him, I pushed aside an unfinished Monopoly game and sat at the table, drinking through cups of tea. Felix was curled up by the stove – he'd fallen asleep.

Hita was crouched beside him, watching like a mother with a newborn. Her head bobbed like she was trying to convince herself of something, an internal dialogue at work. When she stood up and stared out the window, her gaze was thin – as though everything in her line of vision were stretching close to the point of breaking. I could hear Klaus overhead, stomping on the floorboards.

Eventually Hita piled more wood onto the fire and sat down at the table. She'd lost her air of resilience – maybe she was getting tired, maybe she'd imagined too many possible scenarios for Jack in her head. Her voice was quiet. 'Clouds are coming.'

'He'll be back,' I said.

'I've tried and tried. No one told me it would be this hard.' Her German accent forced the syllables into a different alignment so it took a moment to translate them. She continued. 'And maybe I'm not a good parent. But I do my best. What can I do if he lies?'

She raised her arm to scratch the back of her head and for a brief moment I saw her resemblance to Jack. Looking across to Felix, she sighed. 'Could this be avoided?' She wasn't talking to me, she was addressing some invisible judge. 'We can't carry him out. And the radio's still down.'

I thought of Wolfe and his conviction that we could hike out through Cerro Negro – surely Pedro wouldn't keep us here if Felix's health were at risk? What were Pedro's circumstances, I wondered, that would keep him here at the refugio? And how would Wolfe know? I glanced towards the kitchen – a place synonymous with Pedro – but the lights were off.

Emma came through the room, hovering for a moment. Her jittery hands irritated me. She was flexing them, stretching each finger back towards her wrist. Sit down, be still, I wanted to say. But just when I opened my mouth, she stood up and slipped back upstairs.

Hita stared out the window like the answer to all of this hovered just beyond the jagged horizon. 'I don't like that sky.'

The sunlight had been clean and direct when I was walking with Wolfe but Hita was right, a grey haze was taking hold outside and it was weighted with snow.

She glanced down at her cards. 'Children never believe their parents love them as much as they do. It doesn't seem possible, but we spend our whole lives inventing new ways to love them. Sometimes we have to when they disappoint us – it's in the contract.' She pressed both hands onto the table. 'I'm angry but anger comes from fear and love. With children, love always wins.'

She was talking about Jack, trusting me to pass on some message to him, but I only heard what she was saying in relation to myself. My voice jumped in too quickly. 'What about evil? If someone – a parent – is evil. Are they capable of this love?'

Hita made a sound in the back of her throat. 'If we believe in an evil that's not human, then we never take responsibility for ourselves. I think that's why I stayed with Erik's uncle down in Bariloche – I was interested in him as a human, how a *human* could hold values so different to my own.' She sighed. 'And I am too polite, Jack is right about that.'

It had begun snowing outside and the flakes were large – covering the landscape as though nothing should be allowed to breathe.

When the sun dropped over the mountain, Jack still hadn't returned. The door creaked open but it was only Erik, back from searching. He crossed the room and rested his hands on Hita's shoulders. She turned around like he'd scalded her, hissing at him in German. All of her sadness had evaporated and, beneath it, a brittle layer of fear had begun to crystallise. It made her vulnerable and beautiful, but when Erik reached out to hug her she stood up. The motion seemed to relieve her of the need to talk and she dropped another log into the fire. Ashes scattered around the stove.

Pedro stood in the kitchen doorway. He was wearing fingerless gloves and they made his hands look small. He leaned against the doorframe, and I realised he wasn't worried. Jack had only been missing a matter of hours. I wanted Pedro to take the Germans' situation more seriously; I wanted him to understand the tension in the room. If we had to choose a leader, Wolfe was more erratic, but maybe that made him a better judge – this was an erratic place.

'He has to come back.' Erik was pacing.

Pedro cleared his throat. 'He will. No one would stay out there. Can't survive.'

'What are we going to do?' Hita's blue eyes were darker, greyer than usual, as though they'd decided to reflect the heavy sky.

'He will return,' Pedro said.

She was staring at him. 'And if he doesn't?'

'We can't find him in the dark,' Pedro said. 'If he's not back, we'll organise a search party in the morning.'

I appreciated the new look of horror on Hita's face: it was something I could understand. I knew about search parties and trying to map someone else's mind. Where would they go? Where would their instincts take them? When Samuel disappeared, I waited by the telephone table in our living room. I'd taken the blanket off his bed and curled it around me as if his smell could bring him back. It did – for the nights. My dreams were full of him and I began to look forward to sleeping because it was time we had together.

At the refugio, with the night settling in, Hita began to resemble my mother. They looked nothing alike – Hita with her pale features and my mother with her diet-thin waist – but the

German began wiping her eyes even when they were dry and gnawing at her cuticles.

Just as dinner was being set on the table Wolfe turned up, shaking his head. No luck there, either. We were eating leftovers, masquerading as risotto. It was the same meal Jack and I had helped Felix to eat the night before. But now, Felix spooned the rice into his mouth without question. I squeezed his arm when he cleaned his plate and he shrugged at me. When the dishes were cleared, Hita and Erik went outside to call for Jack, and I stayed with the boys.

'Try the lake,' Wolfe said. 'He might have doubled back. Carmen and Jack hiked around there.'

'Really?' Hita asked.

It was the kind of question my parents had asked me with Samuel. They thought I knew where he was, that he'd run away with his girlfriend and told me to keep it secret. He and his girlfriend had broken up but they were right: I did know where he was.

'Whatever happens, don't tell our parents,' he'd said.

'I promise.' I was twelve years old and desperately loyal: when my mother took me into her bedroom that first night and made me swear on her icon of the Virgin, I said I had no idea where he'd gone.

The second night my mother glared at me – she knew I was withholding something, she could see it in the way I scurried along the hallway. And at midnight, she sat in front of her vanity, applying make-up and pressing her eyelashes into tight curls. 'Dress warmly,' she told me and then ordered my father to drive us to a police station four suburbs away where he still had contacts.

Our responding officer was a man with a beige complexion who seemed to have little else to do. He was middle-aged, with a square wedding band on his finger. A layer of glass on his desk protected a couple of tattered photographs. In one, a pair of boys grinned towards the camera, hanging from monkey bars. On the wall over his head, an old photograph of an officer receiving an award watched down over us. It was stark on the wall, emphasising the empty space. The room was too big, as if it had been built for furniture that never arrived.

I sat close to my mother, watching the officer's fingers as he typed our information into a computer with a hard drive the size of a large suitcase. He asked questions, keying in our answers with his pointer fingers before printing it all out for my father to double-check.

My mother sat on the edge of her chair, her purse clutched between her fingers. 'He's been missing for two nights.' My father hushed her, placing his hand gently on her arm.

'And no one has any idea where he might have gone?'

'No.' My parents' voices chimed over each other. The officer looked at me, his grey-green eyes zeroing in on my secret. I only shook my head.

A few days later the phone rang and I picked up the extra extension in the living room to listen in. Someone from the police station had called my father about a body found down near the ports. I snuck out and ran through the city, catching a bus for the last stretch. I was still wearing my school uniform.

A military pontoon fished his body out of the water in Puerto Madero. I watched from a floating bridge while traffic zoomed behind me. Yellow cranes were poised on the other side of the muddy water, waiting to resume work, and the air smelled of beef *asado* from the nearby restaurants. A woman with a Canadian flag stitched to her bag jostled past me for a better view but I didn't need to follow her. I knew it was Samuel, I could feel it. I didn't have to see his body to identify him.

His body had been dropped near La Boca and floated down to the next wall. He had been visiting a dealer to sell a car load of unregistered weapons. Police said he'd overstepped his mark in a turf war. We're a country with a history of missing people, our hills are packed with secret tombs. A whole generation of ghosts. But Samuel wasn't one of them. There is honour in being disappeared – mothers and grandmothers will march for you – but there was nothing honourable in his death. Double-crossing Los Tigres doesn't inspire pride. Samuel should have made better decisions.

❄

When the night searching was called off, Hita and I sat together while Erik played Monopoly with Felix and Klaus. Pedro was hiding in the kitchen, worried. He'd gotten it wrong with Jack and now could have another missing guest. Jeremy and John were bad enough – but a missing kid? No one said it but he'd made a serious mistake. He should have started a full-scale search immediately.

Emma hadn't been speaking to Pedro and I liked her more for that. She'd been falsely accused of stealing the money and wasn't going to let it be glossed over. Her silence wasn't overt – when he asked her a direct question, she'd nod – but she was avoiding the kitchen. If the dining room felt cramped before, it was constricting now.

Hita moved to the fire, pulling at her hair, while Erik and Pedro lectured the boys about mountain safety. Emma and Wolfe looked at each other like the tension was unbearable and left.

A bit later, Hita stood up, watching her other sons. 'Time for bed,' she said. Felix and Klaus began to gather up their things.

'You can keep playing in the morning,' I said. Klaus raised his shoulders like it didn't matter anyway; it was just a game. Then he turned around to hug me. His arms gripped my waist like he was leaving it to me – I needed to bring back his brother.

I was surprised. I hadn't thought of them as close. But it didn't matter – you don't have to be close to be family, I thought.

❉

The next morning, Emma and I crept into the dining room early. Hita and Erik were already eating, the quiet between them heavy as an argument. Erik hadn't wet down his hair – cowlicks were spinning in different directions – but he was wearing his outdoor coat, ready to start searching. Hita's lips were chapped and bleeding – she must have been biting them in her sleep, if she'd been able to get any. Her eyes looked puffy. The boys were tucked into the corner playing another round of chess. My presence held a certain gingerness, like I was afraid of weighing too much and cracking through the floorboards. Emma put another log on the fire.

I grabbed a Diet Coke from the kitchen cooler for breakfast, swallowing it too quickly. It tasted like Buenos Aires and I wanted another but there weren't any left.

'We need search parties. We'll divide into areas,' Pedro said as I threw the can in the recycling box. His voice had a reassuring air of efficiency.

But Hita didn't care. Her voice was severe. 'We should have done this yesterday.'

Pedro swallowed. 'I know. I'm sorry.'

Wolfe was standing by the fire. 'Jack could be dead.'

I got the sense he didn't believe this but was enjoying Pedro's discomfort. Whatever his issues with the Argentinean, though, it was unkind to Hita and Erik. 'He's going to be fine,' I said.

Pedro studied Erik. 'Would he have known to dig an ice cave?'

The German nodded.

'I'll go with Carmen.' Wolfe's voice sounded confident. I turned to him; he was flexing his good hand as though making sure it was still there. For all that I liked him, I didn't want to go with Wolfe – he'd want to leave the safe circle around the refugio and all his talk about snow and avalanches scared me.

Wolfe coughed. 'We'll handle the trail.'

Pedro shook his head. 'Too dangerous.'

Wolfe slid his gloves on but he was still flexing his hand. 'Test pits.'

Pedro was rubbing his temple like he'd given up trying to control anything but the last thing he needed was to lose another guest. He couldn't risk us to find Jack – but he also needed Jack back. I felt sorry for him.

Pedro was watching me, concerned. 'What do you think, Carmen?'

'She's fine.' Wolfe shoved a crust of bread at me. 'Here. Eat something before we go.'

I'd been expecting more of a discussion but Pedro cleared his throat. 'Hita, Erik, Emma. The rest of us need to cover the lake again, but someone needs to stay here in case Jack returns.'

'I will. I'm looking after Felix,' Hita said. He was doing better but she was still worried.

Erik cleared his throat. 'We'll meet back at the refugio in four hours.'

As soon as we were outside, Wolfe reached into his jacket for a cigarette. He lit it, dragging in low, long breaths so it didn't last to the river. He mashed it out on a snow-covered rock, leaving a trail of ash, and pocketed the offending butt. When we'd crossed the river, we followed the path to the right towards Cerro Negro.

Finally Wolfe spoke. 'I knew he was the thief.'

'Is that what you care about? Being right?'

He looked at me like I'd missed the point. 'Even you knew it wasn't Emma. It was obvious.' Then, with only a slight pause: 'Must be hard for you without your boyfriend.'

I thought I'd misunderstood him. 'Excuse me?'

He fished for another cigarette and lit it without slowing down. 'He's a little young for you but, still, I would have thought that he'd tell you where he was going. Thick as thieves, you two. Did he mention anything? Any place where you'd think to find him and no one else would?'

Wolfe reached for my arm. He was only trying to get my attention, to impress on me that this was important, but I shoved him. Both my hands pressed against his chest and knocked him off-balance. It was an impulse – something that I'd never have done before Jeremy and John. He stumbled back in the snow, his arms flailing out for leverage. 'What was that for?'

I watched him, surprised that he'd touched me and surprised at my own strength. My brain picked through my words. 'I'm sorry. The Americans – they scared me one night out by the toilets and I'm a little edgy.'

'Must have been fierce.'

'It was.' I didn't want Wolfe getting the wrong idea. 'It didn't, I wasn't . . .'

'Hey, I never met them but what kind of a guy starts sizing up to Pedro because he's trying to save his life?'

I stopped walking. 'He told you that? I can't imagine Pedro telling you anything.'

Wolfe turned around and started coughing. It took a moment before he could talk. 'I know a lot about Pedro, unfortunately. Now Jack's another story. I know nothing about the kid except that he skulks around with the same book reading it again and again, and he looks like a ratbag. You tell me: on your secret lover walks, where would you go? Did he mention some place? A secret hideout?'

The Snow White cabin came to mind. Jack had known about it – he could be sheltering there. The main track that I'd followed with Pedro was prone to avalanches but there was another way, behind Cerro Negro. Jack would have known that. If I could find him, he'd need to be coaxed back and it'd be easier if I were alone. I needed to get rid of Wolfe.

I stood still and wriggled my toes. 'I don't want to walk with you.'

'You can't separate a search party.'

'Watch me.' I trudged uphill, along a trail to the right. The falling snow had left a pristine overcoat along the ground but the ice beneath was slippery. I slowed myself to avoid sliding, looking up every few steps to see how much distance I'd covered.

I was willing to bet that Wolfe wasn't the kind of man to take directions well and he didn't disappoint me. 'Wrong way. Pedro's already covered that.'

'You'd better go back then. See you at the refugio.'

❆

It took an hour before Wolfe deserted me. I'd been climbing a rocky patch, my hands gripping the uneven grooves and ledges while my feet slipped on the ice. It was a clumsy attempt, and I was embarrassed that Wolfe, or anyone, might witness it so I didn't turn around. When I scrambled to the top and stood up, I was expecting his voice to buoy up, jibing, but he wasn't behind me. My singular path had been scraped into the snow – awkward and inefficient but ultimately successful. I'd made it: a *porteña* scaling the Andes. Below, the refugio was just visible through the cloud-haze, a lighted beacon with its blood-orange shutters, and maybe this gave me a false sense of security. Or maybe it was my tilted view on the range – my elevation made the peaks seem smaller, more manageable. The distant cloud cover helped; the misty-grey gauze blunted the sharp angles.

It was also the first time I'd been alone all week. I felt liberated – an escape artist who's picked the locks and negotiated free from an underwater chest. I could hear my heart tripping over itself, blood rushing to my head. But heading downhill and into the forest, I wished I'd grabbed some food from Wolfe's pack. I wasn't sure how long the trek would take. Walking without snowshoes was difficult. I was light enough to stay on the surface most of the time, but occasionally I misstepped and plunged down, the icy powder cutting up to my thighs.

The snow lightened when I dropped in elevation and entered the relatively flat terrain of the forest. I should have felt safer – the trees provided a wind barricade – but the exposed branches seemed suspicious and unfriendly, the limbs barnacled with knots. It was like the trees were scowling: if I got lost, they wouldn't help me. I kept track of landmarks that wouldn't change and stored them in my brain like artefacts: a jagged rock face that resembled the silhouette of a dancer, a round boulder that made me think of football, a dying tree that looked like the throat of a woman.

I only had three moments of doubt – all at points when the trail forked. The first time I followed the left-hand trail for about fifty metres until it looped around to the east and I had to retrace my steps, and at the second junction I followed the left one. Then left again.

'Right-left-left.' I muttered to remember the paths I'd finally taken. At the last one, between the two trails, a tree loomed with snow-heavy branches bent into an extended heart.

And then, ten minutes later, the cabin came into view. It looked cleaner with the new snowfall and I wondered if I'd imagined its squalor. The brown shutters were closed and the rock-face graffiti subdued with a layer of chunky ice. I felt relief as the open clearing gave space for the sky. The cloud line was heavy and grey but less claustrophobic than the trees huddled around the meadow. They looked like they were listening to a long-kept secret. The field felt beautifully abandoned and the wooden Virgin was striking against the white landscape: it was all so peaceful I didn't expect to find Jack. My stomach murmured and I imagined trudging back to the refugio, arriving in time for a late lunch.

But when I gave the door a good shove and eased it open, Jack was sitting against the far wall, his knees drawn up before him on the floor. He was hunched in his down jacket, arms and legs burrowed in the main body of his coat. He may have been out of the wind, but the walls seemed to radiate frost and, despite his hat, he was shaking. I took this as a good sign – he was alive – and stepped over the frozen garbage and faeces to the small patch he'd cleared for himself.

'Jack—' I slipped on the icy concrete and almost fell into him but he didn't move. His eyes were settled on the floor, entranced by a frosted titanium-orange wrapper. I stood in front of him, hesitant, afraid to touch him as though ghosts were circling, waiting until he was distracted. 'Jack, look at me. Are you okay?'

His eyes were glassy, his face pale and blueish, and my first thought was hypothermia. He began rocking and I tried again. 'Jack, it's Carmen.'

He watched me like I were a phantom he'd pulled from his consciousness. I needed to be strong and grounded to centre him back in the reality of the cabin, but my voice sounded flimsy. 'We've all been searching for you. Your family is worried.'

He closed his eyes. 'How did you find me?'

'Remember – places we imagined, places we felt safe?'

He smiled then, and it felt like he was coming in; I was pulling him back to the present and we'd stand up and begin the hike back to the refugio. He nodded his head as if agreeing with me and then, as though considering the matter further and arriving at a different conclusion, he stopped. 'I can't.'

He lifted his hand. At first I thought he meant to silence me but he pulled at his trousers to reveal his leg. The angle seemed okay – not broken – but his coat was crusty with blood and a frozen pool had formed beneath him. 'I was running – as much as the snow would let me.' He laughed like everything was against him. 'There was a ledge; I didn't see it. I slipped and landed on a rock. I was coming here—' He glanced behind me. 'But it isn't quite how you described it.'

His voice was reassuring. Jack was there. At the refugio he'd warm up and everything would be fine but my stomach was churning with the feeling that we needed to get moving, onto the trail, back to the warmth of the fire. The snow was falling fast. I reached down to his leg. 'We have to return.'

His nose was dripping and he wiped it with the back of his hand. 'I can't.'

I was testing his thigh, probing it with my fingers. 'Does that hurt?'

He didn't say anything so I kept working further up. My scarf would act as a second bandage. He could lean on me and, if luck sided with us, we'd be home before darkness set in. 'We can walk together.'

He pushed me away and I thought I'd found a tender place but he was shaking his head. 'I almost killed my brother.' He said the word 'almost' with jarring tenderness and I realised he was asking me a question.

'Felix is fine. And your leg is not broken.'

Jack shook his head. 'You didn't see it. I almost killed him. I don't get to come back from that.'

'You made a mistake and your brother had an asthma attack. He did not die. Everyone is worried about you.'

Jack's lip twitched but he didn't move and I realised I didn't have the strength to force him. His back was wedged against the wall, his feet locked against the concrete.

My eyes were watering in the cold. 'Jack. *Por favor*. You're wasting time.'

He clapped his hands. It was a muffled sound but it seemed to signal some inner resolution on Jack's part because he turned to me, his voice low. 'You wouldn't do that. You'll go back and you won't mention seeing me.' He was bobbing his head like the motion would lull me into agreement and I realised it wasn't Jack's voice I was hearing. It was someone else talking to me, someone close and familiar. I looked again – my brother Samuel was staring up at me.

'What are you doing here?' Surely I was imagining this. When Samuel died, I begged God to let me see him. I played with Ouija boards and locked myself in the bathroom with the lights turned off, spinning in front of the mirror. But he'd never come and now, when I'd given up, he appeared. For a quick moment Samuel morphed back into Jack and I tried to concentrate on his face but before his features were fixed, Samuel had reappeared.

I stepped back. My vision was blurry and I knew I wasn't strong enough to handle this alone. I needed to get help from the refugio.

Outside, the icy layers meant my progress was slow. The snow had erased my footprints but I remembered my chant 'right-left-left' at the first intersection and followed the trail to the right. My breath came in hollow gasps but I only stopped to rest twice. The next junction arrived quickly and I turned left. Then left again. It wouldn't be long, I told myself, and I'd be standing at the top of the mountain with the refugio blinking below me. Pedro and Wolfe would be waiting, ready to follow me back to the cabin. I just needed to get to the lookout.

But it didn't come. I hurried to the next bend where the forest should have started to thin but the tree line was growing thicker until the light began receding altogether. I stopped, looking along the trail, searching for something familiar, and my foot dropped down, through the layers of snow, and icy wetness reached up to my thigh. Pulling my leg free, I realised I hadn't seen the jagged rock face of the tango dancer or the boulder in the shape of a football. I'd been walking for at least forty minutes and had passed none of my landmarks. That's when it dawned on me: after leaving the cabin, I needed to change my directions – the way back to the refugio was right, then right and left. I began to wheeze with panic and told myself to turn around.

But after returning to the last intersection, I couldn't be certain which way I'd come. My tracks were visible beneath the falling snow but they weren't on the trail I remembered. I would have sworn that I'd come from the other direction and for a hysterical moment it seemed the footsteps had been planted to confuse me, to test my faith in myself.

I followed the rational option: the path with footsteps. But after fifteen minutes, I passed the same rock twice or maybe I just thought I'd passed the same rock twice. There weren't any trail markers – they were all beneath the snowline and my sense of direction was getting shakier. I needed to veer out of the forest but I was afraid of avalanches. I didn't know how to test for one – dig a hole, Wolfe had talked about that, but how deep and where? What would the layers of snow show me? My legs felt shaky and I staggered to a rock, sitting down.

I was panting – the wet air coated my throat and smelled of evergreens and ice. A limb cracked under the weight of the snow – the sound echoed about twenty metres behind me like a prolonged shout. The cloud cover had sunk into the branches – everything was coated with the hazy lightness of snow and the flakes were large and buoyant. I'd follow the path back to the first intersection and take the other arm.

But I couldn't find the first intersection, the one with the tree branched into a heart. Panic was beating through my chest, collapsing my lungs into tight fists. I took stock of the sun – it was tilting close to the tree line: soon I'd start losing light. I needed to conserve energy but tears were seeping down my face. I would be no help to Jack. I'd lost my chance for redemption.

❄

It was about half an hour later that I heard Wolfe's boots squeaking against the snow and my first thought was that I was hallucinating. His figure was like a slow mirage, growing bigger and bigger, and then he cleared his throat. 'The cabin's two hundred metres away. You've made a giant circle.'

My shoulders collapsed with relief. 'Oh, *Dios mio.*'

He pulled a tin of corn out of his backpack and threw it to me. Then a spoon. I fumbled with my gloves so I could peel the lid back and shovelled the watery kernels into my mouth, barely stopping to chew. 'Thank you.'

He glanced over my shoulder at the trees as though they were admiring witnesses, and I wondered how long he'd known I was lost – if he'd left me a bit longer so I'd appreciate him. But Wolfe only coughed and turned back to the trail. 'Finally a bit of respect. Now come on.'

I followed Wolfe, and when he shoved the cabin door open, Jack was still there. He looked up, his gaze shifting between me and the American like this was a turn of events he hadn't foreseen. Wolfe paced across the room, reminding me of a doctor or an aid worker in a disaster zone and I wondered where his work had taken him. Had he covered earthquakes in El Salvador and Afghanistan? The war in Iraq?

Wolfe was at Jack's side, pressing on his limbs, peering into his eyes, touching his face. He yanked up Jack's coat and checked his pulse. 'Jack, listen to me. Can you walk?'

He asked the question again, louder, and when Jack still didn't say anything, he slapped him across the face. 'Jack, you fucking asshole. Answer me – can you walk?'

Jack nodded and Wolfe sat back for a moment, appraising. 'Carmen, get his other arm. We're taking him back to the refugio.'

The word 'refugio' startled Jack and he squirmed away so neither of us was touching him. 'I can't go back.'

'Listen to me,' Wolfe said, his face directly in front of Jack's. 'You're going to hike back and you're going to apologise to everyone and this will pass. One day, you'll remember being stranded in the middle of the Patagonia with a family that you loved and hated, and it will seem a long time away. And you know what? You'll be fine. In fact, you'll probably do something worse one day and this will seem like nothing. That's the thing with life: we just get to keep learning what we're capable of.'

Jack twisted towards me. 'Do you hate me?' His face was pale and I was reminded of how young he was.

'Of course not.'

Wolfe grabbed his arm to hoist him to his feet. 'Don't be melodramatic.'

Jack glanced at Wolfe and, even though he was sitting on the ground, Jack owned a sad confidence I hadn't seen before. 'I could have killed my brother.'

Wolfe prodded Jack's leg. 'It's in the second chances that we prove the world can change.' Wolfe and I hoisted him up; we were crutched beneath his arms. Jack could stand but needed help to walk. We edged out of the cabin and hiked across the open field. Each step was like wading.

'I don't deserve the refugio,' Jack said.

I shifted his weight across my shoulders. 'It's not about you. Think about your family. If anything happens to you, Felix will blame himself for the rest of his life. Your mother and father, they're worried.'

Jack laughed with a seamless anger that surprised me. 'What would you know about my Nazi-loving family?'

We were on the trail now but I stopped walking. I've always been careful with words. A confession can't be taken back and I was trusting Wolfe and Jack. 'My father was a pilot for the military.'

Jack sniffed. 'So?'

'During the Dirty War.'

Wolfe let out a low whistle. 'All the skeletons are coming out of the closet, aren't they?' He peered at me as though he'd thought I looked familiar and had just figured out who I was.

Jack was turning his head to watch both of us, unsure of what had been admitted.

My voice was croaky. 'My father helped "disappear" civilians. He flew planes that dropped people into the ocean.'

Wolfe was shaking his head and Jack was staring at me. 'What?'

'Drugged. They were drugged and thrown into the ocean. You want to talk about family shame ... Mine is more direct than a distant uncle you've only met once.'

'That's why you didn't know whether to visit your father?'

I nodded and we started inching forward again. 'I think he's only sorry he's been caught. And he's afraid that when he dies he's going to be forced to answer to the people he "disappeared", but I don't think he's sorry for what he's done.'

Wolfe cleared his throat. 'Most people can forgive their parents for a lot. But he was a bad father: that's what you're really upset about, isn't it?'

I blanched. Wolfe was trying to badger me but he was right: I was angry Juan Gonzalez had been a bad father – he was too preoccupied with his own demons, too busy being hospitalised. I'd been taught a father was someone to respect, the head of a household. It was hard to hold reverence for a man who murdered people and then, when threatened with jail, started informing. If his confession hadn't been born of such weakness – crying at the dining table, begging God to take pity on him because he wasn't the kind of man who could go to jail – perhaps I could have found more compassion.

Each day of his trial, I sat in the back of the courtroom, leaning forward on the hard wooden bench to hear him recount new crimes. My mother never came – it was all a government conspiracy, she told me, he'd been framed. But I was there, watching when the courtroom lawyer produced logbooks with his signature, and a nervous tick shuddered beneath his eye. Under oath, he cleared his throat and sat forward on his chair. He said he usually went up with Guillermo, and Guillermo would unlatch the heavy door to heave the bodies out. Five, six, seven at a time. Sometimes more. One man, my father said, knew what was happening. Even though he was drugged, even though he wasn't supposed to be conscious, he'd grabbed Guillermo's hand and almost pulled him out of the plane with him. My father had to reach back for Guillermo and thank God he did because he saved his life. What would have happened if Guillermo had fallen into the ocean, my father wondered. Would he have been held responsible?

Our pace was steady now. Wolfe was waiting for me to say something but I couldn't be flippant about this. 'The worst part is wondering if that evil has crept into my genes. Wondering if I'm capable of the same thing.'

I used to go to the Plaza del Mayo and watch the mothers in their kerchiefs. They'd laugh and gossip until they formed a line, beginning their death-walk. I couldn't understand what they'd endured. Laminated photographs of their children hanging around their necks – wedding-day daughters, driver-licence sons.

Wolfe tilted his head, his eyes careful as if weighing up a confession of his own; and I wondered what his family was like, what compromises they'd been forced to make. But he averted his gaze, staring up at the dark-etched trees. 'Nazi descendants and children of the death squads. Aren't you two just made for each other?'

Jack's eyes bugged out and he laughed, a funny gust of sound. Wolfe took advantage of his distraction and increased our speed. But the further we went, the heavier Jack became. His weight was digging into my shoulder, rubbing against my coat. I'd begun to sweat and the moisture made my wool sweater heavy and scratchy on my skin.

'Jack, you've got to help us out here,' Wolfe said, propping him up when we stopped to catch our breath. Jack had started to lose coordination, his legs splaying out as he walked.

When he pitched forward, I clutched him and turned to Wolfe. 'Is he losing blood?'

Wolfe had taken off his gloves and was holding Jack's face to stare into his pupils. 'I don't think so. Jack, say something.'

Jack was facing Wolfe but he was talking to me. 'I finally get the crossover step, Carmen. I understand the tango.' His words were scattered, but his feet jigged through the movement and then, as though the effort exhausted him, he began to sway, his feet planted but his knees unlocked.

I hoisted him higher on my shoulder. 'Come, Jack. Let's go back.'

Wolfe watched him, assessing. 'This isn't good.'

Because of the cloud cover, we were well down the incline before the refugio came into sight. At first, I could only make out the idea of warmth, a vague lightening of the snow-mist, and then finally two windows appeared, glowing. Jack's gaze was focused on them, his eyes bluer in the dimming glacial light. I looked down, concentrating on the steps right in front of us: one-two, one-two.

And then, like we'd stepped out of a slow-motion mirage, the front door was before us. Wolfe pounded on the heavy frame and, a moment later, Hita was beside us, dragging Jack inside.

The dining room was overwhelming: dry warmth, forceful voices, the stale-salt smell of cooked meat. It all seemed sudden and unreal after the barren snow. Pedro ducked into the kitchen for a pan of hot water to clean Jack's wound while Erik ran upstairs for a foam mattress that he dropped beside the fire. Dust motes and ashes shot up from the ground. Hita slammed the first-aid chest onto the bench while Emma looked around, trying to figure out what to do.

Wolfe eased Jack onto the mattress with surprising care, his hand resting on the German's quivering jaw. 'Hard to know what we've got here. Could be hypothermia. To be safe, we have to strip him down and get him into the warmest sleeping bag. Klaus, that'd be mine. In the closet.'

Klaus darted out of the room and Pedro began unzipping Jack's coat. Jack was mumbling, pushing him away but Wolfe held his hands and Pedro slid Jack out of the coat. The two worked with a common rhythm, easing Jack out of his sweater, untying his shoes. Wolfe stripped off Jack's pants and surveyed the gash on his leg. 'We've got to get this clean.'

Pedro doused the leg with soapy hot water. Jack yelped and struggled but Erik gripped him by the shoulders. Biting his lip, Erik nodded to Wolfe, who mopped the gash with antiseptic. It was about eight centimetres long, stretching across the top of Jack's thigh, but it didn't seem too deep. The bleeding had stopped.

'It won't need a splint,' Wolfe said, taping a loose bandage onto Jack's leg.

Klaus pushed open the door; he was holding a dark-orange sleeping bag. Hita grabbed it and began loosening the strings.

Wolfe glanced at her. 'Get inside. Warm it up while we take off Jack's clothes. We have to get his core temperature back up.' She slipped her shoes off and scooted into the bag.

Klaus shuffled to Felix in the kitchen doorway and held his shoulder. Emma joined them. Pedro held Jack while Wolfe eased him out of his shirt.

'I'm sorry, Ma. I'm sorry,' Jack called out.

'We're here,' Hita whispered, pushing forward in the sleeping bag to cup his face.

'I'm so sorry.'

'Carmen, his socks.' Wolfe said, nudging Hita away.

I pulled them back, exposing Jack's blue ankles. His feet were awkward – long and thin with narrow arches and gawky, over-sized toes.

Jack was in his underwear now. His body was thin, his chest skeletal, caught in the middle of a growth spurt. He looked old and young at the same time, as though an elderly version of himself had been superimposed on his adolescent frame.

Wolfe nodded to Hita. 'We need the sleeping bag. We're going to slide you in now, Jack.'

They eased the mummy bag over his feet and Wolfe lifted Jack so Pedro could pull the quilted fabric up, along his body. 'Who's going to get in there? Warm him up?'

Erik was already taking off his clothes. He had Jack's long slender legs and torso. His backside was barely there, his spine tucking right into his legs. I could hear Jack in my head, 'Look at that butt. Look at it. Is that what I have to look forward to?' I pried my eyes away as Erik eased into the sleeping bag, holding his oldest son in front of him. He pulled the sleeping bag over Jack's head for warmth; only Erik's face peered out. He looked like a giant caterpillar.

Erik was crooning a lullaby in the upper registers of his voice, whisper-singing in German. Hita was on their other side, rubbing the outside of the sleeping bag, reminding Jack of the outer limits of his body. She began singing with Erik and their voices joined in harmony.

I thought of my father. The human body was mortal and it was family who took care of it when we teetered between worlds. My mother was probably bathing him and helping the nurses change the bed linens – if he was still alive.

❉

Early the next morning, I read beside Jack as he slept. His core temperature had risen and his vital signs were strong. 'He's nearly well recovered,' Erik said.

Jack's arm was stretched out of the sleeping bag, over his head. His mouth was slightly open and I could hear a whisper of air trailing along his throat. I was reading his copy of *On the Road* – a small hardback, missing its cover jacket.

Outside, the snow was tumbling through the air and I wondered if we'd set our fears on the wrong thing: maybe an avalanche wasn't our worry, maybe it was the onslaught falling from the sky. It seemed impossible that something as delicate as a snowflake could break a roof or barricade a door but the snow was piling up. We could be trapped in the refugio, and food supplies were low. How long could we last? I wondered.

Jack opened his eyes, stretching both arms out of his sleeping bag.

'You okay?' I asked.

He watched my face. It was an inquisitive, familiar look as though he'd misplaced something and was looking for it. His voice was hoarse, his words methodical and clearly pronounced. 'I'm sorry. For everything I said, for stealing the things, for running away. Something could have happened to you. I'm so sorry.'

I wasn't expecting this. An apology is powerful because it is permanent. It is spoken and can never be unspoken, a testament that we are responsible to each other as human beings. By honouring the break, you honour what's been broken.

I was unsure of what to say.

'I'm going to apologise to Emma, too. For hiding the envelope in her pack. That wasn't cool.'

Jack grabbed a t-shirt from the floor and stretched it over his skinny elbows, popping his head through the neck as Felix came padding in. The six-year-old crossed the wooden floor and pressed his hand against his brother's forehead in a pantomime of a doctor. He said something in German and Jack sat up to hug him.

They were whispering. Felix was apologising but Jack shook his head. I couldn't understand what he was saying but the meaning was clear. Felix carried no blame; he couldn't have controlled an asthma attack. Jack drew back so their eyes were in line with each other. He was repeating something. Felix finally nodded.

I saw Felix's guilt and fear as clear as if they were my own. And I heard Jack's words as though they were Samuel's – even if I'd told my mother everything I knew, that wouldn't have changed things. According to police reports, Samuel had died that first afternoon, before the alarm had even been raised. Unless I forced my brother to stay home, there was nothing I could have done.

'It's not your fault,' I said.

❄

I spent the day with Jack, moving between the dining room and the upstairs dormitories. His younger brothers helped Pedro dole out dinner onto each plate. Two spoons of tinned beans, a rock-hard piece of bread and a few dates. Apparently Pedro and Emma had reconciled: she was back in her usual place, up on the kitchen counter, offering advice on the portions. Pedro had dark bruises on his neck but no one mentioned them. Wolfe had a black eye and sat at the other end of the table.

Dinner felt like a parody of a family celebration. The Germans were at the centre and the rest of us were distant relatives. Little things irritated me – the way Klaus tapped his plate with his fork, the lack of grace. I was remembering my own family dinners. When I was a kid, my mother would prepare beef *asado* on Sunday nights. I'd set the table, carrying a large tray, stacked with cups and a water pitcher. The settings would be ordered – polished silver, white china – and the meat would be sliced into thin pieces, salty and tender. Maybe there'd be a side salad of tomatoes, glistening with olive oil. After dinner, my mother would fill the teapot with loose leaf English Breakfast and my father would be the first to pour a cup.

Klaus had shifted onto his knees and was leaning over Felix, picking things off his plate, until Hita tapped him on the arm and he slunk back down. He saw me watching him and grinned. I forced myself to smile back but as soon as my plate was clean, I excused myself for some fresh air. I envied Jack his family.

I shouldn't have been surprised that Wolfe was already standing in the porch light; it was one of the few protected spots for smokers. He was holding a cigarette between his thumb and first finger and tapping his foot against a frozen puddle of water. 'Hello Miss Argentina. Hiding from your admirers?' The bruising around his eye was purple in the porch light.

I wrapped my scarf over my ears peasant-style and stepped out into the falling snow. It felt dry and static. 'How old are you, Wolfe?'

'Forty-three.' He was younger than I would have guessed but sometimes the years aren't kind. The lines from his nose to the corners of his mouth were heavy and his hair was gently receding. His eyes, though, were ageless – they were a persuasive shade of blue that dominated his face.

I took a deep breath – the air was cold in my lungs. 'Does it get easier?'

'What?'

'Life.'

'For the lucky ones, yes. In my experience, no.' He held the cigarette to his lips and pulled the air like he was trying to draw something deeper than the nicotine through the filter. Then he ground his cigarette against the windowsill, dropping it in the tin can by the door.

A bolt of wind rushed along the side of the refugio, rattling the shutters overhead. Wolfe was still staring out at the thick darkness with his hands in his pockets.

Another gust rushed over the refugio and I pulled my coat closer. I felt a collapsing sensation in my chest and saw my father, hooked to a heart monitor, tubes packed into his nose. If he was still alive, he'd be waiting for me. After Samuel died, he'd gripped me with both hands and told me I was the only thing he had left. The only thing he'd done that might balance his sins. I'm so sorry, Carmen. I'm so sorry. It was clear to me now: forgiveness would be an act of compassionate practicality. I couldn't forgive him for anyone else – the Mothers, the Grandmothers, they'd have their own reckoning. I could only forgive him for Carmen Gonzalez and it would be an act of self-preservation so I wouldn't have to carry him with me. My own necessary tango of apology and forgiveness. I followed Wolfe's gaze along the dark haunch of the mountain.

He turned to the door, grabbing the handle. 'We'd better go back in. Pedro wants to have a meeting.'

'Why?'

'Group of people, trapped in an avalanche zone, radio's down, they're low on food: I don't know, Carmen. Sounds like the kind of thing we might want to discuss. This is an emergency.'

I stared at the snow, hoping it would continue its patient descent and cover his words. The power of naming should be taken seriously because it can determine everything. 'How low on food?'

'Are you serious?'

Wolfe led me to a second door I didn't even know worked. He grabbed the handle and jerked up. We were standing in the kitchen. Wolfe tapped his lips to keep me quiet, and I nodded. Everyone was in the dining room and only the beaded curtain separated us. Entering the refugio like this, stealthy, made the building feel vulnerable. The sink was full of soapy water for dishes. The broken radio was sprawled on the counter, Pedro's tools beside it. Wolfe grabbed a screwdriver and tiptoed to the cellar – it wasn't much, just a door tucked into the wall, on the other side of the sink. He began jimmying the lock.

'Wolfe—' I whispered.

He gave me a fierce look and I closed my mouth, keeping an eye on the doorway. After about twenty seconds, the lock budged and he opened the door. It creaked. 'This is everything we have.'

It was a tiny grotto dug into the earth. The walls weren't lined so it smelled like dirt. Pieces of timber had been propped up as shelves but they were empty. Everything was in a small pile, right at our feet. A case of wine, a couple of tins of food, a jar of chocolate-hazelnut spread, a bag of potatoes and some flour. That was all. With Hita and Pedro in the kitchen, taking stock, I'd assumed there was enough food to warrant an inventory but that had been wishful thinking.

Wolfe let out a quiet breath. 'Pedro won't listen – we need to get out of here. We've got two days if we're lucky.'

4

Pedro Carimán

Of course Wolfe found me – the real surprise was that it hadn't happened sooner. It had been wrong to buy the concession and hide in the wilderness but I'd needed it. Before I'd walked the full length of the trail, before I knew there was a building beside a lake, I stood in the yellow grassland and slapped at the flies, and it was obvious. The only thing that could take care of me was the mountain.

My first year was slow, with an uneven trade. Fewer visitors hiked up the mountain in the winter, and though I should have planned for this, I didn't. Refugio Frey also needed repairs. The roof was falling away a shingle at a time and the foundations had shifted. I didn't mind the work but the materials, and getting them up the track, were added costs I hadn't foreseen. There are only so many hours of daylight and so much a man can carry. In the end, horses carted most of the construction supplies. They were well-worked animals, urged along by their owner, Julio. They would leave Bariloche on morning light, arrive at the refugio after lunch, only to turn around for the return trip. They also carried my food stores – I had a standing order in town and radioed in a list for extra supplies. Usually the horses would come twice a month in summer to stock supplies for winter. This proved costly but I sold my truck to pay the bills and was just able to renew the concession when it came due.

The refugio was a paradise for collectors. Nothing that could be used was ever thrown away. I was comfortable with this idea that out of salvage comes salvation. My childhood home sat right behind a spare parts car yard. They were cars whose spirits had been broken – rusted bodywork, ripped upholstery. I used to play hide and seek, flattening myself in their empty bellies and holding my breath so my older brothers wouldn't hear me. In the afternoons, I helped Uncle Jorge tidy the yard and haggle over prices. He'd grip his belt and tell owners *they* should be paying *him* to take the old beast off their hands. It made me sad. As soon as they'd leave, he'd walk around the vehicle, sizing up the mint-condition rear-view mirror or the gleaming door handles. 'You've got to play hard in life, Pedro. You're too soft.'

At home, we had dogs. Seven of them corralled in a fence of greying timbers. The posts, the house, they only stayed standing out of loyalty to my mother. She farmed the back plot for vegetables, which she'd sell in town with the eggs from our scrawny, overexcited chickens. The birds liked to fuss in front of the kitchen stove, leaving the yard to the mutts. This was probably wise as the dogs were creatures that showed affection by baring their teeth. They weren't beautiful, fleas and mange saw to that, but they provided a devoted barrier. My mother didn't let anyone into the yard unless they could get past the dogs and this kept most white people and all the missionaries away. We'd been raised on a mythology of Catholicism and Mapuche folklore but my mother was tired of all the words white people used to talk about God. She was the kind of woman who liked to cover her bases but when we were sick, it was the *machi* we visited.

I loved how remote the refugio was – like growing up in my mother's house, only the determined made it through my door. And while some tourists were rude and some of the mountaineers placed too much faith in themselves, I was able to be with the land. It often happened that three or four months would pass before I trekked into town. And as I spent more time away, it became more difficult to follow the path to the road and hitchhike to the main street. The lines at the bank made me uncomfortable and the artificial lights at the grocery store made everyone look sick. My conversation slowed and I was at a loss when the teller told me I should consider changing bank accounts. The noise of the traffic and the street vendors was too loud and I realised the mountain quiet had settled in my head like a heavy snowfall in the middle of summer.

In the refugio, I slept on the kitchen floor. And if I needed to be alone, Alberto – a friend from the next refugio on the circuit – would leave his place in the care of his wife and watch over my guests while I disappeared into the wilderness for a night or two. Even in summer there was snow on the higher peaks, drawing attention to the spirit-faces in the rock. Overhead, the condors would glide in soft, silent arcs as I slid down the scree and moved across the marshy puddles.

In winter, it was different. Snow was the great equaliser, covering everything in thick powder. After the season's first big fall, the lines of the earth would be suddenly visible. I'd build an ice cave at night and watch the cloud cover. A colder night meant I had the company of crisp stars.

Snow is like harvest, it follows a cycle of abundance and retreat. My people place our faith in the landscape and we've never been disappointed – but we are very careful. The avalanche with the Americans was not a surprise. I'd lived in the refugio for four years and had watched the weather through its seasons. The trail was built by white people in summer: they didn't understand the dangers that arrive with winter. With the rocks – the steep incline above and the sharp cliff below – the mountain was impatient. I always dug test pits before allowing anyone to leave after snowfall, and Club Andino would call on the radio to discuss whether the path should be open. When there are layers of snow, and warm patches followed by deep freezes, there will be risks. You can't see them, the instability takes place well beneath the surface. But no one is bigger than the mountain.

In my first year, Club Andino told us to stay in the refugio on two different occasions. Most travellers were unhappy about this news but we had no choice. I'm a person of careful nature and I don't like risk. Death has had his sights set on those around me and I wouldn't want to give him any opportunities. There were benefits, though – the beer and wine sales alone meant I would survive each month with ease.

The risk of an avalanche could not have been clearer with the Americans but there was little I could do if they chose to ignore me. How could I have stopped them? They were both solid men who stood taller than me. If the snow had carried them down the mountain, there would be a search and paperwork and interviews. I'd stayed awake at night, imagining this. The lines in the police station would be long because they were always understaffed. The recycled air would pant through the air-conditioning so you could smell what the man behind the counter ate for lunch long before you reached him. When I finally did step up, I'd have trouble looking directly at the officer. My voice would fall to a whisper and I'd act like a man hiding a secret. The more urgent the situation – and losing my refugio was now the most urgent thing I could imagine – the less capable I'd become.

Of course I had existed before the refugio so it would follow that I could exist again, without it. But it seemed my life before the mountain belonged to someone else. The journey to Bariloche began at my mother's house. I was twenty years old, trying to bring a brand-new stereo to life for my mother. I'd bought it with my brothers as a gift. We weren't rich – only two of our rooms had cement floors and the electricity was never faithful – but Uncle Jorge had found the surround-sound machine for a good price and we all decided that Mama should be able to hear Ástor Piazzolla as loud as she wanted. It was a gesture meant to pacify: my two older brothers Diego and

Nahuel had moved to Buenos Aires for work and she wasn't happy about this. Though she never said anything to us, she stormed around the kitchen, shouting at the chickens. The hearth was covered in a fine silt of grey feathers.

The stereo had arrived the day my brothers returned to the capital so the task of assembling it had been left to me. 'Fitting,' my mother had murmured as they'd walked down our driveway towards town to wait for the bus. She looked back at me and the worried expression did not leave her face: she knew then – before me – I was about to leave, too.

The next morning I waited – until she loaded her vegetables into the back of Uncle Jorge's truck and drove down the driveway – to unearth the stereo from the cardboard container. It was the original box but the instructions had been lost so I separated each of the cords and laid them in front of the three shiny levels: the main power station, the double cassette, and the CD player. The speakers were soon connected: one on the shelf next to my mother's altar, one on the ground and two on either side of the table. When I pressed the power, the radio roared with such force my uncle could have heard it. But Ástor Piazzolla wouldn't play from the CD. Just a gentle whirling.

That's when the dogs started barking outside. I paid them no attention – they were always full of energy and noise, especially when anyone passed by our house. But then I heard someone call out and the gate swing open, and instead of shouting even louder, they were quiet. Either my mother had returned or, and this was just hope on my part, my brothers were back.

I shuffled to the door and pushed the screen open. A white woman – with brown hair, faded like her jeans and flannel shirt – had leaned her backpack and guitar against the fence and was lying on the ground, wrestling with our dogs. Scratching their bellies, rubbing their ears, kissing their noses. She was calling out to them in English and they were dancing around her.

She even gave happy pats to Mora, the silliest of them. The dogs were hungry, squirrelly things that'd never been bathed. Their fur dropped off in clumps and two of them had eye infections.

She glanced up from the ground and smiled. 'Hola. My name is Rosie.'

I had been the strongest in my English class – I understood her – but I just stared, thinking her face was serene like the ocean on a windless day. I'd never been to the coast but as a kid I'd found a pile of postcards in the glove box of one of my uncle's cars. I'd poured over those careful rectangles, wondering how the ocean could be so big. Rosie had that same soft intensity – unbounded and open. Part of it was her blue eyes, but it was also her clear pale skin, her wide cheeks. She stood up and reached down for one of her sandals that had fallen off with the dogs.

'I'm lost – and there's no one out front, in the car yard,' she said, laughing, walking towards me. My English was strong; I knew what she was saying. I also knew she had a guitar and that translated into the idea that she could help me with the CD player.

Her hair was parted in the middle and curled around her face. She pushed a strand out of her eyes and smiled. Gentle lines eased around her eyes and this told me two things: she was older than I was and she smiled often. I motioned inside and she nodded, walking back to pick up her guitar. I followed and grabbed her pack.

Inside the house, she set down her guitar and gazed at the small living area. Stucco walls painted bright blue. Two rocking chairs and a couple of stools set around a 1950s laminate table. A woven rug covered most of the concrete floor. And then, to her left, my mother's shrine. In the middle of the plastic flowers and sacred rocks, two burned-down candles stood in front of a photograph of me with my brothers. To the right, a portrait of the Virgin. On the other side, a *Duwekafe* weaving. The only thing she didn't seem to appreciate was the stereo. I willed her to look at it – the shimmering case and smooth buttons. But she was more interested in the picture of me standing with Diego and Nahuel. I had to point at the speakers and hold up the spare cord, shrugging at its uselessness, for her to nod slowly in understanding.

She pressed 'play' and tilted the stereo at an angle, listening. Finally she looked at the back of the machine and her hands moved quickly, unplugging one cord and plugging in another, turning knobs. In a big crackle of sound, a giant sway of music rolled into the room. A wistful violin being followed by the skip-skip of a *bandoneón*. The steady piano bass line shifting between the two. It was a dramatic tango, a sad one, and I should have seen this as a warning but Rosie had closed her eyes in easy delight. The corners of her mouth dropped and her chest was rising and falling with the swell of the music. On the crescendo, her wrists lifted ever so slightly.

The music was so loud the bass notes itched out of the speakers and I turned the knob. The volume fell and Rosie opened her eyes like she remembered where she was: in my living room, in a town, in the south of Argentina. I was self-conscious – my intrusion into the music, my simple home – but I was also fascinated. I'd never been alone with a white woman. I'd never seen someone so eagerly self-content. And I was young enough to think this combination of embarrassment and awe meant I'd fallen in love.

When the song ended, I asked Rosie where she was going, if she needed a ride into the city. I said this as much to let her know that I was someone who had access to a vehicle – that I could borrow my uncle's truck – as I did to prolong my time with her.

She laughed. 'I suppose that's a good idea.' But then she asked for a glass of water and sat down at the table like she wasn't ready to leave. The next song began and she drew her legs up so she was perched on the chair. When I set the chipped mug in front of her she nodded thanks, and I lowered myself opposite. We sat, without speaking, for the rest of the compact disc.

When quiet descended, it felt like we'd been sitting in my living room for hours – days, even. So when she stood up, stretching her arms above her head, and said 'Incredible', I was surprised by the sound of her voice. I assumed she meant the music but maybe she was talking about the experience of travelling, of arriving in a place you've never been and appreciating silence and music with a stranger. I told her then she was welcome to stay – I'd sleep on my mother's floor.

❋

One night became two, which turned into a week. Rosie had taken a semester off from study and was travelling the mountains. When she left, walking down the drive, guitar swung over her shoulder, I thought I'd never see her again. But she returned two weeks later and then again. She always had a little gift for my mother.

I suspect Rosie was enchanted with my house, my mother's open fire, the chickens and the dogs. I represented another shape that life could take and this, perhaps more than me, was what intrigued her. We were on uneven ground. She had seen my family home but I had no understanding of hers. I couldn't imagine the wealth she'd left in New York City. Perhaps she felt guilt because of this and wanted to make up for the world's unfairness by loving me. All I know is that I smiled easily for her in those days and she seemed eager to make me smile as often as possible.

Because of Rosie, my passion for the English language grew stronger and this did not sit well in our household. Unlike my brothers, I was not full-blood Mapuche. My forefathers were famous because they held off the Spanish for three hundred years but my mother didn't have as much skill with my *gringo* father, an off-duty soldier consumed with drink. I was mixed blood – too dark to be white, too white to be dark. *Champurrea.* The word hovered in the wind, neither rising nor falling, just hovering behind me as I walked home from the markets. I looked Mapuche – round face, broad nose – and when I was little that seemed proof my mother's blood had won. But I know my mother wondered at the whiteness that Rosie and I shared, wondered if it was part of Rosie's appeal.

My mother wasn't silly, she must have known what was happening, but Rosie and I weren't open with our affections. A few times we went on weekend excursions along the border to Chile when Uncle Jorge didn't need his truck and it was on one of these that Quidel was conceived. When Rosie discovered she was pregnant, we moved to Córdoba – in part to avoid my mother, in part to be closer to Rosie's friends – and my longing for home and the mountains was overshadowed by the excitement of my own family.

I began studying English at the university. It was a language of confidence and my posture changed for the new words that I learned. I sat taller and learned to be more direct when I spoke. With Rosie's friends, I had to forget they were rich – that their watches and sweaters could be sold to feed my family for a month. And perhaps I was a traitor, but I enjoyed that forgetfulness. Rosie paid for everything. We were living off the generosity of her father but I didn't know where his money came from and I don't know that it would have made a difference if I had.

We met when business brought him to Argentina. The idea of Mr Goldberg scared me but Rosie insisted on introductions – and how could I refuse? He was my son's grandfather and our benefactor. A man who decided his place and insisted the world agree with him. He would not have been an easy father.

He commanded his family as he did his business. Dinners were run with the efficiency of meetings. Discussions were tabled. As he aged, gravity pulled at the corners of his mouth so that even when he was talking, he offered the impression of being bored. But it was a wary boredom and I made sure to think through even the smallest remark in case it revealed something unpleasant about my character. He'd made fortunes by reading his rivals and I was under no illusions he could be bluffed.

Rosie's brother visited too, but never with their father. He resembled Rosie around the eyes and mouth but he was the kind of man most comfortable when irritated or angry. Rosie told them I was studying to become an interpreter and I was glad to know I had prospects – or more specifically, glad to know Rosie thought I had prospects – but they both looked at me with the same dull expression as though they were willing to wait me out.

Their patience was rewarded. When Quidel was three, Rosie began to miss home. It began with journeys to the United States. We went with her the first time, travelling on top of the wind in an airplane. I didn't understand how large the world was or what was waiting for us. In New York City, the buildings were so tall they blocked out the sun. Subway ships sailed beneath the earth. People spoke over one another – the voices weaving like a tapestry and I could never see the picture they were making. My English had improved – I was fluent – but what stories could I share with lawyers and journalists? My village didn't seem real to me so how could I explain it to anyone else? And most of all, I missed the trees. The cypress, the coihue, the lenga. Rosie thought Central Park would impress me but I had to wear a false smile as we walked alongside runners and bicyclists – it was more of a garden than a wilderness.

Her brother made sure to visit when we were in New York. He was working overseas and flew in for three days. I was wary but Quidel took no notice of my nerves, asking him for coins and speculating on the things they could purchase. After much debate, the two decided a donut was a more realistic purchase than a cloud, and I realised that our kids are not extensions of ourselves. They are different entities entirely and that while I might not be popular in the Goldberg household, the same couldn't be said of my son.

Rosie made more trips to the United States and then, three years later, she returned for Hanukkah. It was supposed to be a brief trip to visit her father. His lungs had been troubling him: pneumonia. Her brother wasn't able to look after him – he was having a hard enough time holding himself together. It made me angry, how she acted as caretaker for the two of them. Quidel had become used to her absences but he still counted down the days until her return. As a distraction, we were going to Buenos Aires to spend the holidays with my brothers. Rosie telephoned as I was packing his things. I remember sitting on his bed and staring at the Maradona poster on the wall as she told me she'd be back but it was only temporary – she was leaving me. Moving to New York. Taking our son.

I concentrated on that final fact because I couldn't believe she was leaving me. I had never loved anyone else; I didn't know *how* to love anyone else. So I ignored her departure and thought only of Quidel. He was six years old then and his passion was football. He played every afternoon with boys from our neighbourhood. I couldn't imagine him in New York. Where would he play? That was my first thought as I hung up the phone.

When Quidel ran onto the field, he was the smallest and most ferocious kid there. His legs worked through the air, taking two steps for every one step of the older boys. Getting that ball mattered to him more than anything. He would have gladly lost friends for a free run to the net. Scoring points was an afterthought – what he loved was passing other players to get to that open space. That round *pelota* adored my son and Quidel loved it back. It was the strongest relationship on the field.

Quidel and I had plans to go to the World Cup in 2002 and Rosie told me on the phone that she'd still pay for that. But after our trip, Quidel would move to New York with her. That would give me a bit of time to 'come to terms with it all', she said. I wasn't sure what she meant, how it would be possible to come to a point where any of this could make sense. I told her I didn't want her money – I'd take more translation work. The World Cup was going to be held in Japan and South Korea, and the peso had equal footing with the American dollar then. I could just manage it. Flying across the world to watch a game of soccer was an act of foolishness, especially when my mother's house still needed a concrete floor in the second bedroom. But I convinced myself that I worked hard and, because of that, my son and I deserved this indulgence.

Quidel had already been studying Japan – any school project (birds and their nests, cities and skyscrapers) offered an opportunity to learn about the Orient. We searched for sushi in Córdoba. Quidel would unwind the seaweed and eat the rice, then the nuggets of avocado and cucumber. '*La copa mundial. La copa mundial*,' he would chant as he finished the meal. The World Cup.

We booked our tour during the last week of school and made copies of the itinerary: we were going to fly out on 8 June. After Rosie's phone call, it seemed like an ominous countdown but I didn't say anything to Quidel. We'd see six games of soccer in ten days, including two semi-finals, and our names would be in a draw for tickets to the final. I paid the deposit: the rest was due at the end of January.

But that was the year the peso was devalued. A condor falling from the sky. Quidel and I didn't understand what had happened as we travelled the nine-hour bus ride to Buenos Aires to see my brothers. When we got off the bus at Retiro station, Quidel was holding my hand and pointing at all the double-decker buses lined up, nose to curb, glinting and waiting. The sunlight seemed sudden after the tinted windows. I took a careful breath – the air was humid with smog. 'We'll have to get money, little friend.'

Quidel ran up to an automatic teller and smashed an invisible soccer ball with his right foot. I pulled out my wallet. The buttons on the machine had been pressed so many times the numbers were gone. I slid my card in and it was pushed back before I even punched in my security code: sorry, no funds available.

I looked for another set of automatic tellers and a man in an expensive suit began laughing behind me. 'Our money's in the *corralito*, my friend. You won't be withdrawing anything today.'

Someone had pissed nearby and the smell made me sick.

He waved his hand. 'The banks are frozen. The peso . . .'

I didn't believe him. There'd been talk of the economy but we weren't a country that devalued its currency.

The man spat on the ground. 'Why do you think it's so quiet out here? Everyone's either marching or watching the television.'

It was true: Retiro bus station was the busiest in the city and I hadn't needed to wait for a teller. The passengers from the bus had dispersed too quickly.

The man stepped back, bumping into the wall behind him. 'I've lost my business. Fifteen years in textiles. Forty-five employees I can't pay. I'm just drinking to a better day and hoping when I wake up, this will be over.'

Quidel took my hand and flattened it out, sliding his fingers between mine. 'Come on, Papa. We'll walk to Nahuel and Diego's.'

At my brothers' apartment, the television was so loud we could hear it from the street. Diego was sitting in an overstuffed lounge chair with his feet propped on a pile of newspapers. Nahuel was lying on the couch, holding a bottle of whiskey. The television was showing protestors banging pots and pans, chanting.

'*Hola, hola,*' Quidel said and jumped up on Diego's lap like he did during La Boca versus River Plate soccer games. Diego squeezed him to his chest but looked up at me. 'What are we going to do?'

On the television, a crowd of people was pushing a bus onto its side. Behind them, looters were pouring into a bed linen shop.

'We didn't see this coming into town,' I said.

Diego sighed. He'd gained weight since I'd last seen him. 'Bus avoided it, I imagine. It's all near the Plaza del Mayo.' I realised this wasn't a surprise to him. He'd been making gentle withdrawals and converting to American dollars for weeks now. Nahuel had made fun of him on the phone, telling me our big brother was a conspiracy theorist. Maybe that's why Nahuel was so quiet on the couch – he wasn't good at being wrong.

'What does it mean?' I asked.

He pressed the remote control and the television went quiet. We were both staring at the silent box – a news reporter who looked painfully young was standing in front of a restless crowd. Diego cleared his throat. 'If we're lucky, we can withdraw our own money. But they're going to devalue the peso, which means a hundred becomes twenty-five or thirty.'

'But that'll happen to everyone, right?'

He looked at me like he couldn't understand how someone who'd studied at university could be so stupid. 'You were going to Japan?'

I thought of the agent sitting behind the plywood desk and the receipt for my down payment. 'Yeah.'

'Well, if your travel agency even exists next month, you're lucky. Then, you'll have to find three times as much money to pay for your trip. You think you're going to be able to go to one of the most expensive countries on earth now? No way.'

Quidel sat up. 'What?'

Diego squeezed his little arm. 'You can watch the World Cup here on our small screen, Quido Mosquito.' My brother knew about Rosie's phone call. Tactfully he let the possibility slide that Rosie could pay for our trip. Instead, he reached for a pair of pink, sequinned sunglasses with feathers and slid them onto his big face. Diego and Nahuel leased a sunglasses store in Palermo and brought home the silliest glasses for Quidel, who was now watching his uncle, unable to decide if he should cry or laugh. Mouth quivering, he looked up. '*La copa mundial?*'

❄

Rioters had ransacked Diego and Nahuel's store so we spent the Christmas holidays packing up what was left of their stock. After three days of cleaning, we boarded the windows and sat in their apartment, drinking beer and whiskey like mourners. Diego never turned the television off and so we watched the *cacerolazo* crowds. Banging pots. Pulling down billboards. Lighting fires in doorways. One afternoon, Nahuel said he had had enough and reached for his shoes: he was joining them. Diego nodded but I was scared to take Quidel into the crowds, so we stayed inside under a self-imposed house arrest. Quidel sat cross-legged in front of the television, watching the screen for any clues that might lead us back to the World Cup and I kept replaying the phone conversation with Rosie in my head.

That's when I began to make plans for Bariloche.

❄

When we returned to Córdoba, I had no work and the travel agency was boarded up. My deposit gone. I took the rest of my savings and bought a truck so Quidel and I could set off for the Patagonia. I told him it was a long vacation and his mother would be joining us when she returned from America. Later when he asked after her, I changed the subject.

Bariloche seemed like a good place to hide – it wasn't home, but I knew the area. When I was a kid, we visited friends from the *asentamiento* who'd moved there, but they'd since left. I was hoping to find work at Club Andino or on Cerro Catedral at the information centre, but instead found myself selling cheap t-shirts in a tourist shop on Bariloche's main street. My boss was an elderly woman who smelled of coca leaves and sour milk. She liked to open an hour earlier and close an hour later than everyone else on the street. This commitment didn't mean many sales but her mouth quivered with excitement whenever a customer arrived during those twilight hours.

Quidel and I lived in a one-room apartment beneath her house on the western side of town, and most mornings I walked the five kilometres to work. Usually I took the high road: Avenida de los Pioneros. It was not as direct but I liked the views of the lake. Even though it was a thoroughfare the two lanes were plagued with potholes and loose gravel. No one cared for the roads in the south. Most of the crossroads hadn't been paved so dust covered the houses and dogs sitting alongside them.

Quidel began at his new school and the secretary pushed forms at me. She was a thin woman with a patient face who looked like she had spent much of her life waiting. I didn't fill in any information about Quidel's mother and when her gaze stopped at that line and she looked up at me, my throat trembled. She asked how long it had been since my wife passed away. I should have corrected her but didn't. If people assumed Rosie was dead, we attracted less attention.

During our road trip to Bariloche, I had promised Quidel a bicycle. A sudden growth spurt meant he was too big for his old one; he was now almost the same size as other boys his age. I was proud of this and proud to be starting over in the Patagonia. Quidel could still learn the mountains. I'd found a compromise – I may not have been full blood and I might not be living at the *asentamiento* or with my mother in Neuquén but I wasn't giving up the earth. I was returning from the city and my time in Córdoba hadn't come to nothing – I had a beautiful son and I'd become fluent in English. I could be a guide. How a bicycle came to represent this sense of opportunity, I'm not sure. But Quidel and I needed something to focus on after the collapse of the peso, and all of the news about the World Cup now reminded us of a trip we weren't taking, so we focused on bicycles.

The store smelled of rubber and sweat like a gymnasium. Our sales assistant was a high school student who crouched beside Quidel as he tried each model. Quidel seemed relaxed talking to him and I realised my son had inherited a sense of ease with the world that came entirely from his mother. Rosie was as comfortable in dirt huts as in expensive hotels. When she was in a room, nothing mattered more than the face of the person she was talking to. Place lost meaning and it was as though a much deeper conversation were occurring. It wasn't flirtatious, it was more honest than that, and this sincerity was something even my mother responded to. Rosie was the only white woman I'd seen my mother share a *maté* with.

In spite of myself, I thought Rosie would have liked the bicycle for the yellow and orange flames along the frame – she'd decided on the name Quidel because it meant 'burning torch' in Mapudungun, my native language.

'How far can your foot reach?' the assistant asked and Quidel pushed against the pedal.

Quidel squeezed the plastic grips and looked up at me with an uneven grin. 'I think it might be the right size.'

The rest of the frame was silver and red, and the handlebars were upright, the seat low. I could imagine him pushing as hard as he could, wind ruffling his hair, and in the last instant, he'd whip on the brakes, skidding to a dusty halt.

❉

It happened on a Saturday, the kind of late-summer day that makes you appreciate the changing of the seasons. I was standing on the gravel's edge of Avenida de los Pioneros and Quidel was on his bicycle, riding towards me. I was on the lower side of the road with Nahuel Huapi Lake behind me. I'd been staring at it seconds before. The long stretch of water. The surface like a piece of blue stone. I'd been thinking I should call Rosie – I should do it that afternoon and set things right – when Quidel yelled out. His hands were gripping the handlebars. His face bright with accomplishment.

The bicycle gleamed in the crisp sunlight as flames chased his pedalling feet. Pride overwhelmed me and for a brief moment my son was a stranger. He was so beautiful and separate from me it was hard to believe I'd helped create him. I watched him bounce over a rock and shriek with laughter, hair flying around his face.

There were no cars behind him and he didn't seem to be moving too fast. Of course he was, I've walked that stretch of road over and over again, and it's deceptively steep. He was shouting out to me, his eyes watching my face instead of the road in front of him. The pothole was maybe seven centimetres deep. It had a thick ring of cement along the border. The wheel must have hit that lip and lurched forward because suddenly Quidel was airborne, stretched over the handlebars. I didn't understand what I was seeing and for the briefest instant, the moment of impact, I didn't see anything at all. I just heard his head hitting the asphalt. And there he was, sprawled at my feet.

He was yelling out for me and Rosie, and this seemed like a good sign. I asked him to move his legs but they were shaking and pale beneath his satiny black basketball shorts. I couldn't tell if there was damage to his spine. I tried again, asking him to move his arms this time but he just wailed and asked where his bicycle was. It had fallen in the gravel – the back wheel on the shoulder, the handlebars pointed at us.

Quidel's red, scuffed tennis shoes were shaking. He'd sat at the table that morning fastening and unfastening the Velcro, the sound scratching through the kitchen until I'd said, 'Enough'.

'Quido, talk to me. How old are you?'

His eyes rolled back into his head and he began convulsing.

I shrieked. My hands ran along his chest to steady him.

A car stopped. Surely it was the first, I don't remember any others. I shouted for an ambulance. I couldn't see if it was a man or a woman who made the call. Time was dreamy and though it couldn't have taken long, it felt like we were waiting for days alongside that road.

Quidel was howling, white foam spilling from his mouth. I stroked his arms and pleaded with him to stay still. The cries were too much, he was too loud. He was thrashing now and it was the firemen who arrived first. Two thick men and two trainees sirened their way through the stopped traffic.

The younger trainee held up a blanket for shade. The older ones checked Quidel's heart rate and breath before strapping him to a board. His neck must be okay if they can move him, I thought. That has to be a good sign. Their hands were thick and capable, but Quidel had stopped crying. The quiet was almost as frightening as the uneven circle of blood on the pavement where his head had been.

I was standing over Quidel when the ambulance pulled close. His cheek was grazed. His elbows and legs were embedded with gravel and he was still bleeding out of the back of his head. Two of his front teeth, grown-up teeth, had broken off. As my son was loaded into the ambulance, I searched the ground for pieces of teeth. Anything pale that caught the sunlight. Rocks. Chipped glass. The clasp from a broken watchband.

'Do you want to ride with him?' one of the firemen asked.

Of course I wanted to ride with him but I had to find his teeth. I couldn't just leave them there. I was still scanning the gravel when he grabbed my shoulders and pushed me in.

Someone else was picking up the bike. A neighbour.

As we pulled away, the ambulance stammered with the heavy vibration of the dirt road.

I was aware of the ambulance as a car. But I was also aware of it as a room, a tiny room with four people in it, moving towards the hospital. I pressed myself against the wall, but nothing would have interfered with the officers. They were unstoppable. Injections, oxygen, CPR. But none of it mattered. I knew when it was over – Quidel's face relaxed and there was a lightness in the air. I could feel an embrace trailing away and my chest was empty. My son was gone. The officers didn't stop. Maybe they didn't know, maybe they were pretending he was still with us. A tribute of respect to a grieving father. But I knew as I stared over them, through the darkened window, at the road behind us. I was quiet. There would be facts at the hospital, I didn't need them straight away. I'd have the rest of my life to hold onto them: Quidel's neck had suffered damage on the impact but it was the blow to his head that killed him.

❄

Death arrives in the most ordinary moments, common as a bicycle. The only place I found peace in the days after Quidel's death was up the mountain, at a shrine honouring the Virgin of the Snow. The altar was wooden, built off the trail like a secret waterfall. Along the surrounding rock wall, a few plaques offered gratitude.

'Thank you for saving our son.'

'Thank you for returning the good health of Felipe.'

'Thank you for saving my marriage.'

I touched the gold plates, envious of their strong fortune. Candles waited in the middle, in front of her. Some were burnt stubs, others tall and new. Sometimes I'd light them all into a blaze while I prayed. A couple of weeks after Quidel's death, I wrote my message to the Virgin on a thick piece of white paper and folded it tight, leaving it with a bundle of fresh flowers: 'Please tell me what I'm supposed to do now.'

The Virgin watched me from her wooden pedestal, draped in her blue robe. I didn't mind her pity. She knew what it felt like to lose a son.

❄

In a few weeks, the concession came up for the refugio. I hadn't told my family I was in the area. I'd planned on writing to them when I was established – a happy surprise – but then there was the accident and I needed time. Telling my mother or my brothers would have made it real. I thought I would be closer to Quidel at the refugio – mountains are the closest place to heaven – but it wasn't enough. I would dream about travelling back in time. A month before and Quidel would have been wearing a helmet. A year before and I could have made Rosie stay. I still hadn't written to her – she didn't know where I was or that Quidel was dead.

I never saw Quidel or his ghost in my dreams. But sometimes I heard him yelling outside the refugio's kitchen window. It was always in the final moments of a soccer game played on the street in a city I couldn't name. I'd stop whatever I was doing – set down the saucepan, rest the dish towel over my shoulder – and close my eyes. Sometimes I heard the score: one-all or two-all. Always, Quidel was shouting for the ball and, after hearing his voice, I could see him weaving towards the goal. The defence had been caught unaware and no one would reach him with all that open space. There was a pause, a moment of shared quiet as everyone waited: Quidel and the goalkeeper measuring each other. The goalie overconfident, thinking height could save him in this afterlife contest. A strike against the ball and then an eruption of applause. Teammates calling out my son's name.

So when I heard yelling outside the refugio, a few days before the avalanche, I thought it was Quidel. I was fixing one of the benches in the dining room and the front door was held open with a brick for fresh air. It had been a few months since he'd visited and I'd wondered if this passing of time meant I was forgetting my own son.

When I heard the soccer game, I closed my eyes. He was back. But something wasn't right – the voices were unfamiliar. In the four years since he'd died, he'd stayed the same age in this dream and he was always playing with the same team. So for the first time, I stood up gingerly and made my way to the open front door just in time to see Jack pass the ball to Felix. They'd arrived that morning. The field was the open area between the refugio and the toilet block. Two sets of goals had been erected out of broomsticks and Klaus was guarding the one furthest away. None of them noticed me. They were too absorbed in the game. And then Klaus began hooting like a chimpanzee and Felix slipped on the ice. Felix was wearing a blue and yellow Boca jersey over a sweater, the same team Quidel had supported. This coincidence was not a surprising one. Tourists either cheered for La Boca or River Plate, but the colours seemed so beautiful and painful to me I wondered what message the Virgin was sending.

I could imagine Quidel in his jersey – sitting on Diego's lap in that lounge chair, the two of them shouting at a televised referee – and I felt faint.

The following day I hiked down to Bariloche for more supplies. I didn't like leaving guests alone but Alberto, from the next refugio, was worried about his wife – she'd twisted her ankle – and the German family seemed trustworthy. They spent the day outside, hiking and skiing around the lake, and I was back before nightfall. I wouldn't have gone but it was urgent – the horses couldn't make it through the snow and we needed food. I was limited to what could be carried in a pack. Potatoes. Flour. Butter. On the way back, at the Virgin altar, I found Carmen. She was hunched over a camping stove, staring at the alpine cabin. I didn't want to alarm her but she could have trouble hiking back if she waited until morning, especially if a warm snap took hold. This was the case for the refugio, too – both trails had avalanche-prone areas – but I figured she was safer with people who knew the area. I invited her to the refugio, glad to have another paying guest, and she packed her things.

Early the next morning, Felix and I hiked out to the far side of the lake with his father to climb the ridge. It was so steep all we could see was the incline ahead and the sharp blue sky. When we reached the crest, Felix shouted out at all the distant peaks. And then, as we stopped to find our breath, an avalanche slid down one of the banks to our right. It was Cerro Felipe, notoriously moody. I pointed but Felix was already staring at it. It was so far away it felt like we'd seen a falling star. Felix's eyebrows shot up and he gripped my palm so he was holding both my hand and his father's. 'I like climbing.'

'Really?'

'You're responsible for your height.' I wasn't sure exactly what he meant, if he'd lost something in translating his thought to English, but I nodded. It was the kind of thing Quidel would have said and it made sense the more I thought about it. There was something compelling about Felix – maybe it was his age. Almost-seven-year-olds enjoy a fearlessness that's like rewarded faith. I remembered Quidel leaping off my neighbour's house to see if he could fly. He'd swear to me that for a second his body had lifted in the air, and he knew he was one-eighth condor. I could imagine Felix stretching his arms out in the same way.

Erik grabbed his binoculars from his daypack and disappeared over the ridge to study a rock formation, and Felix stooped down to tie his boot. 'We stayed at a hotel in Bariloche and two kids lived there, both older than me. Do you have any?'

'Kids?' I asked.

He nodded.

'I did once – a son. But he died.' The words crept out of their own accord. I focused on breathing and how the cold air filled my chest.

Felix thought about my words. 'What was his name?'

'Quidel.' It was the first time I'd spoken his name to a guest at the refugio. You could learn a lot about someone in a few days and I shared friendships with some of the travellers but they always felt transient to me – not the travellers themselves, but the friendships.

I didn't look at Felix but he took my hand. 'He's lucky. He gets to spend time with my *oma* up in heaven. I miss her.'

'I hadn't thought of that.' It took effort to keep my voice calm.

Felix didn't seem to notice, he was rocking his head from side to side. 'You know, you're my first friend in Argentina.' He said the last bit in Spanish. His words swayed with his head and he grinned at me.

I squeezed his hand and answered in English. 'I'm glad.' I felt like a thief caught outside a window and didn't trust myself to say any more.

❋

That evening, Emma and the Americans arrived. I heard her laughing before I saw her: an uninhibited sound, almost musical. It reminded me of the fat man on the train in Buenos Aires, walking up and down the aisle, playing Elvis Presley from a boom box and selling '*Lo Mejor De Rock y Roll*' homemade CDs for three pesos. He was always grinning, like he had everything he wanted, and her laughter had that same combination of self-deprecation and exuberance.

When I came around the side of the refugio, I saw her: standing on a rock, staring away from me. I waited for her to laugh again but that was the moment Jeremy climbed out of the tent and John appeared on the other side of the toilet block. I watched the two men, but Emma was still gazing out at Cerro Blanco, more in love with the mountain than with either of them.

I walked up to the tent. Jeremy stood in front of me but I was watching her. 'How long will you be staying here?'

The American cleared his throat. 'One night.'

Emma slid down the rock and Jeremy introduced us. She was already smiling, her cheeks flushed from the cold.

She stared at me like we already knew each other. Her brown eyes dominated her face. 'It certainly is a refuge, here. It must be hard to leave.' Her words were like a code I'd been waiting for without knowing it. I wanted to ask her inside. I wanted to share a *maté*. My mother would have been disgusted: not another white woman, surely?

John shuffled over, kicking at the snow, and Jeremy shifted the conversation to daily rates and amenities. He reached for

Emma and she swatted him away. She was polite but her gaze was distracted – she was staring to the horizon like she couldn't believe the physical mass of the mountains. I appreciated that abandon: our lives were breathlessly small. We did and we didn't matter.

I asked how long the three of them had been travelling together.

'A week.' Jeremy's tone was defensive.

'I hope you enjoy your time here.' Even then, I wanted to be friends with Emma – I could imagine her leaning against the kitchen counter, laughing as I chopped the vegetables for dinner – and I knew that wouldn't sit well with Jeremy.

❋

The Americans had arrived just before the warm weather and this meant it wasn't safe for them to hike back to the main trail and continue to the next refugio. On their second night, when I told them they still needed to wait, Jeremy punched my arm as though he could bully me into relenting. I should have been flattered; it seemed he thought the snow would take orders from me.

It was late and we were standing in front of the refugio. He leaned into me. 'You just want us here for the cash.'

It's true, I needed money. The more guests I had, the easier it would be to renew the concession – the bill was due at the end of the month and every bit helped. In fact, I was desperate: there would be no postponements this time. But I shrugged like the American was nothing to me. 'You're paying camping rates.'

I was calling him cheap and he didn't like that. I stepped back but the space between us was still charged. 'Just wait until the snow pack's stable.'

'Thanks, bro. But we'll be leaving tomorrow and we won't be paying our bill.'

He enunciated each word like he was speaking to someone who had difficulty understanding English. It was belittling and stupid but hardly worthy of the deep-seated rage that erupted within me. It happened sometimes – pent-up, wild energy came upon me suddenly. Anger that wanted to tear doors off hinges and smack into bone. I went for Jeremy then, shoving him hard. He wasn't expecting it and fell back into the snow, legs in the air like a giant insect. It was glorious, how silly he looked. But John was right there, grabbing my arm and pinning it behind my back.

'You can leave,' I said. 'Risk your life. But you're going to pay me what you owe me. Otherwise, when you're swept away or lost on the trail, you're going to look for something important – your compass or your granola bars – and you're going to realise that something vital is missing from your pack.'

Jeremy was standing up, dusting the snow off of his coat. 'Is that so? Well, John, we'd better give the man his money.' I could feel John's surprise as he released me. We both stood there for an awkward moment, watching Jeremy. He opened his wallet and pulled out a wad of bills, dropping them onto the snow. 'You shouldn't give people ideas, Pedro. You're more vulnerable than we are. Tell me: what matters most to you out here?'

They left the next morning – before I found the broken radio. The irony was they were the ones who needed it most that day. But you can't control the risks other people are willing to take. I was glad they were gone. Of course I made it clear they should stay, but the atmosphere in the refugio lightened with their departure. Emma beamed as they walked away. Even when we were searching for John and Jeremy's bodies, I was impressed with her composure. She was so capable. And in that sudden urgency, I felt awake for the first time since Quidel died.

Back at the refugio, I tried to keep everyone calm but it was likely the Americans had been swept away. I understated this for Emma's benefit – they were her friends, after all. I worried for her when she didn't appear at dinner. But the next morning she came down and that afternoon, when we shared a *maté*, she seemed stronger.

Then, after dinner, Wolfe's knock sounded on the door. I was in the kitchen trying to repair the radio, hoping the wires could be argued around. I knew the person at the door wasn't a current guest – why knock? But it didn't seem likely to be Jeremy or John, either: I imagined their souls were either climbing into heaven or, more likely, crash-landing into the underworld. Whoever it was, they must have been very experienced or very inexperienced to be trekking through a blizzard. This was the kind of thing that should have inspired a professional interest in me – where would I sleep them, how would our food stores hold? I moved to the doorway as the traveller came in.

It wasn't until he took off his hat and I saw his face that it became clear: Wolfe Goldberg, Rosie's brother, had tracked me down and he was after Quidel.

He watched me for a curious moment and, for the first time since I'd moved into the refugio, I felt embarrassed by how shabby it was. The tables were uneven, the curtains faded. But as he scanned the room, he seemed more interested in the guests, as though they were scheming with me to hide Quidel.

'You alone?' I asked.

Wolfe's eyes were the same shade, the same shape, as his sister's and this resemblance made her seem nearby, as if she might be waiting outside or upstairs. My ears were listening for footsteps.

He nodded and I wanted to ask where Rosie was. Instead, I asked which way he'd come.

'Cerro Negro. Off-trail. What about some dinner?' he replied.

I disappeared into the kitchen, bewildered by the idea of heating up leftover pizza for my dead son's uncle. When I first met Wolfe, I was expecting a male version of Rosie: a jovial man who gave the world the benefit of the doubt. But Wolfe reminded me of a racing greyhound hungry for victory. There were almost six years between them and Rosie explained Wolfe's unbending nature as a consequence of timing. He was an adolescent when their mother left the family for a wealthy Australian and moved across the world. Wolfe and his father fought during that summer. Continual spot fires that could never be put out. Wolfe eventually left for boarding school.

Perhaps because she was younger, perhaps because she was a girl, Rosie was never asked to carry the same expectations as Wolfe. When Wolfe refused his father's order to run the business, he was exiled from the family for two years. When Rosie announced she was travelling instead of going to college, her father called her an adventurer and offered to pay for her airplane tickets. In Córdoba, though, she enrolled in classes, talking herself past entrance exams and prerequisites. But she wasn't concerned with earning a degree – Rosie only took subjects that interested her. Before we met she'd studied for four years and her transcript was so chaotic she wasn't close to graduating.

But Wolfe didn't earn my respect for standing up to his father. A man doesn't deserve reward for following the only path his nature would allow. What impressed me was the fact he was devoted to Rosie despite their father's favouritism, and he adored Quidel. Even when Quidel was a baby, Wolfe would hold him over his head like a trophy. 'This is my nephew. Right here, my little man,' he said. Wolfe travelled to Argentina frequently and always had a small gift for Quidel. On his last visit, Wolfe brought walkie-talkies and they tested them in the neighbourhood by spying on the neighbours. Later, as I was putting them away in Quidel's room, I realised they weren't toys – they'd once belonged to a convoy.

Back in the refugio, Wolfe kept eyeing Felix as though he were a spirit that might take the shape of Quidel, and I realised Felix was the only one in the refugio, besides me, who knew my son had died. I watched, horrified and hopeful, as Felix shifted over to Wolfe and asked him about his hand. It would all come out, I realised. Just like that. Felix would make an innocent remark and the demons I'd been hiding from would burst from under the floorboards and flatten the refugio. But then Felix asked Wolfe his name and the danger lifted. Wolfe was gruff with him, and Felix tilted his head like such grumpiness was something to be pitied. He moved down the bench with his pens and paper.

I watched Felix drawing, and realised I'd wanted him to say something. I wanted Wolfe to know about Quidel.

When everyone shuffled off to bed, Wolfe declared that he'd sleep on the floor in the dining room. His voice was firm. He was ready for me.

Emma watched the two of us, and Felix hugged his arms around my waist. They knew something was unfolding and I wanted to smile but didn't know if they should be reassured. I nodded and they moved upstairs.

Wolfe was sitting in the same place where Jeremy had been. 'How about a *maté*? After all, we're family.'

I moved into the kitchen like it belonged to someone else and searched for the gourd. Eventually I found it in its place, on the shelf over the stove. Rosie had bought it for me in the week after we left my mother. 'To honour new beginnings,' she'd said, picking it up from a market stall without looking at any others. Decisions were easy for her. The gourd was about the size of my fist and beige, with right angles etched around the oval base. I loaded it, shaking the *yerba* so its fine silt coated my fingers, and then filled the thermos with hot water.

Wolfe pulled his chair closer to the table. Sitting opposite, I filled the gourd with water and passed it to him. Wolfe took the *bombilla* straw in his mouth and drained the *maté*. If he found it sour, he didn't show it.

It wasn't until I'd finished that Wolfe spoke. 'You're a hard man to find.'

'I'm sorry for that.'

'I bet you are. Even your family's looking for you.'

I tried to nod.

Wolfe coughed, the sound shaking from his chest. 'About Quidel . . .'

My heart was sick at the sound of his name.

'We have you on kidnapping charges. Lawyers have been called. Police. There's a private detective waiting in Bariloche.'

'We?'

'Rosie's there, too.'

'In Bariloche?'

'Yeah.'

'How is she?'

'How do you think? She wants her son back.'

My expression must have given something away because Wolfe shook his head. 'Look, she wants to handle this diplomatically. You fucked up, we all know that. But you are Quidel's father.'

He was waiting for me to say something. After a moment, he continued. 'She didn't go to the ashram, if that was worrying you.'

I didn't know what he was talking about. An ashram wouldn't have impressed their father. I'd never known him to go to synagogue but he was committed to the idea of his Jewish family. He had shaken his head when he heard I visited a *machi* instead of a doctor. A Catholic or a Protestant son-in-law would have been troubling enough, but a pagan who defended witchdoctors was alarming.

Wolfe was still talking. 'She was taking care of our father.'

'Condolences.'

'These things happen.'

I wondered how his death had affected Rosie. She adored him. Outside it was too dark to see the falling snow except for the flakes that drifted into the soft light from the dining room.

I was about to tell him. I took a deep breath and opened my mouth but Wolfe interrupted. 'So where's Quidel?' His hands pressed down on the table like he was about to stand. 'He's down in Bariloche, I take it?'

I nodded. He *was* down in Bariloche. I'd buried him alone. My landlady had offered to come but I'd told her to watch over the store. I wanted her to refuse but she'd clicked her tongue like life moves on.

'Boarding school. Well, that's something then,' Wolfe said. 'Tell me, where's the bathroom in this place?'

I grabbed a flashlight and showed him outside.

❄

The next day I wanted to escape the things I needed to tell Wolfe, and I asked Emma to walk with me to the ice waterfall. I'd been thinking about her. And when we set off, I wondered if we might make a habit of walking together. But that night the refugio money disappeared and my anger was not calm or thoughtful. That money was the only thing that could keep me safe in the refugio – without it, I'd have to forfeit the concession. Of course the concession was the least of my worries – Rosie was waiting in Bariloche – but I was too edgy and confused with Wolfe's arrival to think clearly. Instead, I'd been counting and re-counting the crinkled bills, smoothing them, calculating how many more I'd need. Things might have turned out differently with Emma if I hadn't accused her so easily. If I'd taken time to think through the logic of the situation. But I was obsessed – someone in the refugio was a thief, someone so privileged they could fly in an airplane still needed more. And Emma was in the kitchen – she'd watched me store money in the cigar box, she was the only one who knew the hiding place. I wanted to doubt her guilt but when the envelope appeared in her pack it seemed irrefutable. And worse, it seemed a sign of my own stupidity. Hadn't I learned my lesson with Rosie – nothing good could come from placing your faith in a white woman.

Wolfe considered the missing refugio money like it was a matter of arithmetic. He wanted to know about each of the guests. Carmen, Hita and Erik, their sons, Emma. He mentioned her name last, carefully. I was cautious with my words and he pretended not to notice the extra time it took to form my answers. Then he asked about the Americans and her relationship to them.

I lied. I said they were friendly. Likeable enough if a bit dumb – wouldn't listen to common sense.

I was too hesitant. Wolfe shook his head. 'You would have stopped them.'

I bit my lip and stepped back. 'I tried. But they were ready for a fight. And there were two of them.'

'Doesn't sound very friendly.' He was staring at me.

'I guess not.'

'Why lie?'

'Why tell the truth?' I wanted to keep Emma, and anything to do with her, to myself. Not that it mattered – we weren't talking to each other. And when the refugio money appeared, I was such an idiot, I still thought she was the thief.

There were larger issues to face, too – when I discovered the radio in pieces, I pretended it didn't matter so everyone would keep calm in the refugio. Usually Club Andino kept a radio log but it was a beat-up notebook that migrated across volunteers' desks. It could easily go unnoticed that my calls had ended – and even if someone did notice, they had no way of knowing we were low on food.

The guests were beginning to irritate each other: they found the cabin confining. People from the First World are peculiar with matters of space – they cannot have enough. Emma and Carmen took shifts with their dormitory room so they could have time alone. Jack would disappear into his books. Klaus and Felix fought louder in their afternoon chess games. Erik began digging in the snow to collect rocks, polishing them as exhibits for the dining room table, and this irritated Hita. Her annoyance was new, something I attributed to our detention, and when Erik was upstairs, she'd throw his rocks out the kitchen window.

Hita was the most generous and competent person in the refugio. She realised we were gliding towards an emergency like a tiny boat nearing a waterfall. But she didn't panic and she didn't let on to anyone how dangerous things had become. She helped take an inventory of our supplies and, when it was obvious how low we were, she added all of her family's food without a word. Of course I'd deduct it from their bill but she just brushed me away when I tried to bring it up.

Ordering from the refugio menu was no longer a possibility – food had to be rationed, so I decided on a flat fee for meals, each one the same size. It was important to maintain a sense of fairness to keep everyone from realising how desperate the situation was.

Hita wrote out the list – every candy bar and soft drink, exact measures of butter, milk and flour. I transferred everything to the cellar and locked it at night. Refugio stores had already been low: if Julio had come up with the horses as expected, we'd have been fine for another month. But he'd developed an infection and kept putting off his delivery – first missing one, then two trips – and the arrival of an early snow meant I had to wait until spring for more supplies. I didn't worry at the time – winter brought few visitors and those who did come usually brought their own rations – but of course I should have been prepared. That lack of foresight meant we could go hungry before it was clear enough to hike down.

There were two trails to Bariloche but neither was safe. The forest loop that stretched out behind Cerro Negro, past Carmen's cabin, had over three kilometres of avalanche danger on the last section to the main trail. We'd be able to hike to the cabin but the final stretch followed a series of couloirs that would be impassable. It's true Wolfe had come that way, but he left the trails and hiked through the back country. The ice climbs alone would be too steep for our party, especially the children. And with the recent weather . . . That left the main trail along Cerro Blanco, the way Jeremy and John had left. It had one unstable area that spanned about five hundred metres, right near the refugio. I wasn't prepared to risk it.

Each morning when there was enough light to see, I'd stand in front of the refugio, smelling for snow with my head tipped back. It reminded me of Quidel, sniffing the sea air for salt when Rosie took us to the beach.

In the first days after his arrival, Wolfe didn't mention Quidel again but every time he offered to help with chores, I worried he was trying to collect information about his nephew. If we were scraping snow off the roof, a bland comment about the distance to Bariloche or the way Felix ran across the snow seemed heavy with suggestion. Of course I'd have to tell him the truth. But the fantasy I'd agreed to – Quidel enrolled in boarding school – had sparked a series of daydreams: Quidel waiting for the next set of holidays, Quidel running up the path to the refugio, Quidel skating on the lake. And if I told Wolfe the truth, these versions of what might have happened would disappear.

When Felix had his asthma attack, I didn't know Hita's purse was missing. I was in the kitchen when she yelled out. As I hurried into the dining room, I saw Felix collapsed on the floor. His mother was ripping off his shirt and pressing into his chest. If anyone was strong enough to frighten death away, it was Hita. Strong even in a moment of panic. Erik ordered Klaus to look upstairs for the purse – his feet pounded on the stairs – but he returned with empty hands. Felix's legs were shaking and I could only think of Quidel.

'Jack. We need Jack,' Hita said, and Klaus ran outside, shouting his brother's name.

When Jack pushed through the door, holding the purse, I still didn't understand he was the thief. I was thinking about Felix, about the importance of his breath. I'd seen emergencies at the refugio – two broken legs, a couple of deep cuts, one fall – but never an asthma attack. It wasn't until Jack fled and Felix was recovering by the fire that I realised Emma hadn't taken the refugio money.

❄

The next morning, we searched for Jack. I didn't understand running from the refugio. There was no sense to it. The temperatures were well below freezing – he could die. And frankly, it was the last thing I needed. It's hard to take care of people who take stupid risks. First the Americans. Now this.

I asked Emma to walk with me. Carmen and Wolfe were hiking near the Cerro Negro trailhead while Erik and Klaus looked around the lake. Hita was staying in the dining room to look after Felix and wait in case Jack returned.

'Please,' I said. 'I want to apologise.'

Eventually she nodded.

We left the refugio, travelling on the same path that led to the ice waterfall. It was impossible to know if Jack had gone that way because the ground was worn with footprints. I let Emma walk in front.

'Watch for tracks that leave the trail.' I was just looking for something to say. It seemed too much quiet would make it impossible for either one of us to speak and we'd be trapped in a grainy silence. She didn't reply.

When I caught sight of the ice waterfall I stopped and, after a moment, she stopped too – but she was still facing the trail with her back to me. I spoke louder than necessary. 'I'm sorry I thought you took the money.'

She turned around, her face more disbelieving than wary. 'It's done.'

Neither of us said anything and I could see Erik's green-grey jacket on the other side of the lake. 'Any idea where Jack might have gone?'

Emma shook her head, her breath escaping like fog into the air. She wasn't going to be distracted. 'I'm surprised you thought I could be the thief.'

'It was ridiculous.'

She tugged at the bright blue beanie on her head. 'Why would you believe that?'

What could I tell her? That I thought she could be a thief because she'd spent time in the kitchen? That I'd loved a white woman who didn't love me? That I'd had bigger things stolen from me – my son, for instance – and I was susceptible to the comforts of blame? 'It's not so simple.'

'You can tell me.'

I should have given her the story of Wolfe's arrival, what it meant, what was waiting for me in Bariloche. I should have owned that I was a coward, paralysed with the thought of going down the mountain. She would have listened without judgement. That could have given me clarity with so many lives at risk.

'I can't.' This was the literal truth. My chest was so tight I was having trouble with my breath.

She sighed, disgusted, and it was like I was thrashing against a dangerous tide. The words were there, in my throat, but I couldn't find air.

She watched me without blinking, like she was deciding what to think of me. Sometimes there are moments that change everything – like a kaleidoscope tilting colours into a new pattern. We were in one of those moments; I knew it. I needed to trust someone brave with my story. If I could start speaking, the rest would come. I needed to tell her about Quidel so the weight of remembrance could be shared. The only way to walk clearly into the future is to stand firmly on the past.

She turned back to the trail. 'If Jack hadn't stolen that money, everything would have been different. We'd have a brighter picture, wouldn't we?'

I was surprised. Jack had nothing to do with where we were. It was my fault. Jack had provided a circumstance – a way to distance her – but I was my own sweet saboteur. Emma and I shared a link – I'd felt it when I first heard her laughing in front of the refugio – but it couldn't hold my fear; nothing was strong enough to hold that weight. I would have found another way to ask her to leave.

❋

Wolfe and Carmen returned with Jack in the early evening, and he was sick. We bandaged his leg and raised his temperature but it felt like a warning. First Felix, then Jack. And now Hita and Erik had stopped talking to each other. No doubt she held Erik responsible – they would never have hiked to the refugio without his enthusiasm. If the German family – our keystone – was falling apart, how much faith could I have in the rest of us? I was worried: our food stores were almost gone.

Late the next morning, I found Wolfe in the dining room with a miner's flashlight strapped to his head. There were piles

of papers in front of him. He was reading the back of an envelope and making notes. Everyone else was upstairs.

'What are you doing?' My voice surprised him. He tried
to cover the pile in front of him with his arm but I'd already
seen the bank statements and unpaid bills. My filing system – a
wooden crate – stood at the end of the table. He was going
through my accounts.

He propped his chin on his fist and rested his elbow on the
table. 'You're not doing too well up here, are you, Pedro?'

I shrugged, not trusting myself to speak.

'How are you paying for Quidel's school?'

I clenched my teeth together and could feel where I'd been
grinding them in my sleep. The back of my jaw was sore.

Wolfe repeated his question and I stepped towards the table
and pressed my fingers against the wood. I waited a moment to
steady myself. 'I should have told you—'

'Yes.'

He had no idea what I was about to say and for a brief
moment I wanted to protect him. But he didn't understand my
silence; he was angry. 'Where's Quidel?'

I looked down to the uneven grooves in the table and then
back to his eyes, focusing on one and then the other. 'He's
dead.'

'Don't pull that bullshit with me.'

I took a deep breath and glanced down. Someone had run a
ballpoint pen along one of the ruts, where a piece of wood had
splintered. I stared at the uneven blue ink. 'He had a bicycle
accident. Avenida de los Pioneros. He was taken to the hospital
but died in the ambulance. Fractured skull.'

'Fuck you, Pedro. Tell me where he is.'

My head lifted. His eyes, Rosie's eyes, were staring at me; my
chest crumpled as I tried to keep my voice level. 'Wolfe, would I
trust Quidel with strangers?'

He snorted. 'You wouldn't leave him with a babysitter to go out to dinner.' His face went pale as he followed his own logic and then, panicky, 'But he's in Bariloche.'

'Bariloche cemetery.'

'Why didn't you tell me? Why didn't you tell Rosie?' His fist tightened on the table.

'He hit a pothole. I was right there.'

'Surely a mother ought to know her kid's dead?'

'The *bomberos* came first.' The firemen.

'Fucking hell, Pedro. Rosie had a right to know.'

'Then the ambulance. There was a crowd of people standing around us, standing around my son.'

'How long? When, when did Quidel die?'

Of course the date was heavy in my head – every year I went cross-country and drank myself sick on the anniversary – but I couldn't form the words. My throat was too sore. 'Soon after the peso collapsed.'

Wolfe waited while I rocked back and forth on the bench. My face was damp, my hands wiping at my eyes. The room felt suddenly huge, as though the walls had pulled away and there was nothing to fill all the space that had been left behind. I could hear Wolfe breathing, slow and concentrated. I wondered what he could possibly say with that breath.

'That was four years ago.'

'I know.' It made no sense but I was angry at Rosie for not knowing, for not magically appearing in Bariloche after it happened. Surely she could feel the earth shaking underfoot? The air was so heavy with my grief she must have smelt it in New York.

'Four fucking years.'

'I thought he would come back. Maybe not in the same shape, maybe no one else would recognise him even. But I watched kids in the *supermercado*, lining up behind the cash register with their candies, and I was watching for him. I thought if he just came back to me I could explain it all to Rosie then. And when I realised he wasn't coming back—' my chest was shuddering now, '—so much time had passed it seemed wide as a river.'

'You owed it to Rosie.'

'She left me.'

'People leave each other all the time. You watched your kid die and didn't think to tell his family?' Wolfe lunged across the table and seized me by the throat. His fingers gripped the tendons in my neck; his nails dug into my skin. I tried pulling away but he was too strong and I couldn't breathe. The bench toppled over as he pushed me back against the wall. I bit him hard, the taste of nicotine bitter in my mouth. He released me for a moment and then was back. I scrambled against him – punching and kicking. I made contact – again and again – but Wolfe kept coming at me with the strength of a wild animal.

He released me. 'Fuck, you make some bad decisions, don't you?' he said.

I laughed: my voice spiteful, surprising us both. 'You can't talk. Afghanistan? You make bad decisions and people die. How many, Wolfe? Four? Five? What about their families?'

He went crazy then. He lunged at me, grabbing me by the arms and throwing me onto the ground. I landed hard, my skull cracking on the floor. My ears were ringing as the refugio spun above me. He was kicking me, then slamming my head onto the floorboards. This was it, I thought. I'm going to die. And I remembered Quidel's burial, the tiny wooden casket, the sweeping beauty of the cumulus sky that morning. There had been a funeral procession two rows down: a father had died. All his children – at least five or six of them – sobbing and holding each other as if the grief were so strong they couldn't trust their own legs.

'Jesus Christ.' Jack was standing in the doorway, and his presence caught Wolfe off guard. It gave me time to shove him off me. For a moment I thought Wolfe was going to keep fighting but he collapsed onto his knees, his head and forearms resting on the ground. Jack stood in the doorway, waiting.

I pulled myself up. Wolfe looked worse than I expected. He had a gash along his cheek and his eye was swelling. His shirt was covered in blood.

'What is this?' Jack asked.

'Tell him, Pedro,' Wolfe said. 'Let's make this public.'

'What?' The sour taste of iron in my mouth.

'Tell him why we're here.'

The words arrived slowly. I began with the bicycle. Wolfe rolled onto his back and stared at the ceiling. Jack slid down so he was leaning against the wall. I told them about the flying decals above the pedals, the teenager who'd sold it to us, the angle of the frame against the sky as Quidel flew over the handlebars. My voice sounded like it belonged to someone else, like it had been recorded and was playing back to me. The intonation was unfamiliar, with strange pauses, but I kept going. The visits to the Virgin Mary. The letters composed to Rosie in my head.

Jack gingerly stretched his leg. I wouldn't have chosen him as a confidant but he understood the fatality of stupid mistakes. We all have our rites of passage.

Wolfe lay there, arms sprawled over his head, staring upwards, like he could see beyond the beams and the roof to the sky and the heavens.

'I'm sorry, Wolfe.'

He shifted to his side, weight moving slowly, and stood up without looking at me. His hand hovered over the ground for a moment. Jack was hunched against the wall, his knees in front of him. Wolfe nodded to the teenager and walked out of the room.

❀

I didn't see Wolfe for three or four hours. When he strode into the kitchen that afternoon, his face was red and blotchy. A large bruise was forming around his left eye. 'I think it's time.'

I looked up from the scouring pad in my hand. 'Time for what?'

'I've dug two test pits and the slabs have bonded to the other layers. I thought that wouldn't be enough for you so I did a Rutschblock and it held my weight. All seven levels. The outlook is clear but cold. If we wait, it could get warmer and that's the kind of avalanche weather that would leave us stranded.'

I turned on the tap to rinse the saucepan I was holding. 'We can't leave tomorrow. I've been working on the radio. We'll call Club Andino. They'll tell us what to do.'

Wolfe coughed into his hand. His knuckles were grazed. 'You've been working on the radio since I arrived.'

I set the pan in the drying rack and stared at him, speaking slowly. 'It's not safe.'

He rolled his shoulders back and met my gaze. 'We've got enough food for two more days. What other option do we have?'

'People can survive a month without food.'

'They need strength to hike down.'

'It's not worth risking an avalanche.'

'We don't have a choice, Pedro.'

I grabbed the next pot, dropping it into the water. 'I'm not putting nine lives at risk because of your impatience.'

He gripped my arm so I was forced to look at him. 'You have to face Bariloche.'

'I will – but I'm not chancing lives.' My voice sounded weak and I worried he could see all of my fears, perched like birds inside my rib cage.

Wolfe's hand was clenched like he wanted to punch the wall. Instead, he let his fist fall down on the table. 'We'll have a vote.

If the group votes to stay, I'll stay. If they vote to go, you'll lead us down.'

✳

I hiked out to Cerro Blanco. Already Jeremy and John had proven the mountain was capable of avalanches this season. Snow might add weight but temperature worried me more. I dug a pit six feet deep. The layers seemed bonded – the snow wasn't sugary and this was a good sign. But with a shovel shear test, there was a cracking ice lens, a medium shear. That meant the avalanche rating was still yellow – potential for danger. I was wary because your eyes couldn't help you. Everything might seem stable but if that hard case cracked, all the soft and feathery snow could come pouring out.

✳

Dinner consisted of tinned beans, a bit of stale bread and a couple of dates per person – but the atmosphere was so anxious no one complained. Everyone ate their portions in silence and waited expectantly for the after-dinner meeting. We had decisions to make, and that gave a tender panic to the ritual of eating. When the boys finished, they became loud with boredom but it only added to the tension. Klaus grabbed a loose thread on Felix's shirt to see how far it would unravel, and Felix laughed like a make-believe villain. I was glad when Hita hushed them. She sat on one side of the boys and Erik on the other. Both hunched over their plates as though they'd given in to the same interior exhaustion.

Wolfe settled next to me at the head of the table. He glanced over my head and I realised he wasn't talking about Quidel because he wanted me to wonder at what was waiting in Bariloche. He didn't believe I deserved any resolution. I had to focus, I told myself. Whatever I had to settle with Wolfe and

Rosie was separate from hiking down. But that was wrong. The two were linked: in hiding from my son's death, the very place that had offered safety could kill me.

After all of the dishes had been washed, everyone returned to the table. I stood, hoping height might add some authority to what I was about to say. My throat was sore from where Wolfe had grabbed me. 'It's too dangerous to hike down – we need to stay. We wait at the refugio, watch the weather and reassess in a couple of days.'

Wolfe pushed the bench back and stood as well, waiting for me to finish. His left eye had swollen up but he was wearing his hiking coat to give him a sense of authority. 'We don't have enough food to stay. There's a clear window if we leave first thing tomorrow morning. If we miss that, we could be stranded here another week or more and we don't have supplies for that.' It was disturbing how calm he sounded. He was offering everyone the option of death like a logical choice. I scanned the other guests to see if they understood how ludicrous this was but no one seemed alarmed. In fact, Erik was nodding.

I should have kept myself calm. 'We can't go down. It's not safe.'

Wolfe took his time, looking at each person around the table except me, keeping his voice even. 'Even if Club Andino and the Comisión have realised we're stranded, they don't have a helicopter. There are risks but we don't have a choice.'

'We do have a choice. Even without food it's crazy to hike down, after the Americans . . .'

'I think we stay,' Hita said, and I relaxed. People would see sense.

Wolfe cleared his throat. 'I've dug test pits. It's safe.'

I thought of my shovel against the snow, the medium shear. 'None of our options are safe.'

'Safest we've got.' His arm reached around me as though we were teammates but his fingers were digging into my shoulder.

'What do you think, Erik?' he asked.

The German shrugged. 'The snow is convincing. It depends on our weather tonight, of course. But if it holds, I think we go.'

I couldn't believe it. Of the guests, he was the most experienced. He should have known what was at stake. Hita was watching him with a stern expression, her mouth a rigid line. She pressed her palm to her scalp and looked at Erik. 'You would risk our lives? We followed you. We would not come here without you.'

He leaned forward. '*Es tut mir leid.*'

'What?' Her voice was sharp. She wasn't going to let him hide in a language only their family could understand. She wanted him to speak English.

He took a deep breath and lifted his head, peering at his sons. 'I'm sorry.'

She drew a sudden breath and then shook her head. An inward gesture. She didn't look up but her hands turned so they were holding her husband's. 'I forgive you. But I'm scared, Erik.'

'I know. I still think we hike down. We might not find this chance again.'

'I want to stay.'

I was holding my breath. Everyone in the refugio was watching him. It felt like all of our lives were resting on his decision. He looked to the door and then back to his wife. 'Okay. We stay.'

Jack stood up and paced over to the stove.

'Emma?' Wolfe was looking for something that could swing the momentum in his direction. Emma was standing behind the bench, her back pressed against the window so the refugio light reflected a soft aura around her. 'I have no idea. I'm not a mountaineer. I trust you, Wolfe. But an avalanche up close? It's terrifying.'

Wolfe stared at her and I could see he'd assumed she would vote with him. He was territorial of her opinions and I wondered about the friendship they shared. It occurred to me I wasn't the only one drawn to Emma and this didn't sit well. Wolfe scoffed. 'We're not going to join Jeremy and John under that pile of snow.'

Emma shook her head but she was smiling. 'Sensitive, Wolfe.'

'From the sounds of it, Jeremy wasn't known for *his* sensitivity.' He mumbled this but it was clear he wanted Emma to hear. Wolfe was angry with her.

She watched him like she was willing to play along. 'What do you mean?'

'Ask Carmen.'

'I'm asking you.'

Wolfe looked at Carmen, who shook her head as a warning but he'd already said too much. Even if it had been in his nature, he couldn't retrace his steps now. 'Two boys, one girl, out by the toilets. A bit threatening, don't you think?'

'Nothing happened,' Carmen said, but she spoke too quickly. I wasn't surprised – I remembered Jeremy punching my arm, his breath heavy in my face.

'What did they do?' Jack asked.

Emma stood up. For a moment, I thought she was going to smooth over Wolfe's accusation but instead she hugged Carmen around the shoulders. 'Are you okay?'

Carmen's mouth lifted into a bewildered smile. 'I didn't tell you because I knew you were close . . .'

'No, we weren't,' Emma said. She turned to Wolfe, defiant. 'I think we stay.'

Wolfe smacked the table with both hands. 'What a group. A *porteña* who protects a couple of thugs. An Australian plagued with guilt – but for what? That's the mystery. A German family who can't stand up for what they believe in. But Pedro's the real winner here. Let his wife walk away and then watched his own son die. Didn't think to tell our family. Didn't think that might be one of those things you pass along. And now he wants to stay hidden in his little cabin and you all are willing to let him. The only reason Pedro doesn't want to hike down is because the police are waiting for him in Bariloche.'

Hita sat forward and Felix put his arm around her. It looked small against her wide shoulders but she patted his leg. Klaus had moved and was sitting by himself next to the cassette player. Erik glanced at him but the ten-year-old wasn't concerned by Wolfe; he was practising fingerings on the guitar.

I looked at my brother-in-law and tried to steady my voice. 'You're right. All of those things.'

With the bruising on his face, Wolfe looked menacing. 'Don't deny it?'

'No.'

I was hoping my admission would give us a way to end this conversation but Wolfe smiled. His anger was like a hungry dog circling inside the room. 'Look at—'

I cut him off. 'What about you, Wolfe? What about your inheritance?'

He shrugged. 'I'm not responsible for my father.'

I wanted to shove him into the wall. Rage was simmering in my fists. 'You carry guilt if you live off of his money.'

Carmen's head whipped around. 'What guilt?'

Wolfe shook his head like this was a tedious conversation he shouldn't be forced to endure and it seemed such a typical gesture of him that I spoke up, my voice loud. 'His father dealt in arms. From Israel. He supported the Dirty War.'

Jack stepped away from the stove, towards us. 'That doesn't make sense. Why would Israel support a country that protected ex-Nazis?'

Everyone was looking at Wolfe. He shrugged like the answer was obvious. 'Politics of trade.'

'You're unbelievable,' Carmen hissed the words at Wolfe and I was surprised by her ferocity.

He made a face. 'Because people do deals and I happen to be related to them? I'm not sure you can talk.'

'You could have told me.'

'No one asked for your family confession.'

'My father isn't the issue.'

I didn't know what they were talking about but Jack stepped forward in the shadowed light as though he'd been summoned. He stood taller than I remembered. Resilient. 'It's in the second chances that we prove the world can change. You said that.'

Erik put his arm around Hita but he was staring at his oldest son like he was a familiar stranger. Hita nodded towards Jack, and Felix climbed onto her lap.

Wolfe laughed. 'That was bullshit.'

'It saved my life.'

Wolfe's voice lifted. 'What, so you apologise and everything's fine? Wrongs can't be erased. Quidel isn't coming back.'

My hand went to the back of my head, to the tender place where it had hit the floor.

Wolfe wiped his forehead with the sleeve of his jacket and grabbed his lighter like he was going outside to smoke, but Carmen cleared her throat. She wasn't ready to be appeased. 'What happened with the Americans is not ammunition for you to use, Wolfe. It's not a point in a larger argument or a reason that we should hike down to Bariloche. That's my fear you're talking about and you're talking about it without permission. But, even so . . . I think you're right. We should hike down. We all have things to face. The snow is the least of it.'

'Which way is safest?' Jack asked. 'The main path along Cerro Blanco or through the woods with Cerro Negro?'

My voice was frantic. 'We can't hike down. I will fix the radio. We need a few more days. I know we're low on food but—'

'We have no food,' Wolfe said.

Erik cleared his throat. 'We can't follow Cerro Negro. We would have to hike in back country. We don't have enough equipment—' he glanced down at Felix, who was resting his head on the table, '—so we'd have to separate.'

Wolfe grabbed his backpack from the empty table and pulled out a map, unfolding it. It was creased and torn – I recognised it as one from Club Andino. He pointed at an X that signalled the refugio. His finger moved along the contours. 'With Cerro Negro, there're at least three kilometres along the trail that are too risky. Especially here, after the alpine cabin. Erik's right – we'd have to leave the trail, something I'd only recommend for experienced mountain climbers. And even then . . . That leaves the main trail. It's safer.'

Hita's eyebrows lifted. 'How can it be safer? It's an avalanche area.'

'Both are. It carries less risk,' Erik said, resting his hand on her shoulder.

Hita tilted her head. 'To be clear – the best track is unstable and two people have probably died on it?'

Wolfe shook his head. 'No need to sugar coat it for everyone.'

Emma laughed: it was an honest, unapologetic sound that startled everyone in the room. I took advantage of the brief silence. 'We need to be cautious.'

Wolfe shook his head. 'Your caution will see us hungry, Pedro. The snow is stronger. It will hold us.'

It's true, the snow pack had strengthened since Jeremy and John had left. And I was overcautious. But I could sense trouble. The mountain did not like to be taken lightly. We would be punished for Wolfe's audacity.

Hita and Erik were whispering to each other in German. When they stopped, Hita gave him a small nod and turned to me. 'Erik knows the landscape and thinks we should leave. I change my mind. I vote to hike out.'

It was absurd – how well could a foreigner know this terrain? 'We can't. We could die—'

Wolfe laughed, an angry snort. 'You aren't afraid of dying, Pedro. You're afraid of not dying. You're afraid of hiking into Bariloche and facing Rosie and the police. Votes to leave: Carmen, Hita, Eric, myself—'

'And me,' Jack said.

Wolfe cleared his throat. 'That's a majority. I'll test the snow and if conditions are good we hike down tomorrow morning.'

He was almost cheerful and it occurred to me Wolfe might be urging us down the mountain because he wanted an avalanche. He had been daring death his entire life – skiing in dangerous areas, living in war zones – and now he had another chance. Wolfe had a death wish and wanted to take us with him.

I couldn't believe no one in the refugio had seen through him. I should have made his past public – Afghanistan, the missing journalists. But I was angry. It's horrible to admit but part of me wanted to prove how foolish it was to place faith in Wolfe. Part of me wanted to hike down and face a worst-case scenario.

There was a long wait as everyone considered our decision. Emma was watching Wolfe like she was impressed with him and this made no sense – she was the one person who hadn't voted to leave. Then Carmen stepped into the middle of the room. 'Jack and I have been practising the tango. We thought to perform after dinner. If we're done . . .'

I watched her and nodded. Emma was poised at one of the tables, and Wolfe helped her ease it back. Jack and Felix shifted the benches. Klaus had stopped playing the guitar to offer advice that was only ignored. Beyond him, it was a clear night, the snow lit by a moon I couldn't see. The edge of the lake was just visible. I turned off the kitchen light as Hita lit candles. A quiet light fell on the empty floor.

Carmen held her arm out for Jack and nodded towards Klaus, who pressed a button on the cassette player. The song began low and I was reminded of my mother's stereo. The way sound can overwhelm a room. Ástor Piazzolla.

Carmen didn't look at anyone except Jack as she took his hand and glided towards him. He pressed his palm into her back. His face seemed older. At first, he was careful with his injured leg but his fear fell away and it was easy to forget they were Carmen and Jack. They moved like silver birds. They had transformed and all of us watching were implicated. She spun into his bent leg so they were facing each other. His right foot circled the floor behind him and she followed that momentum, trailing his body in the same direction. There was an eagerness to their dancing as if they'd just figured out how strong they were. I was afraid they might brush against the stove, but Jack guarded Carmen. Catching her. Gripping her hand.

I'd been living in the mountains for four years and the dining room was a record of that time. I'd climbed onto the roof to fix the chimney twice. I'd served meals on the benchtops. I'd swept the floor every evening before making my bed in the kitchen. When a drunk mountain climber punched his fist through the furthest window, I bandaged the pane with more care than his hand, taping it with cardboard until I could get another piece of glass. My world had become as small as that room.

The two dancers stopped for a brief moment – Carmen's arm straight back, her leg forward – before they stepped back into the tango eight-step. Their feet followed, keeping exact distance from each other. I could smell their bodies. They were both spinning as the song began to peak and a tremor passed through my chest as though something had been released. I could face the mountain. I could face Bariloche. Whatever happened, I was ready.

After the dancing, everyone prepared for the morning. Because I'd been living up the mountain for four years, I didn't have a backpack that could easily be filled with my things: packing to leave the refugio was like packing to leave a building on fire. What could I carry with me? What would I need for the rest of my life? Even with the money returned, I didn't have enough to pay for the concession so if we did survive the next day's journey, and I endured whatever was waiting for me in Bariloche, the refugio was no longer my home.

I concentrated on folding two sets of clothes to line my backpack. Then I climbed on one of the tables and pulled down the storage crates behind my finances. I found my passport, the papers for the concession, Quidel's birth and death certificates, his La Boca jumper, my tent, stove and sleeping bag, and of course the first-aid kit. When I finished, I realised I'd almost forgotten my transceiver. It was hanging over the sink, in the kitchen. This near oversight drove me back to each room, searching for anything urgent, anything that I had failed to see because it was part of my everyday life.

And then, when it couldn't be avoided, I snuck back to the kitchen counter and began writing. I wrote to my brothers, my mother, Quidel. I told the story of the past four years and asked for their forgiveness. My handwriting was strange and lofty – like skywriting from a plane, transferred onto paper. Blue ink bled over my fingers and I wiped them on a dish towel. Klaus was playing 'Let It Be' in the dining room. There was one more letter. Rosie. I didn't let myself start again or scratch anything out. I kept going for five, six, seven pages. It took the least amount of time to write because it was a letter I'd been crafting in my head for years. A message in a bottle on a mountain. Left on the table in case I couldn't deliver the words myself.

❊

Early the next morning, I trekked out to the mountain to dig one last test pit. It was going to be a bright winter morning – daylight was already shining on the dusted peaks. The sky was cloudless and the temperature cold. My flashlight only offered a hungry circle of light but it was enough to see the path. Crossing the river, I followed the trail to the beginning of the avalanche zone where Emma and I had searched for the Americans. Taking a deep cold breath, I pushed the shovel into the ground and broke the surface layer of ice. When the pit was deep enough, I kneeled down and dusted the wall like an archaeologist clearing sand. The lines were even, the levels clear. I wished again we had a working radio but by my estimation we were still at a grade yellow. Stable but with risks.

When I returned to the refugio, the fire had been lit and the boys were all sitting at the table. I nodded at them and paced through to the kitchen. Chopping boards were balanced under the window. Knife handles rigid in their block. Sink faucet dripping. I pulled out food for breakfast – potatoes and flour for soda bread.

'Please let me keep busy.' Hita bustled in as I was making the dough, and I motioned to the pot and paring knife.

When everything was served on the table, I sat at the head. Wolfe eased in next to me. Spearing a potato with a fork, he looked up. 'We need a plan.'

Everyone was watching me. The choice had been made and we needed the momentum of a group. I nodded like I recognised this, like I was the bigger person. 'We hike together until the path veers away from the river. Then we take it one at a time in case there's a collapse – that way there are people to dig.'

'How was the test pit?' Erik asked.

'Yellow. You have a transceiver, right?' I asked.

'Two of them.' Erik turned to Wolfe. 'And you?'

'Don't use them.'

Erik looked at Wolfe as though he couldn't translate his words and then just shook his head. 'You can have one of mine. We need them on people with experience.'

Wolfe shrugged like it didn't matter to him either way but Erik was right – they had to go to people who knew how to use them. Even so, I was surprised he'd give it to Wolfe – that meant Hita would be walking across without one. I used to have another but someone had stolen it the year before and hiked down before I realised it was missing. It was stupid to take it because a beacon by itself is useless. You need at least two so someone can receive the signal.

By 8 am, everyone was standing in front of the refugio. I waited in the doorway. Klaus and Felix were swollen with sweaters and coats. Felix was flying like an imaginary airplane around his brothers. Carmen and Emma were standing furthest away, laughing and staring back towards the lake, and Wolfe was smoking a cigarette near the toilets. I willed Emma to look at me. I needed her outrageous brave humour.

'Is there anything I can do?' Jack asked and I shook my head, gripping the door handle. Glancing back into the hallway, I paused. It was dark, the door to the dining room closed. A toolkit that had been there when I first arrived, over four years ago, was sitting beneath the empty coat hooks. The refugio's sudden tidiness made it look familiar and foreign at the same time.

'We going anytime today?' Wolfe called out.

I pulled the door closed. The bottom edge scraped against the frame and I realised I wouldn't have to fix it. This idea, that someone else would take care of the refugio, gave me a sense of weightlessness, of flight. Like a premonition of death.

5

Wolfe Goldberg

My father wasn't capable of dying. The guy had a metastasised baseball in his lung but he'd hang on, sucking at his oxygen and patronising the nurses until I was old enough to need the hospital bed next to him. A year ago he took a turn – I was ready to get the party hats out. But they kept operating and he kept surviving. The man was drawing breath to spite me.

Then Rosie called. I was climbing the stairs to 14th Street. Always a treat for the sensory nerves: subway air and sweaty garbage. I was supposed to be meeting a friend for a beer and almost ignored my vibrating pocket. She'd been ringing five or six times a day. We were like parents coordinating day care for our father with nurse rosters and medicine boxes.

Her voice was shrill. 'Who's going to stay with the body? We need someone to stay with the body.'

'What are you talking about?' A wispy guy with a ridiculously large briefcase bumped me and I grabbed the handrail. Something gummy stuck to my hand.

'He's dead.'

'Who?'

'That's not funny. It's been half an hour. I've been trying to call you.'

'Public transport.' I started gingerly to climb the stairs again. A kid in front of me spat on the ground. His pants were at half-mast, surrendering to a band of Calvin Klein red.

'You've got to come home.'

'Can't someone else keep him company?' For some Jews, it was custom to stay with a dead body until it was buried. I'm not religious and neither is Rosie. Our father only attended synagogue if he was in Israel, with other middlemen who cared about Judeo-existential concepts like homelands and heaven. But Rosie wanted to do this one by the book. And that meant reciting Kaddish and honouring Shiva – seven days of mourning.

'Please, Wolfe.'

I sighed into the phone and turned around. Erudite graffiti – 'FUCK the MAN' with a one-eyed penis drawn above it – greeted me as I made the heroic descent. I swiped my Metrocard through the turnstile and took the stairs two at a time down to the 4/5/6 line. A homeless man was shaking a mega plastic cup full of coins and I threw in a ten-dollar note. He grinned at me and I wanted to high-five him and every person scurrying past. On the platform, it required self-restraint to keep from hollering down the empty tracks. Aaron Goldberg had finally died.

✳

Rosie and I were confined to his four-bedroom apartment for a week after the funeral. It was prime real estate, right off Central Park – but Rosie wanted proper mourning so I wasn't allowed outside to enjoy the long-awaited arrival of summer. I wasn't allowed to change my clothes, either. Thankfully all the mirrors were covered, which made the house feel like the set for a horror movie, especially with all of my dead father's faux-Victorian furniture. Love seats with velvet upholstery and wardrobes with hunting scenes carved into their doors. His desk took up an entire wall of his study, with panels that slid out to reveal secret compartments. That's where I'd found the will – which had proved to be surprisingly fair. But of course it was all about subtext. I'd been made executor. Rosie was left property and I was left his business. Fiscally, it was an even split. But it was inevitable my hands would be dirty with his work. Even if the company sold quickly, I'd be his second-in-command until the buy-out could be organised. Make no mistake – the man would still be running things from the grave.

In the dining room, the over-polished table had legs sturdy enough to support a baby grand piano. It was piled with bagels and salads from the city's best delis. It was a sad indictment. All the sympathetic well-wishes had been ordered. The egg salad was my favourite. I ate and organised, ate and organised. One desk drawer at a time. I found the email at the end of the week. Printed out, filed away.

Quidel had been missing for four years. Gone. It was like Pedro had boarded a UFO and settled down on Planet Fuck-If-You-Can-Find-Me. Even his family had no idea – his brothers offered me a pair of Ray-Bans if I could track him down. I wasn't worried, though. Pedro was so taken with Rosie, it seemed like a plea to win her back. And when I did start to worry, I thought wealth would trump desperation. Our resources were absolute: my father had spent a lot of time in Argentina in the '80s – he secured the contracts that made the Dirty War possible, and important people were still hidden in the ranks who owed him favours. But I hadn't anticipated how the devalued peso would complicate things. No one cared about a man disappearing with his son when the capital was rioting. I remember holding a policeman by the collar of his uniform, shaking him, and within minutes I was surrounded by a circle of officers on horses, batons ready, as though I'd been caught looting. It still made me seethe even though it'd been four years ago.

The thing that made it so surprising was that Pedro didn't have a network. Anyone who could help him disappear had been friends with Rosie first. But it seemed he'd pulled off the impossible. Rosie had hired private detectives and followed most leads herself. She gave up the idea of leaving Argentina (oh the irony, considering that's why she was separating from Pedro in the first place) and devoted herself to the search. It was appalling. She lost her kid. But she'd been about to do the same thing to Pedro – the plan was school years in the City and summers on Long Island.

Rosie said she wasn't going to leave South America without Quidel but that changed when my father was diagnosed three years ago. Emphysema and lung cancer. Within hours of my father's phone call, she was lifting her luggage onto the scale and collecting her boarding pass for the next flight out of Buenos Aires.

Now he was dead. The email was only a few lines, dated just over a year before, from a private detective in Buenos Aires. It listed Pedro's full name and an address at a refugio in the mountains near Bariloche. I gaped at the piece of paper, waiting for some other meaning to take hold. But there was only one way to read it: the old goat had known where Pedro lived. He knew where Pedro lived and never said a word to Rosie.

Even I couldn't feel smug. It was too horrific.

'But why? Why wouldn't he tell me?' She was standing in the kitchen with the email in her hand, the fridge door open and forgotten behind her. She genuinely couldn't figure it out. Rosie wasn't stupid but she's always been into buttering her bread and a bit of denial spreads well.

'I don't know,' I said. I was being tactful, something rare for me, because anyone could see the timing was suspicious: our father found Pedro right when his cancer took a bad turn. My bet is the selfish bastard didn't want to give his daughter any reason to return to Argentina.

✲

That night we booked our flights to Bariloche. We didn't know if Pedro would still be there but it wasn't worth making enquiries that might scare him away. Rosie and I weren't always the closest but I loved her kid and wanted to be there when the shit fell from the sky. When she and Pedro first met, I was a war correspondent. I dropped into places where people were being killed and took notes like a mercenary, turning atrocities into stories. The copy I filed wasn't going to inspire the West to take potable water or landmines seriously. Maybe I could direct the big media eye for a moment but it would soon blink and focus on something else. Fact is, that do-gooder stuff didn't interest me. I liked the work. Riding in helicopters. Starting cars that could be wired with explosives. Securing interviews with people so desperate they'd be tempted to take me hostage, and talking myself safely back home. I liked the proximity to death – Charon could be one sexy motherfucker. And sure, the humanitarian thing grew on me, and all the righteousness that went along with it.

I was stationed in the Middle East when Quidel was born so all of my frequent flyer points went on trips to Argentina. He gave me some purpose. I could imagine myself as his contingency plan and I even quit smoking – an effort that lasted for almost a year. As a baby, he'd stop crying when I held him. Belly along my arm, head resting in the crook of my elbow. He grinned so easily when he saw me that I had to return the favour. And I never told Rosie or Pedro, but the kid shared his milestones with me. It was like he was waiting for my visits and then he'd finally roll over. I also got his first steps. Rosie and Pedro were out at dinner and the kid took four steps right in a row and started laughing his head off like we were tighter than Laurel and Hardy. And counting to twenty? That was all me.

Then, after Quidel had started school, I had my mid-career crisis. Maybe it was the incident with the media convoy or the belated arrival of PTSD that Rosie had always been predicting.

But I stopped filing copy. I ignored emails and phone calls from my editors. I just focused on the civilian death toll. It was unremitting, a gliding white shark that only swam forward and never stopped moving. For some reason I linked it with Quidel. I had to be more careful because he was depending on me.

My father enjoyed my newfound occupational listlessness. Aaron Goldberg made his wealth as a political middleman – flying between Washington DC, Israel and the developing world delivering war toys. He wasn't upset by my stories or their implications – he'd argue that if he weren't supplying arms, someone else would. But he didn't like the implicit judgement of his son, demonstrated in such a public arena. Everyone can read newspapers.

❋

I paid for our first-class flights and we left two days later; that gave Rosie the full week to mourn and me a bit of time to get my mountain gear together. Usually I was an economy-class kind of guy but I thought this trip called for celebration. On the plane, I enjoyed the extra cabin room and the open bar but the miniature crystal salt and pepper shakers were a decadent touch that reminded me too much of our father.

Somewhere above the North Atlantic, after watching a barrel-chested blockbuster with lots of exploding buildings, I motioned to the stewardess for another drink. Rosie stopped fiddling with her handset and looked at me. 'What if they're not there, Wolfe?'

'Then we're no worse off than before.' When Rosie was a teenager, she told me she didn't believe in misanthropy and my hostility was a personal convenience that bored her. But even Rosie would have to know there'd be a better chance of getting a pep talk from the aging mile-high hostess serving bourbon than from me. I was jonesing for a cigarette and preoccupied with the thought that in only a matter of hours we might have Quidel.

She rubbed her first two fingers between her eyes as though smoothing out the worry lines. 'It still doesn't make sense to me. Pedro's not the kind of person who would do this.'

'Apparently he is.'

'I'm worried about him.'

'The man kidnapped your son.' This was my way of trying to lighten things up.

Rosie shook her head. 'Things were difficult.'

'Of course they were.' I started flipping through the movies on my screen. I didn't want to have this conversation.

'What was I supposed to do? I was missing home. Pedro wasn't going to move to the States and I had to take care of Dad anyway. You weren't going to.'

These accusations weren't new and I didn't find them any more palatable this time around. 'First off, I'm sorry I had a breakdown. Little out of my control, that one. Second, it's not my fault Pedro's gone AWOL. Third, you didn't have to go back to Dad – and you certainly didn't have to stay for three years. Don't pull that martyr shit with me. You wanted to be in New York City.'

Rosie loved public scenes – I shouldn't have egged her on. She'd get the alcohol cut off for both of us. 'You think it was easy leaving Argentina? Dad needed me. He needed us, Wolfe. And where were you?'

'Gosh, Rosie. I was sitting through all the fucking hours of therapy it took to get over the fact he was my fucking father.'

She laughed. 'Therapy?'

I almost smiled. 'Of course not. I was making a point. You don't have issues with our father? That's fine. The guy knows where your kid is and doesn't tell you. You think, "Huh, that's a bit strange. But I bet there's a good reason for that because our dad was such a swell person." Well, Rosie, I don't care that he's dead. I think the guy was an asshole. He tried to get me fired, Rosie. What kind of a man makes a few calls to fuck over his son? Usually nepotism works to your advantage.'

'You didn't have to push him.'

'It was a difference of opinion. People are entitled to those.'

'Wolfe Goldberg. The great hero of Modern Democracy. Mr First Amendment.'

'Fuck you, Rosie.'

'Sophisticated, Wolfe.' Rosie had a sugary voice that made even her sarcasm sound ironic. Like she was laughing at herself as she laughed at you.

She pushed her hair out of her face – two frown lines were etched between her eyebrows.

I took her hand. 'I love you.'

'I know. Mixed blessing, that.'

'Quidel is going to be fine.'

'You don't know.'

'I do. We're going to find them and these last four years are going to fade like the shitty nightmare that they've been. Quidel is going to be fine.'

She squeezed my palm but her eyes were worried. 'God, I hope so.'

❄

We caught our connecting flight in Buenos Aires and flew to Bariloche in a bashed-up plane strapped together with duct tape. After forty precarious minutes, circling above a snow-storm, we were finally allowed to land. From the airport alone, you could tell we'd arrived at a tourist haven. The terminal looked like a giant gingerbread house. Log cabin doors. Fancy flags. It wasn't the kind of place where I'd imagined Pedro. He was too unadorned for all the restless money there. Which got me thinking: Rosie was right. It didn't make sense that Pedro would keep Quidel for four years. Not here.

When Rosie first introduced me to Pedro, I liked him. He wore wool sweaters with holes in the elbows: the kind of thing that would make my father uncomfortable. That bit of flesh shining through said more about wealth and excess than any diatribe I could deliver. Pedro and I had little shared ground so there were often long silences between us when I stayed in Córdoba, which I didn't mind. I appreciated that he didn't pretend we were closer than we were.

When Quidel was born things changed and Pedro spoke up more. I think he was in awe of his son's enthusiasm. There was nothing hesitant about Quidel, even as a baby, and this seemed to rub off on Pedro. And I appreciated the sardonic expression Quidel wore, like he was loving everything and making fun of it at the same time. Even soccer. He'd practise and practise and then bob his head and roll his eyes when he missed a perfect shot at goal. '*Que será, será . . .*' he'd say.

The thing I liked about Quidel – and maybe this is common to kids in general – he didn't pretend he was a nicer, kinder, happier version of himself. If he was pissed off because I won checkers four times in a row, he'd let me know. When Rosie had her thirtieth, he told me he'd decided it was actually his birthday, and I should bring him a big present. He wasn't concerned with seeming gracious, like adults, which meant you always knew where you stood. I loved that.

I didn't let on to Rosie, but I was excited to be in Bariloche. The last four years had been bleak. Living in Manhattan, waiting for news of Quidel. I was working infrequent shifts as a sub-editor on the *New York Times* and recovering. Flashbacks would hit me like panic attacks – sometimes once a week. Eight vehicles in the convoy, travelling between Kabul and Jalalabad in the eastern Nangarhar Province. I'd organised it, recruited journalists at the

Inter-Continental Hotel. Official protection was a note, written out by the militia commander, but we had armed guards. The goal was to get closer to Tora Bora, an Al-Qaeda encampment in the mountains. Hilltop caves and bunkers. Some reports claimed there were four hundred fighters, others two thousand. Someone nearby had to have a bit more information.

This was before embedded journalism took hold. Before Iraq. Before reporters were cocooned with the military, carrying press passes and printed itineraries. The 'in-beds' can't be objective: they're eating with soldiers, sleeping beside them. It's not a war they're witnessing, but a PR exercise. Thing is, it's got to be safer. And maybe that matters more. It can't be a good idea, leaving journalists to their own devices in a place with no government, no police. Back in Manhattan, my chief editor at the *Times* would start pointless arguments about embedded journalism. And, even though I agreed with him – theoretically, anyway – I'd pipe up as if actual experience counted for something. It's easy to have conviction when you're sitting behind a desk.

The thing with New York: it smelled of hometown. Manhattan was only twenty-three square miles. So even though there were a million and a half people living there, I could be accosted by my high school lab partner at the bar. Ex-girlfriends from NYU, now fashion editors or children's writers, would touch my arm in the bank. 'Is that you, Wolfe?' Nothing makes your life feel more pointless than having to see your past in your present when you're forty-three years old. To look at a woman who appears remarkably as you remember her. Except that because of all the Botox pumped into her face, her features don't move, so it's like she's suffered a stroke on both sides of her brain. You look at that pale zombie skin and think, we had sex. Huh. After my prodigal return to the States, my relationships were confined to one-night stands or sporadic dates with Brandi – a girl with a nice personality who took Visa.

Sometimes I'd fly down to Argentina when Rosie had leads, which happened with less and less frequency. Then she came back to New York and we lived together until I accused her of knowing more about Quidel than she was letting on. She moved in with our father and didn't speak to me for six months. An unfortunate way to test a hypothesis, really. And now, after years of Promethean waiting, our father was dead and we were within hiking distance of Pedro and Quidel.

Outside the airport, we were lucky to nab a *remise* taxi driver. Rosie did the talking and I piled our stuff into the trunk. I was suspicious of anything that had vacancies during the ski season but we didn't have much choice. The bed-and-breakfast proved to be a bed-and-no-breakfast but it was surprising tidy with plaster walls painted pale blue and white bedspreads embroidered with *gaucho* cowboy scenes. The most irritating thing about the place were the heaters: they all operated at full-blast, so you could choose between sweltering dry air or frigid cold. In our room, Rosie left the heater on and propped open a window.

I checked the thermostat: it wasn't working. 'You know, I think we're close to Club Andino. I might see if they're still open. You want to come?'

She pressed her fingers against her temples. 'I'm not doing so well. But yes, I think I will.'

I trudged outside and lit a cigarette while she gathered herself together. She was impossible in this regard: it could take her half an hour to put on a pair of shoes and find her purse. And when she finally appeared on the stairs, she sighed like she'd been the one waiting for me. 'Ready?'

'Whatever,' I said.

The crazy thing about Bariloche was it looked like someone had transplanted a town from the middle of the Alps into the Andes. The houses had window boxes and brown shutters peeled back. Rounded doors. There was a Disney aesthetic to most of the buildings that gave the town an aura of creepy innocence. Uneven mounds of ploughed ice blocked the street, so we had to cross at the corners with the streetlights.

Club Andino was packed with posters of wilderness scenes and pamphlet racks full of outdoor advice. Someone's ski gear had been tossed in a corner. I stood at the counter, waiting as a guy with a Canadian accent gave his colleague a blow-by-blow description of some recent snowboarding triumph. He was leaning back dangerously in an office chair that had seen better days, and eventually turned to me. 'What can I do for you?'

Rosie took a deep breath. 'We need to hike up to Refugio Frey.'

'Refugio Frey? Yeah, I think that trail's closed.' He spun around to look at his colleague. 'Hey Carlos, Refugio Frey, that's closed, eh?'

Carlos nodded. 'Avalanche danger.'

The Canadian shrugged. He wore an irritating thin ponytail like it might help him seem older but he was going to look twelve until he was older than me – ponytail or not. 'It'll probably open in a week, man.'

Carlos spoke again. 'Two or three weeks.'

Rosie smiled her accommodating smile but I decided to shortcut the conversation. 'There're a few ways up there. We have crampons, ice screws, that kind of thing. I used to be stationed at Thule Air Base in Greenland. If I get worried about avalanches, I'll test the snow. I'd just like a rundown on avalanche zones and a detailed map of the area, if you have one.'

The advantage of working as a war correspondent was that I knew a lot about the US military and sometimes it was easier to be an officer than a civilian.

Carlos watched me sceptically but the Canadian was convinced. 'Wow, intense,' he said and peered at Rosie. 'You have experience?'

'Enough,' Rosie said. This wasn't true. My sister would have been fine on the trail but she'd never been ice-climbing in her life.

The Canadian cleared his throat, a pompous sound. 'You'd know to be careful then.'

I held up my hand with the missing fingers. 'Trust me, I'm aware of the dangers.'

'Shit.'

I smiled and he saluted me. Truth was, I'd suffered frostbite hiking in the Adirondack Mountains when I was a teenager. My father had decided to host his own tough-love version of Outward Bound and, as usual, things went awry. I wouldn't leave a fourteen year old without a compass in the middle of a national park come January, but there were a lot of things we disagreed on.

Carlos walked up to the counter and tore off the top page of a notepad. It was a map of the Nahuel Huapi circuit. 'I'd wait. If you need to head off, I'd go this way, past the old alpine cabin. You might have to go through back country here, though. This stretch is notorious. There are some steep ice climbs but otherwise you should be fine.' He reached under the counter for a bigger map with more detail.

'What kind of grade are we talking about?'

The Canadian piped up. 'They're M6 – vertical to overhanging. Not a lot of rests.'

We were fucked. There was no way Rosie could handle that. Even something gradual would have tested her. It was shitty luck but I'd have to go without her, and bring Quidel and Pedro back when the trails cleared.

Carlos handed me a form. 'Before you leave, you want to register with us, get a permit.'

I slid the maps into my backpack and glanced up as if I'd just remembered something. 'Oh, and a backpacker said I should look up Pedro Carimán. That he runs a refugio along here and it's a good place to stay. Do you know if he's still up there?'

Carlos nodded. 'Pedro? Yeah, he's up at Frey, the one you're headed to.'

Rosie stiffened beside me. 'Thank you.' The two words sounded prim coming from her mouth but neither of the guys seemed to notice as she forced a grim half-smile.

❄

Rosie headed back to our room while I grabbed us some dinner. She was sprawled on top of the covers when I returned with veal *milanesa* sandwiches.

I handed her one of the rolls and she peeled back the paper. 'I'm trying not to eat meat.'

'It's vegetarian – by Argentinian standards, anyway. They added some lettuce to the veal.' She needed some food. Her jeans were too loose, even layered over a pair of long johns.

'Very funny. When do we head off?'

'You can't make those climbs. They're crazy.'

She sat taller on the bed. 'We don't have a choice.'

'We do. We can wait for the trail to clear or I can go up myself and bring Quidel and Pedro down.'

I didn't mention the possibility of back-up. Our experiences with Argentinean police over the last four years had been less than constructive. My incident with the police on horseback was nothing – Rosie had been arrested.

She clicked her tongue against the top of her mouth. 'I'm not going to risk losing him now.'

I agreed with her. There was no knowing what Pedro's plans were and we were too close to let him slip away. I sat down at the foot of her bed. 'I'll head up.'

She stared at me, unblinking. 'I'm coming with you.'

I knew what would happen. Rosie wouldn't make it past the first ice climb and we'd have to come back. I'd lose a good day or two. It wasn't worth it.

She stood up and closed the window. It took a bit of effort – the wooden frame was finicky.

I cleared my throat. 'I'm going alone.'

'Not if I follow you.'

'Have you ever climbed ice before?'

'Doesn't matter.'

'It's dangerous, Rosie.'

'Oh well.' Her tone was pure I-don't-give-a-fuck. She was my sister. She didn't just push my buttons – she twirled in, all unassuming like a ballerina from a jewellery box, and produced a giant cartoon hammer to pound into them.

'Fuck, Rosie.' I hit the trim along the top of the bathroom door and took a deep breath.

'He's my kid, Wolfe.'

'Fine. You win.'

I opened a bottle of Mendoza Malbec and poured the red wine into two water glasses I'd found in the bathroom. The absurdity of the stout cups made Rosie smile and we clinked them half-heartedly. 'To Quidel.'

I'm a jerk. I know that. But I organised my pack, wrote a placating note to Rosie, and left early the next morning. If only I'd waited – Rosie and I would have hiked up in a couple of weeks, Pedro none the wiser. Carmen, Emma, the Germans: they would have waited for better conditions that may or may not have arrived. Hypoglycaemia would've knocked them for a turn – Emma and Carmen, especially. But they would have coped. What's the saying: three, three and three? Three minutes without air, three days without water, three weeks without food. But I'm impulsive and convincing: a bad combination.

I took a *remise* taxi to the trailhead and tipped the driver extra for being on the roads in such shitty weather. He was a fat man who left the windshield wipers flapping even when the wet snow had stopped falling on the glass.

'You sure you want to be left here?' he asked in Spanish.

I had gear and food and half a litre of Scotch. My sleeping bag could go to minus forty and my tent was built for Arctic conditions. I nodded, slamming the door closed, and he hit the gas, slowly at first, but the taxi just skidded in place. I gave him a shove and the car squealed forward, spraying snow and mud. He honked as he circled the parking lot and I waved, grateful to be alone.

It took two days – and eight vertical climbs – but eventually I was standing in front of the refugio. Light spilled out onto the snow, and smoke from the chimney hung in the air. I circled the place so I'd be ready if things turned slippery. There were two doors – the main entrance and another one from the kitchen. I propped a chair that had been left outside under the second doorknob to jam it.

I was standing in the shadows when the front door opened and two people trudged down the steps. One was tall and thin, maybe a teenager. The other was a kid – about six or seven years old. He was bundled in a padded coat and swayed as he walked. Adrenaline revved through my body, and my mouth went dry as tissue. His feet creaked in the snow. He pointed at a cluster of stars and murmured something. I'd found him. We'd leave as soon as it was safe and Rosie would forgive my eagerness. The fact they were speaking German didn't register. The fact time had passed and Quidel would be ten didn't even occur to me. I was enchanted by the darkness and the idea the search was over. I waited, breathing in the cold air and flexing my hands inside my gloves. They finished in the toilet block and ambled back to the refugio. The door closed behind them and the night air was still.

I needed a cigarette. After one, I still wasn't ready so I lit another.

Finally, I took a deep breath and knocked on the door.

❋

The refugio was smaller than I imagined – ceiling lower, walls closer. A bit Lewis Carroll. Pounding heat emanated from the wood stove and claustrophobia clung to the guests. It took a moment, searching the faces, to figure out Pedro was standing in the kitchen doorway. He'd aged in four years – his face was loose under the cheekbones, his eyes sad.

And Felix. I remember thinking how useful that Quidel had a friend his age to play with. It didn't occur to me that it was Felix I'd just seen scampering across the snow until he asked me about my fingers. He shifted towards me on the bench and I recognised the cadence of his voice. Immediately I looked up at Pedro. I was ready to be angry – it felt like Quidel had been kidnapped again – but my brother-in-law forced a wistful smile. The screwdriver looked so pitiful in his hands. And I knew I didn't have to worry about him trying to leave. He'd been hoping for this. He was grateful I'd arrived.

Everyone else in the refugio was stirring the crazy pot that night, fixated on the missing Americans. I was keeping an eye on Pedro, who was proving to be an unconvincing villain. Felix was caught with his Nazi artwork and Jack was forced to apologise. Erik's plasticine shock was wonderful to watch – there's nothing better than when a solid well-meaning family joins the rest of us at Dysfunction Junction. And Emma, with her hazel-brown eyes. She stared at me with an intensity that was bewildering and appealing in a three-night-stand kind of way.

She didn't like me but that didn't have to stop us. I'd talk her round.

When all of the guests had gone to bed, I asked Pedro for a *maté*. Hiking up, I'd plotted so many ways of frightening him into confession but now that he was finally sitting in front of me, my orchestrations seemed artificial and petty. He was too eager for news of Rosie. His reverence was off-putting. I kept prodding him about Quidel and his answers were vague but it didn't feel like he was withholding information on purpose. If this was an interrogation, he was a compliant but confused witness. He sat across from me, fingers tracing the designs on the *maté* gourd, and I wondered if he'd suffered some kind of breakdown. Maybe Quidel wasn't attending boarding school at all, maybe he'd been taken into care.

Despite my impatience, I had time. The snow meant no one was leaving anytime soon. I could let the story of the past four years emerge. But Pedro didn't mention Quidel over the next couple of days. I followed him through his chores – passing a shovel as he cleared snow off the roof, leaning against the counter as he swept the kitchen. In the dining room, I made sure to stand slightly too close. He'd edge backwards and I'd step forwards. Backwards. Forwards.

The refugio inmates offered their own intrigues. First, Jeremy and John. I'd never met the cowboys but if they thought hiking into an avalanche zone was a theme park adventure, it seemed only right to let natural selection have its way with them. Then the disappearing money – Jack was the only one capable of such a pointless and banal crime. Yeah I was a little forceful, grabbing him outside, but I think teenagers need that – they need to know someone cares, and their actions have repercussions. Then Pedro – so certain that Emma was the thief. That's what I found interesting. His reaction had 'high stakes' written all over it and I would have bet five hundred bucks he wanted to sleep with her.

I wondered how things would have gone down if the trail had been safe and Rosie had made it to the refugio. She would have burst through the dining room door as soon as we'd arrived, shouting for her son. No need for diplomacy. No talk of being a regular. And maybe Pedro would have offered up Quidel immediately or maybe he'd act as confused and frightened as he had for me. I couldn't work it out.

The night after Jack ran away was tense. Carmen and Hita sat in the living room as though battle lines had been drawn and they'd realised they were on the same side. Erik took care of Klaus and Felix, playing games and escorting them to the bathroom. He knew better than to interrupt Hita; she was busy with her fear. Pedro had three missing people to worry about and I wasn't giving him any slack. Everything I said to him was nuanced with Quidel. The only person who wasn't agitated was Emma. It wasn't polite to be in good spirits but her name had been cleared. She'd braided her hair into two thin strands and the ends were tied with bright yellow yarn that had been sitting on the games shelf. I sat next to her, maybe a little too close. She didn't move away.

Pedro was trying to play the leader, talking about search parties and Jack's strong chances of surviving the night. But the more he talked, the paler Hita's face became. It hadn't occurred to her in such plain terms that her son might not survive the night. A nicer person would have interrupted him – instead, I nudged Emma, rolling my eyes. She smiled in spite of herself and finished her beer.

'You think he's okay?' she whispered in my ear while Pedro's voice droned on. Her breath was warm.

'Pedro or Jack?'

'Very funny.'

'Both are creeps.'

Her shoulders lifted into a half-shrug. 'I have a soft spot for creeps.' Fuck, she was cute.

'That could put me in good stead,' I said.

She looked at me like she'd already gone out with me and knew she could do better. 'What are Jack's chances?'

'If he knows what to do, he could be fine. But the longer he's gone, the worse it is. I've got some whiskey in my pack. Want some?'

'Oh yeah.'

We made separate clumsy excuses and left Pedro and Erik, who had started a tag-team effort to bring Mountain Survival 101 to the cooped-up refugio audience.

The dorm rooms upstairs were too cold so we ended up in the stairwell. The light was pale and diluted. A low watt bulb in a Chinese lantern shade. Someone had painted a patch of the ceiling with Van Gogh star swirls. It was rough – the paint was peeling away in chunks the size of my hand – but the billowy nightscape gave us something to look at.

'I never noticed that before,' Emma said. She was sitting two steps above me. We were facing each other, backs to the walls, legs sprawled. Even rugged up in leggings and a sweater you could see she was fit. She was a decade younger than me – maybe more – and had no idea how beautiful she was. In ten or twenty years, she'd look back on photos of herself and marvel.

I took a drag from the flask. 'An inconvenient place to get inspired. Imagine a ladder in here.'

'It'd be tricky.'

'My father died two weeks ago.' My observation came out of nowhere like a blizzard in the Florida Keys. Didn't even know I'd been thinking about him.

'You okay?'

'The guy was a jerk.'

'Even so.'

'I guess.' People don't change, I knew that. But when Aaron Goldberg died so did any chance that things might ease between us. Some bastards mellow with age but I wouldn't know with him. Sitting in my father's apartment with Rosie, all the mirrors covered, reciting Kaddish, I realised I was next in line. Every time a generation dies, the next one steps up. The patriarch had vacated the throne but I wasn't up for the job – I didn't have a family to preside over. My life was pretty fucking useless.

Emma cleared her throat. 'I like that you can spend all this time here – days and days of waiting – and there's something like this that you didn't notice.' She was talking about the ceiling.

I passed her the Scotch. 'It's not enough for me.'

'You know anything about Australia?'

'Bit.'

She took a deep swallow and let out a short huff of air. 'Well, there's the Stolen Generation – all these Aboriginal children who were taken from their families and adopted out or put into government care. Regular practice until the '50s and '60s, and later, too.'

'Ah, White Australia. Assimilation. Government knows best.' I grabbed the flask.

She shrugged. 'I never thought about it. Not really. Rationally you know it's monstrous – and I went on marches for reconciliation – but I couldn't imagine it. And because it's unimaginable it's like it's not possible.'

'But it is.'

'I know, I know.' She laughed – a wry sound.

I shifted my weight, resting my arm on the stair beside me. It was dusty. 'Something similar happened here, you know. Not on the same scale by any means. And it was more about politics, less about race.'

Her head tilted to the side. She was watching me. 'The Dirty War orphans.'

I nodded. 'I know a family in Buenos Aires. They had a son, bright young man, year or two younger than you. He puts it together that he's adopted. Figures out it was illegal. But his adopted family – they're big. Dad's wealthy, a big-time judge: that kind of thing.'

She leaned towards me, elbows on her knees. 'What did he do?'

Maybe I'd already said too much – I had to be careful, secrecy was everything – but I wanted to impress her. 'Used a negotiator. The Grandmother in question, she agreed to keep it quiet – that surprised me but there you go. There's still a chance it could blow up and the media will get word of it. But so far so good.' Fact was, I'd been the negotiator. The man was a journalist, a friend of mine.

'And he trusts a newspaper hack like you? Huh.'

'You'd be surprised how trustworthy I am.'

Emma reached for the flask and took a sip of whiskey like it was nothing more than iced tea. 'I'll keep that in mind.' She gazed at the starry ceiling and then, like she'd seen more than she wanted to, she cleared her throat. 'What are you doing here?'

'Existentially or physically?' I asked.

'At the refugio. Climbing up with all that snow. You're the one person who can leave – go back the way you came – but you don't.'

I waited long enough so she was forced to look at me. 'What do you think of Pedro?'

She laughed. 'What do I think of Pedro Carimán? That's the million dollar question, isn't it?'

I didn't get why this was funny, but I waited and she continued. 'He's damaged goods. Don't know if he'll recover, that one.'

'You think so?'

'Yeah.'

I had a horrible thought. 'You in love with him?'

'What? No.'

I breathed a sigh of relief. 'Well, something's going on.'

'What do you mean?'

'Long story cut short: he's my brother-in-law. He kidnapped my nephew. We've been after him for four years and I've tracked him down, up here of all places.'

'What?'

'Weird, huh?' My tone was disbelieving and offhand – like it was some kind of sick joke. Maybe it was, maybe the joke was on me. All the years of waiting and now that I'd found Pedro I was still waiting.

'Where is he, your nephew?'

'That's what I'm wondering. Pedro says he's down in Bariloche, at school, but something doesn't feel right about it.'

She pulled on one of her braids. 'Pedro's never mentioned a kid. You sure he's the one you're looking for?'

My tone was too sharp. 'He was in my family for six years. Think I'd know what he looks like.'

Her gaze settled on the ceiling. 'I'm just saying, it doesn't make sense.'

'What, you think you know Pedro?' I was baiting her. I wanted her to look at me.

Finally she did. Her thin lips pressed together. 'Yes, actually. I do.'

I scoffed. 'Because you've stayed at his refugio for a few days? You're not his friend, you're a paying guest. A business opportunity.'

She was irritated. 'You can still have friendship—'

'Not when money changes hands. As a musical sage once said, "money changes everything".'

She smiled, cutting through all my shit. 'You think capitalism always trumps friendship?'

'Of course.' I didn't agree with this. I was thinking of my driver in Afghanistan – Omed. We loved talking about Persian poetry.

Kabul was such a shithole it was easy to forget that we were in the heart of civilisation. Omed invited me to his house once a week to eat with his family and we had intense conversations with his wife Mehri about the epic poem 'Book of Kings'. It was one of the few times I got to debate with an Afghani woman, and I took this to mean Omed trusted me as a brother. He was the best friend I had there and he was on my payroll.

Emma tapped her fingers on the stair. 'I don't think Pedro's a bad guy.'

'He thought you stole the money.' I wanted to shake her – I was the one who defended her. I was the one who took it to Jack to clear her name. 'You're being a fucking idiot.'

Her eyebrows lifted. 'Thanks. Anything else?'

'No, just that. A total fucking idiot.' That was really going to impress her. Wolfe Goldberg – a man with a knack for the ladies. I wanted to punch myself in the head.

'Good night, then.' She stood up, taking my flask of whiskey, and disappeared upstairs.

❄

Waking up, a bit foggy from the Scotch, I wanted to talk to Emma. But Erik and Hita had hit the panic button – they were desperate about Jack. I figured Carmen was the only one with a shot at finding the teenager: she was the only one he'd talk to. So I partnered with her and – surprise, surprise – Jack turned up at the alpine cabin. He had no idea how lucky he was. Felix's asthma attack could have gone down some other way or Jack could have fared a lot worse. One night on a mountain and I paid for it with two fingers. I suppose my father's test put me in good stead, though: after the emergency services found me, I joined Scouts and learned wilderness survival.

Jack recovered by the fire that night; Carmen and Felix sat beside him. When Hita wasn't with them, she was combing through all the cupboards with Pedro like more food might magically appear. Emma kept her distance from me. I didn't think it was possible, but the refugio was becoming even more tedious. I was tired of waiting. Emma was right: I wasn't stuck in the refugio like the rest of them. All I needed was Quidel.

Late the next morning, after all the excitement had died down and Pedro was up shovelling snow off the roof, I cased the kitchen and tore through the recipe books and expense journals to see if Quidel's name was listed anywhere. I stood on plastic crates and pawed through the uppermost cupboards. Nothing. In the living room, I lifted down boxes one at a time. The first offered up a mouldy sleeping bag, a single ski boot and someone's chunky set of keys. The second held old sweaters ravaged by moths. The third, though, was pure jackpot: Pedro's finances. To use the term 'books' would be misleading: the cardboard box was filled with envelopes of receipts and handwritten notes. Scribbled reminders. It was obvious the guy hadn't done his taxes since he'd moved to the refugio. From what I could tell, he didn't have the cash to set things right with the tax office. That's when it occurred to me that Pedro didn't have the money to pay for Quidel to be in school. My nephew had to be with a relative. Pedro, that fucker, had lied.

When he came into the dining room, I was ready to beat the shit out of him. 'Where's Quidel?'

Pedro's hands gripped the table and I had to repeat the question.

Finally, he stared me in the face, his lips barely moving. 'He's dead.'

'Don't pull that bullshit with me.'

He kept talking but I couldn't handle it, all the waiting and dancing and fucking around about Quidel. He was droning on and it hit me: Pedro never trusted his son with anyone, not even a babysitter. There's no way my nephew was in boarding school.

I don't know why that didn't register before. Quidel's death was the only thing that made sense. Rosie and I had been searching for a kid when there wasn't a kid to find.

You asshole, I thought. The flights down to Argentina. The police. The private detectives. And it happened four years ago. Four fucking years ago. We'd reached some kind of threshold and just like that my hands were around Pedro's throat and I was shoving him against the wall. I liked the feeling of release; I'd been craving it since I arrived, but his teeth clamped into me and I thought he was going to bite my fucking thumb off. I shoved him away. But he wanted the fight, he wasn't ready to give it up. Why taunt me? Why bring up Afghanistan? Pedro was kicking and punching, fighting like he wanted to give me something to remember. But I was bigger and had more prac-tice. I was ready to kill him. I had it in me.

But then, thank God, Jack interrupted us. I made Pedro tell us, I made him take ownership of his weak, sad story and he started talking like he was narrating a slow-moving dream. Pothole, fire truck, ambulance.

I'd done a few death knocks in my time – turning up on a doorstep with bad news, hoping for a quote before the afternoon deadline. One elderly man with a birthmark on his face invited me in for a cup of tea. An aspiring model threw her mobile phone at my face. A middle-aged woman the size of a truck just shook her head like she'd been getting shitty news her whole life. And now it was me. It makes sense: if you live long enough, someone you love will die. But I couldn't be in the same room with Pedro. The guy was messed up, no question, but what right did he have to be upset now? He'd had four years to grieve.

Outside, I pushed past Emma, who was sitting on the front step, knees drawn to her chest. 'You thought I was fucking with you? Wish I had been. My nephew's dead. Pedro didn't tell us. Pedro didn't fucking tell us that my nephew's been dead.

For four fucking years.' I was yelling at her. Everything I couldn't articulate inside was now gasping out of me into the cold air. I kept repeating the word 'dead' like if I said it enough times the meaning would register and I'd know what to do.

Emma sat up. She was staring at me like I'd become suddenly dangerous. Maybe I had. And you know what? I liked the fear on her face. I wanted everyone in the world to be afraid. I was standing in front of the snow wall that I'd shoved Jack into. Even though my hands were bare and the ice must have been hard as cement, I started banging my fists onto that top layer. Slamming them down. I couldn't feel a thing.

Emma's face was pale.

'He was such a good kid. So funny. Smart, too.' I was ranting.

'What happened?'

My hands had split and blood was seeping into the ice but I kept pounding. 'Bicycle accident. Who dies in a bicycle accident? There wasn't even a car. Just a pothole. A fucking pothole.'

Emma stood up and walked through my anger. One step at a time, slow and deliberate. She stood beside me and grabbed my shoulders so I was facing her. I stopped and she reached for my hands, seizing them. It was hard for me to control my anger, but I didn't shove her off. I let her hold my hands. After a minute, she released my palms and hugged me. Her whole body holding me close, uncomfortably tight. I was gasping and crying but she wouldn't let go.

❄

I climbed Little Cerro four times that afternoon. On the final ascent, before the peak, my knees buckled and I sat in the snow. I cursed every road that had ever been built and every bicycle that had ever been ridden. I screamed at the watered-down sky and sat staring at my bashed up, bloody hands. When I finally came down, Emma was waiting outside.

❋

Even in grief, I knew it was gutless to blame God or fate for shit luck. And even though it made me feel better to hate Pedro, I couldn't pin Quidel's death on him alone. It's true – if he'd made different decisions my nephew would probably be alive. If they hadn't left Córdoba, Quidel couldn't have been riding his bicycle on Avenida de los Pioneros. But something else could have happened. Rosie would have taken him to New York where he could've fallen out of a window. Been hit by a taxi. Drowned in the Hudson.

And Pedro was right: I knew the guilt that comes from not being careful. In Afghanistan, four people had died on my watch. I was too eager to get to Jalalabad. I thought it would be safe because an anti-Taliban coalition had chosen a governor for the Nangarhar Province. Of course the authorities didn't have full control of the area but I talked over any concerns. If you want the story, you have to go get it, I'd said to Daniel and Juan, a couple of journalists at the Inter-Con Hotel. The big white building had a hole in one side four storeys tall from a misguided rocket but it was the only accommodation in the capital. We were sprawled across the two single beds in my room, sharing a flask of cognac Daniel had smuggled into the country. Daniel was tall and solid like a Scottish warrior. His feet were hanging off the end of the bed.

'Find your balls, boys,' I said, toasting them both.

Daniel had natural talent and a gut instinct for good stories. Just three years earlier, he'd been a produce manager at a Melbourne supermarket and thought there had to be more to life than stacking apples. So he took off to East Timor to cover the Indonesian occupation as a freelancer. Just him and his camera. He was taken hostage in the Fiji coup the year before I met him, and shrugged it off. 'No biggie, mate,' he'd told me.

I wasn't expecting to round up enough interest to get out to Jalalabad but Daniel was the kind of guy who takes you on your word whether you've been drinking or not. So there we were, a couple of days later, heading east towards the Pakistani border on the worst fucking road. My head kept knocking against the roof of the car and I'd had to ask Omed to pull over more than once so I could puke.

Omed and I were the last car in the convoy. Daniel and Juan were ahead of us with two more journalists. It was late morning. I was sitting in the back seat – I'd given up the front to humour Omed. He'd watched too many American movies, and fancied himself a chauffeur. Truth was, he was more of a courier service. Whenever I needed a ride somewhere, he'd take advantage of our destination to deliver something to or on behalf of his relatives. That day, it was chickens. He had a rusty wire cage on the front seat with four hens in it. They looked like skinny Rhode Island Reds but he told me they were some Afghani native. Good layers, apparently. Another six were crammed in a cage on the back seat, next to me.

I was leaning forward, my elbows on the bucket seat between us, talking chickens, when Omed slowed down. We'd been trying to make up space with the car ahead of us after my last pit stop.

'Get down, get down,' Omed said.

The road was blocked. Not a good sign – we were in the middle of nowhere. There was grey rock slicing up into a mountain on one side of us and scruffy outcrops on the other. It wasn't going to be a military checkpoint.

I scrambled behind the seat, crouching down while Omed pulled a blanket over me. He shoved the cage so it was on top, jamming into my shoulder blade. I could smell oil and chicken shit.

'It's bad,' he said. 'They have guns. They're taking the journalists.'

I wanted to look over the seat but restrained myself. 'Taking them where?'

'I don't know. Into the bushes. Behind a rock.'

'What about our guard?'

'Shh—' I could hear footsteps. Omed rolled down his window. There was a rapid conversation in Pashto, which I couldn't understand, and the front passenger door opened. The chickens were squawking – someone was hoisting the cage out. The door slammed close.

The deep voice said something else. They wanted the other cage. Omed pleaded, he needed the birds for his family. The back door opened. And then four gunshots – from Kalashnikovs, I could hear that much – rang out in immediate succession. The door slammed shut and I heard footsteps running away, towards the gunshots. There was shouting. Omed slammed the car into reverse and spun around. I had no sense of how fast we were going – the road was too broken for speed, but my head bounced against the floor with every pothole, the tyres juttering beneath me. Even though it was a chilly November in the mountains, I was sweating.

'You can get up now,' Omed called out. The stopped cars were already tiny in the distance behind us. I stayed there, staring out the back window, even after we rounded a bend.

We didn't get word until late that afternoon. Gunmen told the drivers they were part of the Taliban militia, targeting journalists. Daniel and Juan had been killed, along with a Pakistani photographer and an Italian reporter.

❈

Back in Kabul, I couldn't focus on my assignments. I ignored deadlines, emails, phone calls. If Afghanistan didn't want a free press, who was I to force it? But there were the aerial bombings and every day the civilian casualty list grew, name after name, and I was back to the argument that landed me my first overseas posting: you couldn't let the world ignore what was going on. Someone had to bear witness. Someone had to make my father responsible.

But it couldn't be me. Not then. I locked myself in my hotel room and slept under one of the beds. I didn't respond to editors. Stopped eating. And then, late one night, there was a knock on the door and I heard Rosie shouting my name. I thought she was an apparition, a phantom drawn from my subconscious. But when I let her in, she hugged me close and I could feel she was real.

She scanned the room. 'Let's get your things packed.'

I nodded.

Omed was waiting in his car to take us to the airport. He'd called her.

✳

We arrived back in New York just after Thanksgiving, and the New Year brought its own trouble: Pedro disappeared with Quidel. And then, four years later, my nephew was dead. Of course Pedro was traumatised but he sure as hell should have told us. His crime was buying the concession and withdrawing to the mountains. I would have taken him to task on this but it wasn't my job – Rosie would have to be the one to see to that, I'd trespassed into her affairs enough. But even so, I couldn't leave like Emma had suggested – I had to make sure Rosie got her reckoning. I had to get Pedro down to Bariloche. It's true, that was motivating me when we took a vote. I would have risked trekking through grade red avalanche terrain. I wasn't a good man to trust.

And I had no trouble in getting personal. When Emma didn't vote with me, I was surprised and impressed. But her decision stole my momentum so I played dirty. Brought up the Americans and how they'd cornered Carmen. Attacked the Germans for their passivity. Targeted Pedro. He looked like he'd survived a car crash, bruises on his neck and a big lump on the back of his head. He admitted everything, didn't hide from his crimes. But he caught me off guard, bringing up my father. I thought he'd mention Afghanistan, my record for taking bad risks.

Then Carmen and Jack cleared the dining room floor to dance. The two of them so young, their bodies in controlled unison. They moved like a nuanced dialectic was taking place. Carmen asked a question, Jack answered. Then Jack, and so on. Their arms stretched out as they paced the floor of the dining room. Carmen spinning just outside the circle of light. All of us watching, part of it. If we were talking about moral parameters, Pedro was right – I was living on guilty money. My father supplied weapons to a government that waged war on civilians, Carmen's father was an accomplice in that war, Pedro's family suffered from it – though his people had long been fucked, since the Spanish Crown crossed the Atlantic, really. And then the Germans – Erik's great-uncle escaping along the 'rat lines' to Argentina, all the Nazis bringing their expertise that would prove so useful in the Dirty War. We were in Argentina, but we could be anywhere. I thought of the countries I'd reported on: El Salvador, Sierra Leone, Kosovo, Iraq, Afghanistan. Perhaps that was the human condition: grappling with the wrongs we commit and those committed against us.

❉

I'd decided to shift to the dorm room that night. After the day's events, I didn't want to sleep near Pedro. And Emma was upstairs. Not like I thought anything would happen but a man can hope.

Her sleeping bag was splayed out on one of the top bunks and Carmen's stuff was scattered below. I climbed the ladder and parked myself in the spot closest to the door so I'd be able to turn off the light without getting up. Carmen came in as I was easing into my sleeping bag. She stopped in the doorway and watched me for a disapproving moment.

'The tango. Wow,' I said. My voice was genuine.

'Thank you.' She was waiting.

'About tonight . . .' I didn't know what to say.

'At least you lack prejudice. You seem to hate us all. It wouldn't be easy – your nephew . . .'

Even though I'd been the one shouting it out in front of the refugio and yelling at Pedro, it still surprised me that Quidel had become public knowledge. That I could have a conversation about him with Carmen.

'And your father's death,' she said.

'How did you know that?'

'First night, right when you arrived – you told Pedro.' Her eyes, rimmed in kohl, were watching me like I'd given away more than I'd known when I said that. 'I decided I liked you. I decided to forgive you for your manners.'

'That was lucky.'

'I'm not angry because you kept your father as a secret. I'm angry that you sat in judgement. You implied you were above us.' Her mouth lifted into a smile that didn't reach her eyes. 'What was the funeral like?'

'My father's? He was buried the day after he died. Simple service. The rabbi recited psalms. It was like any other funeral I've been to but this time I had a role I was supposed to fill . . .'

She stepped into the room and I was surprised by how glad I was that she was talking to me.

'Did you feel like an impostor?' She placed the accent on the final syllable so it sounded Spanish.

'Maybe.'

'Are you glad you were there?'

'I don't know. I guess I am. I think a funeral is a ritual for the mourners. Maybe you don't have to mourn the life that was lived. Maybe you can mourn the life that wasn't lived.' I was thinking aloud but it made sense. My father. The journalists in Afghanistan. Quidel.

Carmen sighed. A dreamy, slow exhalation. 'I like that.'

I was thinking about my nephew and the weight of telling Rosie that our search was over. I thought of her on the plane to Buenos Aires, the caution etched into her face as though she already knew.

❄

The lights were off when Emma came to bed. She had a flashlight and snuck up the stairs, easing over my feet. She climbed into her sleeping bag. I could see her rounded silhouette, lying beside me. In the quiet darkness, she shifted towards me. I thought it was an accident, that she mustn't realise how confined the bunks were. But then she rolled closer again and all my pagan holidays arrived at once. She nuzzled in next to me and we slept, spooning, my arms wrapped around her. I wasn't under any illusions – Emma wasn't going to be my girlfriend. But that didn't make me any less thankful. I'd take anything I could get.

❄

Emma was still sleeping when I woke the next morning. Quiet, so I wouldn't disturb her, I climbed down the ladder and hiked out pre-dawn to check the snow. Shear test, Rutschblock test. Because of the steep slope, the trickiest section would start about a mile and a half in, along the Cerro Blanco ridge, where the Americans had been swept away. By my figuring, it seemed stable enough. At least we wouldn't need snowshoes. The ground was frozen – the light dusting less than an inch thick. On my way back to the refugio, Pedro passed me with a plastic shovel.

'Another opinion,' he said.

'Suit yourself.' He could knock himself out. Fact was, we'd be heading down.

Pedro was back within an hour and serving breakfast. Emma sat beside me and let me squeeze her hand under the table. After the dishes were done and final rations packed, we were supposed to meet outside.

Klaus was the first one in front of the refugio, standing at attention like a soldier from an old war movie. The darkness was lifting and there wasn't much cloud cover – we'd have a clear day for hiking out. I dropped my backpack on the ground. 'Ready?'

He saluted me like we could blitz our way down the mountain. 'Yes, sir.'

Jack followed me down the stairs and shoved his brother into the snow. 'You ready? Really?'

Klaus was taking swipes at him when Erik cleared his throat from the top step. 'You need to save energy. We have a full hike in front of us today.'

Klaus pushed Jack off of him and they both brushed the snow from their jackets. They scanned the mountain, exaggerated hands shielding eyes, parodies of Erik.

Hita and Felix emerged from the door next, with Emma behind them. She watched me watching her and smiled. Then Carmen. The only person left was Pedro. I thought I was going to have to go back inside for him.

But then he appeared, waiting on the top step for a moment as though he were completely alone. He surveyed the mountain behind us and turned back to the refugio.

271

'We going anytime today?' I asked, and he shut the door.

I was waiting for a galvanising speech from our refugio landlord but Pedro pulled on his pack and started walking. '*Vámonos* – let's go.'

Hita looked at Erik, who shrugged, and they nodded to the boys. The rest of us filed into line behind them. A discussion about order would have to take place closer to the avalanche site: order was everything. The first person to walk across would face the most danger. If the track wasn't stable, they'd be the one to find out. If the path held, you wanted to be second or third. Anything after that was suspect because the weight of the previous hikers could break down the snow pack. Trouble was, I didn't trust Pedro to go behind me.

Pedro and Jack set a quick pace and soon a gap formed in front of Felix and Klaus. The boys tried to keep up with enthusiastic bursts of running and Klaus stepped on Jack's heels to slow him down but Jack shrugged him off. It wasn't until he reached the river that Pedro turned around and realised we weren't all right behind him.

Crossing the river meant hanging from a heavy cable and stepping over the rocks. Erik helped the boys and when Felix slipped, he grabbed his arm, lifting him to the other side. I followed. Then Emma. She was all bundled up, her small backpack sitting evenly on her shoulders. Behind us, the refugio was taking shape in the morning light. It looked small and unimportant with mountains staggered behind. The fire had already burned out; no smoke drifted from the chimney. Rosie would have said the building missed us, missed Pedro, and I would have told her to cut back on the sentiment. But it did look diminished without a human presence.

I wondered what Rosie was doing. Each hour itching by as she waited for the trail to clear. Maybe my biggest crime was leaving her to face those long days alone. That's when the quarter dropped for me. We had to get down. I wouldn't be able to set things right with Rosie if we were swept away. All of my huffing and puffing about leaving had been driven by the need for movement, the need to feel like I was doing something. I hadn't taken our safety into account. Even digging the test pits, it'd been about supporting my argument with Pedro, not about objectively assessing the circumstances. I'm such an idiot – it hadn't occurred to me that we might not make it across.

I had a moment of panic and almost said something – but Pedro was walking ahead and everyone was lined up behind him. I filed in last. Felix started singing a song in German, and Klaus joined him, their footsteps keeping time with the stern melody. Pedro tried to follow the rhythm but, despite his efforts to keep us together, we couldn't follow the same pace. Pedro would start slow, catering for the younger members, but he'd begin walking faster and, after a few minutes, he'd have to stop again and wait for everyone to catch up.

We made it to the edge of the avalanche zone where the Americans had last been seen. Snow had slid down, covering the trail in a debris field. Everyone shed their packs and stood in a loose circle, gulping from their water canteens. I was going to take Pedro aside. Ask him what he really thought. Forget Rosie, forget Bariloche: can we make it across?

I adjusted my transceiver – it was strapped on, under my arm and across my chest. Pedro and Erik had decided I should wear one – you want to stagger your experience and your transceivers. That meant Pedro, Erik and I would have to be spaced throughout the group. The beacons transmit signals to each other – if there's an avalanche, at least one of them needs to be outside the fall so they can locate those beneath the snow, otherwise they're useless.

Pedro's voice had the monotone drawl of tour-safety videos but I was glad he was taking the role of leader. I didn't have it in me: I had too much doubt. 'Everyone who doesn't have a beacon, take an avalanche cord. Tie it around your waist,' he said.

Erik passed out the bright orange strings, each about thirty yards long. In a worst-case scenario, a searcher could follow one to a body.

Pedro continued, his voice confident. 'We'll walk across one at a time – except for Felix and Klaus. They'll hike with Hita and Erik. Don't stop for any reason. About three-quarters of the way across, there's a series of gullies. Couloirs. Take your time. They might be steep.'

We'd be okay, I thought. It was normal to be afraid. All of the shear tests indicated that the snow pack had hardened. And Eric was a geologist for God's sake – he was the one who'd voted to go. We don't have a choice, I told myself. Imagine all nine of us, without any food. Buck up, Wolfe. No time for nerves.

Erik chimed in. 'If you hear snow cracking above, try to find a tree or something you can hold.'

We looked out along the path – except for a couple of rock shelves, it was barren. There wasn't even a patch of scrub. I shook my head. 'I'd drop your pack and run. How are we going to order this?'

Pedro looked at me like he'd been bracing for this conversation. 'You're the one who wanted to leave, Wolfe. You should go first.'

He had a point but I couldn't risk it. 'I don't trust you to follow. We'll draw straws.'

He waited a moment, then sighed. 'Okay.'

I'd planned on this and reached in my pocket for a stick. I broke it into different lengths, showing them to Klaus. 'One's long and one's short?'

He nodded.

Holding the sticks, I moved my hands behind my back. 'How long will it take to get across?'

Pedro glanced along the trail. 'Depends on the condition of the snow. Maybe ten minutes?'

I coughed, breaking the twigs so they were both the same size. I was cheating, I know, but he was a flight risk. 'We'll make seven trips?'

'Yes.'

'Well, then.' I spoke like we were in agreement on some deeper issue and brought my hands out so they were in front of me. Two twigs poking out. 'The short one goes first. Pick, Pedro.'

He watched both hands for a moment and then pointed to my right. I opened my hand. 'You're off. Walk safe.'

He nodded like he'd expected it. 'The three with transceivers should spread out through the group.'

I disappeared both sticks into my pocket. If anything happened to Pedro, I was going straight to hell – I knew that. But we wouldn't have been on top of that shitty mountain in the first place if it weren't for him. 'You go first. Erik in the middle – he'll have Klaus with him. I'll bring up the rear. Who goes second?' I asked.

Jack shuffled forward, watching his father's face. 'I'll go.'

Erik shot me a warning glance. Jack didn't realise going second was one of the safer positions. He thought he was being brave and I held myself back from making a wisecrack. Erik nodded to Jack, and Hita grabbed Felix's hand as though she could protect all of her sons with the one maternal gesture. I liked Hita – she was the only person at the refugio who wasn't consumed with herself.

Pedro handed Jack one of the collapsible shovels to carry so they'd be dispersed through the group. 'Whatever you do, don't stop.'

They started lining up. First Pedro. Then Jack.

Carmen and Emma were looking at each other like they had no idea what to do.

'Next?' Erik was in democratic organisation mode. But sorting this out could take all day and we didn't have time. If we got to the other side, we still had a good eight hours' hiking in front of us. With the boys, it could take even longer.

Hita had given up her transceiver: it was only fair that she walked across next. I cleared my throat. 'Hita and Felix. Then Erik and Klaus. Then Carmen. Emma. And me. Everyone ready?'

As soon as I spoke, I regretted it. Emma should have gone closer to the start but she was already crunching through the snow to hug Pedro. 'Good luck,' she said.

Pedro almost toppled over with the weight in his pack. I was just willing him to fall but he found his footing. 'It'll be okay.'

He tugged at the straps of his backpack with too much force and then needed to loosen them again. He scanned the group. 'This is it. Goodbye.'

Felix started to cheer and then realised he was the only one so stopped. Klaus elbowed him in the ribs and Erik rested a hand on each of their shoulders to quiet them. Carmen inched towards Jack and held his hand.

Pedro looked at me and shook his head like he couldn't understand how we'd gotten to this point. His face was inscrutable and he gave a bewildered shrug before starting off, scrambling over the debris field. Pedro slipped twice, falling forward onto his knees, and each time we all seemed to hold a collective breath in case the impact was enough to trigger a collapse, but the mountain was still. He reached the path and this seemed like a little victory. He started walking, each step taking him deeper into the avalanche zone. The sun was now streaming across the quiet valley. Pedro ignored his own advice and paused on one of the peaks, scanning the valley below him.

'Keep going,' Emma said under her breath. She was beside me, shifting her weight from foot to foot and staring intently at the mountain.

Pedro began moving again, slower than before. He should have been making better time. 'What are you doing, Pedro?' I asked no one in particular.

He'd reached the halfway point. Smack in the heart of the scariest stretch. If anything happened, he was equidistant from either end: there was no possibility of running to safety. Soon he'd edged along, though. He wasn't moving as fast as I would have expected but he was concentrating on making a clear path for us to follow. Lifting his legs high as he walked and watching his feet. Easy footsteps. I wouldn't have been so diligent.

And then he was on the last section, with the couloirs. There were dips in the path so he would drop out of sight and reappear half a minute later. Down. Back up. Down. Back up. Each time he emerged I found I'd been holding my breath. The couloirs would be an easy place for a small slide. Then he was within thirty yards of the other side. Twenty. Ten. When he made it to the clear ledge, he threw off his pack and waved both arms like he was trying to hail an airplane. He looked like a fool but he'd made it. Thank God, I thought. Whatever I thought of Pedro, I couldn't have handled telling Rosie that something had happened to him.

Jack was next. Hita and Erik took turns hugging him – Hita, then Erik, then Hita again – and his younger brothers offered him gloved high-fives. Carmen stepped back like she didn't want to intrude but Jack grabbed her by the arms and she kissed him on the cheek.

'See you over there,' he said to the group, almost casually, as he headed off. He didn't pause or look around; his gaze stayed focused on Pedro's footsteps as he climbed through the debris field. His shoulders were rounded from the weight of his pack but he moved with care.

Felix was standing in front of his father, chewing on his sleeve, eyes focused on his brother. When Jack reached the open trail, he started clapping, and Erik muttered something in German under his breath. Hita grabbed her husband's hand and he squeezed it back. Jack kept a steady pace through the open area and once he hit the middle, his speed crept up a notch. Pedro had done a good job laying the path. Three-quarters of the way along, just before the couloirs, Jack pulled his hat off and stopped for breath. His father whispered a reprimand in German but Jack was soon moving again, his hat stuffed in a pocket. A few more minutes and he'd made it to the trenches. Without waiting, he dropped out of sight and appeared again about thirty seconds later. Dropping down. Appearing. Every time he emerged, Hita let out a little pant of sound. This happened four more times until he popped up after the last one. His pace quickened on the final stretch so that he was almost running and after about ten seconds, he grabbed Pedro in a crushing grizzly bear hug.

'Hooray!' Felix cried.

Hita and Felix were ready. She murmured something in German to Erik and he kissed her on the forehead. She and Felix were off, both of them trailing avalanche cords behind them.

They took longer than Pedro or Jack. Scaling the first section was slow work. Hita had to climb behind Felix because he kept slipping. Felix would grab chunks of snow for leverage and they'd break off in his hands. On the main trail, it wasn't any easier. Felix had trouble following in Pedro's footsteps. At one point, Hita tried to pick him up but with the clumsy weight of their packs, it wasn't going to happen.

'Be patient,' I murmured.

Erik was rocking back and forth, balancing up on his toes and lowering himself to the ground. Klaus was standing beside him, holding his hand.

Hita set her son down and they pattered slowly across the mountain. Then she stopped.

Emma was kicking at the snow, hands shoved in her pockets. 'What's she doing?'

'Don't know.' But I was willing to bet it was the Americans. It'd make sense with the pack shifting – their bodies were probably exposed. After a moment Hita moved on.

When they descended into the first couloir I thought something had happened – the seconds ticked by but they didn't appear.

Emma gripped Klaus's shoulder, and Erik looked at me, worried. 'What do we do?'

'I don't know. Pedro would have a better view.'

I grabbed binoculars out of my pack to see if Pedro was panicking, issuing orders to hike in, but he was standing still, watching impassively. It was impossible to tell if he could see them or not. Erik reached for the binoculars and sighed as he focused the lenses.

Another minute passed and they emerged, disappearing into the second couloir and then the third. Each time it took longer than it should have. But they appeared after the final couloir and Felix ran ahead to the group. A trip that lasted all of nine or ten minutes for everyone else took them almost double the time.

Erik let out a whoop and said something in German I didn't catch. Klaus was clapping.

Then Erik turned to Klaus, holding the avalanche cord – he was going to tie them together with the orange rope so they'd both have the advantage of a beacon. The ten-year-old jumped away from his father.

'Come,' Erik reached for him.

'I'm going to hike across by myself.'

Erik's nose was dripping. He wiped at his face impatiently. 'Not now.'

Klaus looked across to his mother and brothers. 'I can do it.'

He was balancing on a rock and his father grabbed him by

the front of his jacket, pulling him down. Klaus huffed as his dad tied the orange cord in place.

Erik stepped forward to shake my hand. Emma and Carmen each grabbed him in a hug. And just like that they were off, Klaus strutting like a hero from an adventure movie. If there were a couple of dead Americans down there, I hoped he wouldn't look – he was the kind of kid who'd straggle down the cliff to get a better view. But his father was right behind him, probably urging him to hurry up. They made it to the middle without a problem and I stepped back to have a cigarette. It was too much, watching everyone trek across. I moved to the far edge of our safety zone to stretch my legs, drawing the smoke deep with every inhalation. When I came back, Erik and Klaus were at the couloirs. They dropped down and reappeared like the others. This was the unsettling bit. When they were visible, you had the illusion you could gauge their danger.

'They'll be fine,' I said more to myself than anyone else.

Soon they popped up for the last time and joined the rest of the party. The family all grabbed each other in a big hug, and I could imagine Hita and Erik beaming.

Now it was Carmen's turn. Back at the refugio, she'd caked on the make-up – red triangles on her cheeks and glitter-blue eyelids. An anthropologist might have given her the benefit of the doubt: primitive face paint, a mask to confuse Death. But she looked more like a hooker, ready to lean into Death's lumbering Mercedes to negotiate a few more years.

She kissed me on the cheek and strode up to Emma, whispering something in her ear. Emma grabbed her by the hands and they stared at each other for a moment. When Carmen broke away, she walked straight to the debris field and began climbing. She paused at the top and slid down the rough snow – instead of landing with a weighty thud, she stepped straight off. Her eyes were trained on Pedro and Jack as though using them for balance. She didn't look down until she'd crossed the first trench and, when she did, she stopped. About ten yards from the halfway point. It was the Americans, I was sure of it now.

'Come on, Carmen. Keep moving.' Emma was biting her lip.

The *porteña* started scurrying across the snow, oblivious to Pedro's footsteps. She was running and slipped on an icy patch, her arms flying out.

'Calm down, Tango Princess. Focus,' I muttered as she stood up and started off again, slower this time.

Emma glanced up at the mountain but it was still. A few minutes later Carmen hit the couloirs and dropped out of sight. When she came up after the last one, I could make out Jack punching the air. She was safe.

I needed another cigarette. I took off my glove to flick the lighter and held the warm smoke in my lungs.

Emma adjusted her pack. Her turquoise beanie was poking out of her coat pocket. 'I like you.'

'No accounting for taste.'

'You'd have to stop smoking.'

'You'd have to move to New York.' I was bluffing. I would have moved back to Afghanistan for her but she shrugged like the Big Apple wasn't the end of the world. It was worth considering, anyway. And with that, she started off. No goodbye. Nothing. Just hiking it out across the snow. Grabbing her beanie out of her pocket, she pulled it on. That flash of bright blue broadcasting each time she turned her head. I followed her gaze to the other side of the ravine. Staggered layers of snow. Bright, cheerful sky overhead. Ragged clouds on the horizon. Fuck, I wanted her to make it across.

After the rough terrain at the beginning, she hit the trail and sped up. But after a couple of minutes, she must have caught sight of whatever it was down there. 'You can't stop,' I said aloud. 'Keep moving.'

My hand went to the binoculars around my neck. I wanted to be ready to see what was down there.

She was moving now but not as quickly.

'Jesus, they're dead. No use joining them,' I muttered.

And as though she could hear me, she became more assured and her pace quickened. Within a matter of minutes she was halfway, then three-quarters of the way, along.

Everyone else was perched on the other side, watching. Klaus and Felix weren't wrestling with each other or tugging at their avalanche cords – they were lined up next to their parents. Hita was shielding her eyes from the sun. Erik had his hands in the pockets of his parka, his elbows sticking straight out. Pedro and Carmen were standing a couple of yards away, next to Jack.

Emma started down the first couloir. Half a minute passed and she appeared for a brief moment before disappearing into the second. Then the third. Every time she resurfaced she was noticeably further away. Smaller. And then she was standing on the other side, hugging Pedro.

'Guess it's my turn.' Who did I think was going to hear me? The invisible cameras all poised on my intriguing life? I was under no illusions. In fact, in that moment, it seemed inevitable, my life was too good: there would be an avalanche and snow would entomb me. I double-checked that my beacon was set to 'transmit'.

Scrambling over the debris field was trickier than I'd imagined. Chunks of ice, uneven footing. The backpack shifted my centre of balance so I had to take it slow to keep from toppling over. I eased down a sheet of ice on my butt and my feet landed on the trail. I had Pedro's footsteps in front of me. They were worn from the others. This was the easiest stretch but also the most exposed. If an avalanche was triggered, I'd be carried into the ravine, no question. Every breath clouded the air like smoke, which reminded me of how desperately I wanted another cigarette. My boots jarred into the snow, making little echoes.

And then, while loosening the straps of my backpack, I saw a flash of red below. To the left, about forty yards down. I kept walking, but held my binoculars up with my left hand. An arm with a gloveless hand exposed. Otherwise, whoever it was – John or Jeremy – was well and truly buried. Dead on impact, I'd guess, and suffocated just in case. About twenty yards along from him, another body. Just the back of the head and torso. Buried up to his waist. Same bright red.

It was only when I reached the flat bend before the couloirs that I realised how quickly my heart was beating. My lower back was drenched in sweat. It was like I'd seen the victims of a Sphinx and knew a riddle was waiting ahead: only an idiot would keep going. But what choice was there? I was three-quarters of the way across. Still, I wondered how far the Americans had made it along the trail. Surely I'd passed the point where they'd been swept away, back with the rubble?

The couloirs were bigger than I'd imagined. Not gullies at all but trenches carved into the side of the mountain. Each one was about ten or fifteen yards across. During spring, they'd fill with water, improvised rivers. But now, covered with ice and snow, they were steep, and it was like climbing along the bony spine of a dragon.

I paused on the first point, willing myself closer to the plateau where everyone was watching. For once my fellow citizens didn't seem so bad. I just had to get to where they were. It was a matter of space. The particles that composed Wolfe Goldberg needed to be standing on that same open ledge and we'd be fine. After this stretch, the rest of the hike was straightforward. It would be slow-going with Felix and Klaus, but we'd all take turns irritating each other until we finally arrived at the bottom. I had two peaks ahead of me – less than a hundred and fifty yards. That's when I tripped – maybe on my bootlace, maybe uneven footing, I don't know. My hands took the full brunt of my weight and I was lying there, face planted in the snow. In the grand scheme of the pass, it was only a butterfly flutter but that's all it would take. I stayed for a moment, listening for some kind of movement overhead, but everything seemed still.

I got to my feet. The air was tight in my lungs and, with each step, I focused on the cigarette I'd have when I arrived. I'd light it quick and breath in slow. Savour each breath. That smoke would be the closest I'd get to prayer.

I didn't hear it coming. The first chunk of snow fell right in front of me. It was about three yards square and bounced on the trail, breaking into an icy spray. Fuck, I thought. This is it. Cerro Blanco looked beautiful and terrifying – white against blue, snow versus sky. Pedro was yelling something and I began to run. In my mind's eye I could see the path behind me, slipping away, collapsing into the ravine. My feet were pushing me forward but I wasn't making enough ground. There was no way I'd get to the plateau. I needed a tree or a rock ledge, some kind of protection. I was on top of a dragon spine when the snow began to shudder beneath me. I threw off my pack and the binoculars so I'd be lighter, and when the snow fell on me like a wave I swam through it, thrusting upwards to stay near the surface. The force turned me heavy and spun me upside down but I tried to stay focused on my direction, turning again.

The most critical moments were as the avalanche came to a stop. Debris snow sets quickly and there would be no hope of digging myself out, even if it were a small slide. I punched into the snow around my face to make an air pocket and took a deep breath to expand my chest so I'd have space to breath. Nothing worse than forgetting that one: imagine the snow holding your diaphragm so close you can't move to draw breath.

If my concentration had held, I should be facing upwards. I couldn't be more than a few yards beneath the snow and surely there hadn't been enough force to take me off the ledge? I was still alive – I hadn't died on impact. I hadn't even felt a fall so it had to be a small avalanche. My beacon was turned on. If Pedro thought it was safe, they'd be able to get to me. Emma would be next to him, thrusting the probe down, searching for something solid. I tried to move but was pinned into place like an insect in an entomologist's album. Ice cramped my arms and legs. I concentrated on breathing. Small, shallow breaths. Come on, Pedro. I know I've been a bastard, that'll never change. Come and get me, anyway.

I probably had about fifteen minutes, maybe twenty. After that statistics were against me. But how long had I been waiting? A matter of seconds? Minutes? In the white darkness, it was hard to know. What I did know was that I wasn't interested in making a pact with God. If I survived, I wouldn't attend synagogue or give my father's money to charity. All of the wheeling and dealing people do when they're going to die assumes they have some pull in the barter system. And, even if, in some anthropocentric twist, God was listening, how could he respect someone frightened of something so mundane? People die every day.

My fingers and toes were losing feeling but the cold had a mild euphoria to it. There would be worse ways to go.

And then I heard something overhead. Muffled. Barely audible. Emma? Maybe I didn't hear it at all. There was too much hope in imagining them – Pedro overhead, digging a shear test to make sure the snow was safe. Erik fiddling with his transceiver. Jack, with his collapsible shovel. It took self-control not to shout – I couldn't afford to waste oxygen.

I was thinking about Rosie. I had to make it back for her, apologise for leaving her in Bariloche. I couldn't fix anything but maybe we could travel. Fly to Germany – a World Cup pilgrimage in honour of Quidel. Or maybe she'd want to stay in Bariloche. Have our own funeral at the cemetery.

Everything was silent – a pale silence that could drift all too easily into nothingness – and I began to panic. I needed to stay calm to maximise the oxygen supply but my heart was working so hard I thought it might blow a valve.

Slow it down, Wolfe, I told myself. You can do this. I had to trust Pedro. If it was safe, they'd dig me out – it'd only be a matter of minutes. I could hold on. Surely I could hold on.

Author's Note

This novel is inspired by historical events and real places, however it is a work of fiction. While there is indeed a real Refugio Frey on the Nahuel Huapi hiking circuit, the events I portray are imagined. For purposes of narrative, I have altered the physical terrain at Refugio Frey – particularly the paths to and from the cabin. The characters depicted herein are not based on real people, though four journalists – including Australian Harry Burton – did die on 19 November 2001 in a road ambush between Kabul and Jalalabad.

Acknowledgements

Researching *What the Ground Can't Hold* involved everything from studying avalanche guides to trekking in the Andes. Thank you to all who helped me along the way in Argentina, Australia and the United States – especially Scott Bazley, Serena Cosgrove, Marty Bosworth, Rosa Nair Amuedo, Patty Kistenmacher, Ed and Audrey Shaw, Josephina Schapira and Ignacio Albarracin.

I thank Alex Craig for having faith in what this book could be through all of the re-drafting, and Vanessa Pellatt for her literary nous. I'm indebted to Jo Jarrah for her editorial feedback, and Deonie Fiford and Glenda Downing for their attention to detail. And this book wouldn't exist as a published artefact without Lyn Tranter's support over the seven years it took to write.

As well, thank you for feedback from Joshua Lobb, Nathan Kelly, Beckie Hart, Irene Otis, Anne Cawsey, Cathy Cole, Christine Howe, Tamryn Bennett, Wes Chung, Brodie Bortignon, Sally Evans, Stephanie Drummond, Nicole Thomas, Amber Stewart, Rachel Abrams, Amy Pearson, Bridget Lutherborrow, Michelle Bateman, Susie Lenehan, Yvonn Deitch, Tom Williams and WRIT212. Thank you, also, to Linda Meyns.

And to the literary dining set: Linda Godfrey, Eva Hodge, Ali Smith, Emma Dalton and Deb Young.